New York Times and *USA Today* Bestselling Author

CYNTHIA EDEN

SLAY ALL DAY

SIN ALL NIGHT

DEDICATION

A special thanks to all the amazing ladies in Eden's Agents. I hope you know how appreciated you are!

CHAPTER ONE

The vamps had a new toy. Unfortunately, the bloodsuckers didn't exactly know how to play *nicely* with anything, and if Harrison Key didn't step in and teach them some proper manners, they'd rip that new toy apart.

"Don't even *think* of touching me!"

His eyes narrowed at that fierce shout. A woman's voice had burst from the middle of the vamps — they'd closed in on their prey, forming a tight, hungry circle around the new toy.

The toy…the woman. Their latest snack.

The vampires growled. Inched ever closer —

"Touching you isn't the only thing they have planned," Harrison called out, stepping from the darkness that surrounded him so perfectly. "Drinking your blood, draining you dry — that's more on their to-do list for the night."

The vamps whipped toward him. Four vamps. One terrified woman in their midst. The vamps had their fangs out and their claws were at the ready.

Harrison smiled. "Sorry to interrupt dinner time, boys, but she's off the menu."

One vamp charged at him. Roared and ran right for Harrison. Taking his time about it, Harrison brought up the wooden stake he gripped in his right hand, and he slammed the stake into the vamp's heart.

The vamp fell to the ground, body instantly turning hard as stone.

The movies and TV shows had it all wrong. Vamps didn't explode when they were staked. They just dropped like stones. End of story. End of vamp.

He yanked the stake out of victim number one. Harrison smiled at the three vamps who remained. "Who wants to be next?"

Instead of charging at him, a tall, dark-haired vamp grabbed the woman. Harrison hadn't paid much attention to her until that point. Sure, he'd known she was a victim. He had to save her. Blah, blah. He'd heard the story before. A million times. Just another night's work for a hunter. But when the vamp wrenched her against him, when the guy wrapped his fingers around her throat and put his fangs far too close to her, Harrison actually looked at the toy.

Then he couldn't look anywhere else.

Like vamps, he could see perfectly in the dark. One of his enhancements. So he saw her dark and gorgeous eyes. The darkest and deepest eyes he'd ever seen in his life. Her heart-shaped face was absolutely perfect with smooth, creamy skin. Her lips were full, red, and slick. Her blonde hair was a wild and gorgeous tangle around her face. And her body…his gaze drifted down. Damn. Talk about a temptation. The dress she wore fit her like a second skin, revealing every single curve and dip in her body —

"Excuse me." Her voice was even sexy. Husky and warm and it wrapped right around him. "Are you going to stare at me all night, or are you *going to save my ass*?"

His lips twitched. She wasn't exactly some terrified damsel and that made her even sexier to him. "I'm going to save your ass." Her very hot ass.

The vamp holding her snarled. He yanked back her head, exposing her throat more. But the woman's gaze never left Harrison's. "Then do it, *please*," she gasped out. "Because I don't want to get bit!"

A vamp's fangs going into her delectable flesh? Not on his watch. Harrison tossed the stake in the air, catching it easily as he stood there and considered his options.

The other two vamps hadn't moved. He figured they were either waiting for the right moment to attack or looking for the perfect moment to flee.

"This doesn't concern you," the vamp holding the woman snapped. "Get out of here!"

Harrison took a step forward and tossed the stake in the air again. A slow-as-you-please toss that sent the stake going end over end before

Harrison caught it in his hand. "I'm a hunter. You're a vampire. Killing you is kinda my job so…" A shrug. "Call me concerned."

The vamp closest to Harrison surged forward.

Harrison threw the stake at him. It sank into the vamp's chest, and the vamp hit the ground.

Two down. Two to go.

Except…

Vamp number three turned and fled. Ah, so he *had* been looking for the perfect moment to run. Harrison watched him go with a shake of his head. "There is always one," he murmured as he retrieved his stake. "One who gets scared and runs."

The woman's breath heaved out.

Harrison advanced so that the weak light from a nearby building would fall on him. He wanted her to see that he was human. Well, mostly. He winked at her. "Consider yourself rescued."

"I will *snap* her neck," the vampire holding her bellowed.

Good thing they were alone in the alley. The guy's voice was sure loud. What had happened to the nights when vamps tried to keep a low profile? Dumbasses like this one made it hard to keep the supernatural world secret.

"If you snap her neck, you lose a meal," Harrison pointed out. "Vamps can't drink from corpses. Bad for the digestion. You need your food fresh." He stalked forward.

The vamp's claws pricked her throat. Drops of blood slid over her skin.

The vamp gave a sharp inhale. "What...? *That scent...*"

Harrison saw the savage hunger flare on the vamp's face. The vamp's fangs barreled for the woman's throat even as she let loose a high and terrified scream.

Harrison grabbed her. Wrenched her away from the vamp. Staked him and spun so that by the time the vamp fell to the ground, Harrison had the woman cradled in his arms. Everything happened in mere seconds. Boom.

And that is how you get shit done.

"You can stop screaming," he told her casually. "Don't worry, I won't bite."

Her screams stopped. Her long lashes lifted, and she stared at him with terror plain to see in her eyes.

Okay, fine, maybe he shouldn't have made the bite joke.

And she *was* bleeding. He eased her away. Tipped up her chin so that he could take a better look. Two drops of blood slid down her elegant throat. "Nothing too bad. You'll live." Which was more than he could say for the vamps on the ground.

Once more, Harrison retrieved his stake. One vamp had gotten away, but he'd be catching the guy soon. Time to get hunting. "Stay out of dark alleys. Consider carrying a wooden stake in your purse. And have a nice night." He took a step toward the mouth of the alley —

She jumped into his path. "You can't leave me."

He lifted a brow.

"I need you, Harrison. I need —"

Whoa. Hold up. His shoulders stiffened. "How do you know my name?"

She licked her lips. Looked even sexier. She was about a head shorter than he was, even with those high and tempting heels that she wore. There were a few nightclubs on the street. He figured she must have been in one earlier that night. Before she'd wound up in an alley, surrounded by vamps.

"I know a lot about you," she whispered.

Since most folks didn't know about the supernatural world, her response was surprising. Because if you weren't dealing with supernaturals, there was no need to know about *him*. But then again, he realized she hadn't seemed particularly shocked to find vamps surrounding her. She'd been scared, yes, but not shocked.

He was still cradling his stake. He shoved it into the holster on his ankle and rose to tower over her once more. "Who are you?"

"My name is Elise Aine."

The name meant nothing to him, but it was pretty. Kinda musical.

"I came to Savannah in order to find you," Elise continued in her husky, sexy voice.

If he'd had more time, he could have really appreciated that voice. And her. But work waited. "You're still bleeding." His gaze was on her neck. "You need to go and get those two scrapes cleaned up." He brushed around her.

"I *need* a hunter." Her hand flew out and clamped around his arm.

Heat licked through his body. A surge of awareness that he'd actually felt when he'd first grabbed her moments before. He'd shoved that awareness away, though, because he knew it sure as hell wasn't the time or the place for that kind of reaction.

He glanced down at her hand. Blood-red fingernails. Delicate fingers. "And just how do you know about hunters?"

"I know because I've *had* to learn. This isn't the first time I've been targeted. Monsters are coming after me, one right after the other. They won't stop. It's like—like they're drawn to me. No matter where I go or what I do, they find me."

That was new. He turned toward her, cocking his head, as curiosity stirred within him.

"I went to see a voodoo priestess in New Orleans." Her words came faster as her hold tightened on him. "She told me that I needed a protector. A hunter. Someone who was born to fight the monsters."

Yeah, that was him all right. Born to kill. And raise some hell along the way.

Hunters weren't just your Average Joes who woke up, realized that paranormals were real, and started staking things. Hunters — *real* hunters — were born to the life. Born with enhancements that made them into perfect predators. After all, if you were going to hunt vampires, werewolves, and demons, you had to be on an equal playing field.

Hunters had enhanced strength and speed. Their senses were far more powerful than those of normal humans. And when it came to tracking prey, no one was better.

Hunters were nature's way of balancing the scales of justice. Monsters had to be stopped. Hunters were given the job. End of story.

"The priestess said I needed *you*."

Great. He had a sinking suspicion he knew exactly which priestess she was talking about. You save one old lady from a loup garou, and she tells the world about you because you stopped a big, bad wanna-be wolf. Someone needed to stop oversharing. "Listen, hate to shatter your plans, but I'm not for hire. Consider tonight's save a pro bono effort on my part, and, like I told you before, keep that hot ass out of alleys."

Her gorgeous eyes narrowed. "You are *not* what I thought."

"I know, I'm even better."

Her lips parted, then after a shocked moment, her mouth snapped closed. She seemed to struggle for words before blurting, "I am in trouble! I need help!"

"Then go to the cops. They help people for a living. Or so I've heard." He glanced pointedly at her hand. Still on his arm. "Now, I have a vamp to hunt so..."

"Humans can't help me. They'll just get killed." She brought her body closer to his. Her scent teased him. She smelled delicious. Hell, no wonder the vamps had wanted to take a bite. She was like a mix of strawberries and vanilla. Lush and sweet.

Her gaze held his. That dark gaze...chocolate eyes with hints of gold around her pupils. Eyes that seemed to be looking right through him.

"I will pay you *any* price," Elise promised him softly. "If you don't help me, I'm dead. It's as simple as that."

He couldn't look away. When a beautiful woman brushed her body against his, when she offered to pay *anything,* was he really going to be dumb enough to tell her to move so he could walk away?

He...didn't want to walk away. In fact, Harrison found himself leaning toward her. Toward those red lips and her sexy, sinful body so that he —

He locked his arms around her shoulders and pushed her back, moving in a quick lunge so that her shoulders hit the brick wall of the alley and the front of her body pressed to his. "Who are you, lady?"

"I-I told you, my name is Elise —"

"Maybe I should say...*what* are you? Because a normal woman wouldn't just carry on a sweet-as-you-please conversation while three vamps were dead at her feet."

Her gaze darted away from his, then back. "How...would a normal woman react?" She seemed to be puzzling this out. He noticed she hadn't denied not being human.

"There would be more screaming," he assured her bluntly. "A lot of it."

"I *did* scream earlier. Didn't you hear me? I-I thought you even told me to stop screaming."

"Normal humans would have been running. Not stopping for a chit-chat in the dark. A normal human woman would be hauling ass away from the dead as fast as she could."

"But I can't run. Have you seen these heels?" She blinked, all innocence.

No one was innocent.

"Maybe a normal human would have fainted," he mused. "That's a typical response. I've seen it from men and women. They just pass right on out and hit the ground."

Elise gave a quick, negative shake of her head. "The alley is filthy. No way do I want to faint and fall on this ground. That just screams unsanitary."

Damn, but she was surprising. Reluctantly, his lips quirked. "I'd catch you if you fell."

Her eyes flared. "Promise?" She reached for him.

He caught her hands and pinned them against the bricks. "You didn't tell me *what* you are."

"Yes, I did." Her voice stroked over him. "I'm a woman in trouble. The paranormals are hunting me. They want to take me out. If you leave me in this alley, I might be dead by dawn."

His hold tightened. Her wrists seemed far too breakable as his fingers encircled them.

"I'm lucky to still be alive. My luck got me to Savannah. The priestess said to look for you in the dark, so I started —"

"Wandering into any dark alleys you could find?"

She nodded.

Shit. Was she serious?

Elise sighed. "The vamps found me before you did."

Yeah, he'd noticed.

"But then you appeared just in time. You saved me."

His nostrils flared. Her delectable scent was making him almost drunk. But…this wasn't just about inhaling her scent.

Another hunter bonus — he could smell lies.

So far, she'd been telling him the truth. *That* was why he hadn't left her. He wasn't heartless enough to leave a woman to die.

"I told you, I'll pay any price," Elise assured him in her breathy voice. The voice that stroked over his skin. "I need your protection. *Please*. I will do *anything*."

Oh, the images that came to mind right then. Apparently, he *was* pretty heartless. And horny.

But he wasn't a total dick. Yet.

"All right. I have a survival game plan for you. You ready for it?"

She nodded eagerly.

"Great. How about you stop lurking in dark alleys and offering yourself up as vamp bait? That's a good step one," he told her. "Step two would be to get your ass back home—wherever home is—and maybe pick up some nice, safe hobbies. You know, the kind that don't involve you being vamp bait."

Her delicate jaw hardened. "*First*, you obviously have an obsession with my ass. Nice to know."

His lips twitched. She was so…unexpected.

"*Two*, I don't have a home, at least, not one right now. I'm on my own for the foreseeable future. If I don't get a protector, I'm dead. How many times and in how many ways do I have to tell you this?"

She wasn't lying. Her scent hadn't altered at all. Hell. Harrison didn't know what to do with her. "I think you have me confused with someone else."

"You're a *hunter*." A pause. "You hunt monsters, don't you?" She waited, all expectant-like. Even biting her lower lip.

"Yeah, I'm a hunter."

Her eyelids flickered. He thought she started to smile.

But she seemed to catch herself.

"And you're right. I do hunt monsters. That's my job. I *don't* offer myself as a bodyguard to humans. Not part of my gig. So…while it's been fun…" Actually, talking with her *had* been fun. How screwed up was he? "I have places to go and monsters to kill. You know the drill."

"I-I—"

He thought about kissing her. Her lips were parted, and he wanted to taste her *so* badly in that moment. So badly that he could feel his careful control cracking. That crack sent alarm splintering through him.

Back away, now! An internal roar.

He backed away.

Leave her.

Yeah, that would be his survival instinct talking. The little voice that popped into his head whenever shit was about to get bad.

Sure, the sexy woman before him didn't look bad. She looked gorgeous. Tempting. A straight-up fantasy in those heels and that curve-hugging dress. But…

He shouldn't want her so much. Shouldn't be aching so desperately for someone he just met. He *never* responded that way to *anyone.* "You're still bleeding. Get that checked out." He whirled away. Headed for the alley's mouth once more.

"You are leaving me?" Her angry shriek.

He kept walking.

"You are *such* an asshole! I'm going to die, and you don't care?"

One foot in front of the other. *Keep walking.*

"You're leaving me with *dead* vampires? How can you do this? I thought you were going to save me!"

"I did." He tossed a wave over his shoulder. "You're welcome."

"Ugh! You can't just —"

He put on a burst of speed and shot out of the alley. He could move just as fast as vampires, and he knew that — to the woman in the alley — it might even look as if he'd simply vanished. He kept up his fast speed until he reached the corner and stopped near his waiting motorcycle. His breath heaved in and out. He could still smell her scent. His fingers lifted. They were shaking, just a little.

What in the hell?

Since when had he ever wanted a woman so badly that he started to *shake* from need?

***

Elise Aine put her hands on her hips and glared at the now empty mouth of the alley.

"That went well," a male voice announced from behind her.

"Fuck off," Elise snapped without looking back. There was no point in looking back. No one was there—just a brick wall. A wall and lots of shadows.

"You *found* the hunter, my lady," the voice continued. "That's a win."

"He *left* me in the alley." She stepped forward and nearly tripped on a vamp. Furious, she kicked him. Then nearly broke her toe because staked vamps were hard as stone. "Ow!"

The disembodied voice immediately wanted to know, "What's wrong?"

"I am alone in a stinking alley, talking to a dumbass who isn't *here,* and I am miserably, weakly *human!*" She was so angry that she wanted to scream. Instead, she started leaking. Tears. Elise swiped an angry hand over her cheek. She had never cried, not until a week ago. That was when her banishment had started. She'd never cried, never been weak. Never needed anyone else's help or protection. *Until I was banished.* In fact, the very idea that someone would need to protect her—*her!*—would have been insulting.

"Go after him."

Elise rolled her eyes. "Of course, I'm going after him. It's not like I have a choice." At least she knew Harrison was in the city. That was a starting point.

"Good. Excellent. He will see the error of his ways and fall at your feet."

She glanced down at her heels. Her filthy, now broken heels. Her nose scrunched. "I'm thinking that's going to be a no."

"My lady?"

"Stop spying on me. I've got this." Such a lie. Elise was lost and desperate, and she *hated* for anyone to see her crying.

"I'm not spying!" Now he was all offended. "I'm tied to you, you know that. I'm your loyal—"

"Go get laid or something okay? *I've got this.* Stop peeking at me through mirrors and shadows." She stomped forward, moving on her broken heels and then just giving up on them and tossing them away.

At the mouth of the alley, Elise paused and glanced back. So...were the dead vamps just going to be left there? Or was there some sort of hunter clean-up crew that would arrive?

Yet even as she looked back, Elise felt the wind blow against her. Thunder rumbled in the distance. The wind picked up, and it...it hit the vamps. Only the stone seemed to fade, no, to thin. To become...ash? Or something very like ash as the stone faded away and the would-be ash blew in the wind. It blew and blew, until nothing was left.

Well, how about that? She'd never actually seen what became of a vamp's remains. Sure, she'd tangled with plenty of vamps in her time, but when it came to body disposal, Elise didn't tend to get her hands dirty. She had people for that.

She turned around, stepped forward —

And tripped on her dress. She fell face-first onto the dirty, stinking ground, and her left hand slammed into some sort of goo — the sort that she didn't want to think about too much.

For a moment, she just remained there, all prone and fucked up, but...

Then she rose. Straightened her spine. Lifted her chin. Her hand swiped over the side of the dress as she wiped away that wretched goo. One deep breath, and she headed down the street.

A catcall followed her as she ambled along the pavement.

She ignored the call. Harrison Key *was* her agenda, but, unfortunately, the hunter had left her. But...was he still in the area? Had he gone after the vamp who'd gotten away? If so, then perhaps Harrison would be close enough to come to her aid again.

Another cat call.

This one was closer.

She knew why, of course. Elise was being hunted. She hadn't lied about that unfortunate situation to Harrison. She hadn't lied about anything. She *couldn't* lie.

Monsters were coming for her. Monsters were *drawn* to her right now. If they caught her scent, they'd be pulled to her. Moths to the flame. She was burning bright.

Elise saw a club up ahead. She hoped the fact that she didn't have shoes wouldn't stop her from gaining entrance. She pasted a bright smile on her face even though Elise knew she probably looked like warm hell.

The bouncer's nose twitched —

Oh, no, he's going to stop me —

The bouncer waved her past. "Go on in, lady. Bet you'll find a real good time waiting."

Well, that was nice. After her day — and night — Elise could certainly use a good time. She headed into the club. Lights were flashing. Bodies were gyrating. Music pounded. Oh, it seemed like everyone there was having a good time. Her body began to sway. Her bare toes curled against the cold floor.

And a hard hand grabbed her wrist. She was jerked around and pulled up against the body of —

Werewolf. He's a freaking werewolf. His eyes are a dead giveaway. Golden, feral eyes stared back at her.

"Hey, sweet thing." He grinned at her, flashing teeth that were a little too sharp. "Thanks for walking straight into my den."

Shit. She'd *walked* into a werewolf den? No wonder the bouncer had been all eager to let her inside. But he'd been wrong…being werewolf prey did *not* make for a good time.

The werewolf ran his fingers — tipped with claws — down her arm. "I am going to have so much fun with you." He leaned closer. Put his mouth to her ear. "I know what you are," he whispered.

Oh, really? Elise lifted her left hand. Slid it over his chest. "I know what you are, too."

He backed up a little and smiled down at her. Such a wolfish grin. He thought he was the big, bad predator.

He thought wrong.

Her right hand drove a knife into his stomach.

He howled.

"Silver, asshole," Elise spit out. "Bet that stings like a mother, huh?" Smoke rose from the wound.

Everyone turned to gape at them as the guy howled and howled in pain. Crap. Elise spun and ran. The crowd was made of mostly humans, but if the place was really a werewolf den, the pack would be there, too. When she caught a few growls and angry snarls, Elise glanced over her shoulder.

Oh, damn. They were charging for her. Three werewolves with glowing, golden eyes. They were moving fast, too. Way too fast and she only had the one knife and —

Oof!

All of the breath was knocked from her as she slammed into a brick wall.

She staggered back and would have fallen —

Not a brick wall. Just felt like one.

Harrison smirked at her. A stupid, oddly sexy smirk. "I can't even leave you alone for five minutes before you find trouble?"

"Trouble..." *Heaving breath.* "Found me." That was part of her curse at the moment. It was also why — she suspected — he was back. "Help?" Another heaving breath.

He lifted one dark brow. His handsome face — truly, she hadn't expected him to be so good-looking — didn't show a hint of concern. That face of his was all hand-crafted perfection. A square and strong jaw. Killer cheekbones. High forehead. Straight blade of a nose. His hair was thick but short, and shoved back as if by careless fingers. And his eyes — those bright, bright blue eyes of his glittered with...

Amusement?

What an ass. Did he want her to beg? It was completely alien to her, so very foreign, but she gritted her teeth and managed, "Please?"

Fast as a blink, he'd yanked her behind him. Since he was very muscled — *awesomely so* — and very tall — *had to be about six-foot-two or three* — she appreciated him being between her and danger. He shielded her with his body as she stood on her toes and craned to see around him.

The charging werewolves halted.

"Hunter," one rasped.

"It's great to be recognized by fans," Harrison replied. "Thanks."

"*Get...out!*"

Uh, oh. That bellow had come from the werewolf she'd stabbed. He was lumbering toward them, holding his hand over his bleeding gut, and sending her a look that could totally kill.

"Glad to leave," Harrison inclined his head. "We'll just—"

"*She* stays."

The music wasn't playing any longer. No gyrating bodies. The humans were gaping, and Elise was afraid the werewolves were about ten seconds away from full-on shifting.

"I don't...um, I choose not to stay," Elise called out, voice too sharp. "I'm leaving with him. He's with me. I'm with him. We're totally together."

Harrison swung his head toward her.

She smiled at him. "We *are* together." It would help her out so much if he would just *say* those three little words back.

"Is this true?" The wounded werewolf's disbelief was clear. "You're with *her?*"

Elise held her breath. All she needed Harrison to say in order to seal the deal, so to speak, was—

"No, I'm not with her."

Sonofabitch. Was he just trying to make things extra hard for her?

Elise caught the werewolf's grin. "If she's not yours, then she doesn't leave. She stepped into my den. She *stays*." He lunged forward.

Harrison caught him and wrapped one hand around the werewolf's throat. "You have a crowd of humans watching you. Have you lost your mind?"

The werewolf's eyes glowed ever brighter. "Give...her—"

"You're not getting her. You're not touching her."

Elise held her breath. *Come on, Harrison. Say it. Just say—*

"We're together," Harrison fired out. "As far as you and any other monster is concerned, she's off-limits, got it? So keep your paws, your claws, and everything else away from her."

The wolves backed up.

"Damn straight," Elise heard herself crow. She couldn't help it. She'd just scored a major win. "You back up when a hunter is in town."

Harrison looked over and frowned at her. "Are you...quite sane?"

Some might debate the issue, but she just went with... "Yes."

He nodded. Then he glanced at the werewolves. Voice low, he growled, "I'm not killing you because there are humans around. Consider yourself very lucky, Gustave."

Gustave? That name was vaguely familiar. It nagged at her mind.

The bleeding werewolf narrowed his eyes. "You're a fucking *fool*, hunter. You picked the wrong side."

"Yeah, well, any side you aren't on feels *right* to me."

Oh, damn. The name clicked for her. Gustave Etienne. He was an ancient werewolf. One of the strongest out there. And, goody, it appeared he was her new sworn enemy. No wonder he'd known what she was the minute she walked up to him. He'd met others like her before.

She needed the wolf to shut the hell up before he said too much. Elise slithered closer to Harrison and wrapped an arm around him.

He immediately stiffened and his blue eyes swung back to her. "What are you doing?"

"Hugging you?" It felt like that was what she was doing. "We need to leave. Now."

Harrison grunted. Grunted — at *her*. Had she picked a winner or what?

She tugged on him.

He wrapped an arm around her. His arm was strong and warm and when he touched her, a little tremor shook her body. *Oh, hello, unexpected treat.* She'd felt a similar tremor when they'd been back in the alley. Her response to the hunter was unexpected, but not unwelcome.

Especially since…

We're together.

She had to stop herself from actually bouncing with glee, but a little happy hum did escape her.

"Are you humming?" Harrison asked with a foreboding frown.

Shit. She hummed when she was happy. "Um…let's go. They look hungry."

Mostly…Gustave looked hungry, and his hungry gaze centered on her.

"I would have taken the job," Gustave announced.

The job?

"We could have been on the same side," he told her. "Now you've made us enemies."

Elise winced. "Was it the silver knife to the stomach? Because, in my defense, I could've aimed for your heart. I was being nice."

He blinked.

"You're welcome." Once more, she tugged on Harrison's arm. "Let's go." He didn't move. The guy was like a giant stone statue.

His bright glare was on the werewolves. His body was tense and battle-ready as he snarled, "Follow us, and you're dead."

Oh, she liked that warning. "Yeah." Elise gave a hard nod. "Stone-cold dead."

Gustave laughed. "You're outnumbered, hunter. Have you looked around?"

"Sure have. Saw all the humans. That's why I haven't already put silver bullets into all of your werewolf hearts. Because I could. I could fire them before you even shift."

Sweat appeared on Gustave's brow.

"I didn't come to kill you tonight. Word in hunting circles was that you were being peaceful. That you kept your hands off humans." Harrison shook his head. "Then I find you going after *her*."

Gustave's slightly thin and beast-like face purpled with fury. "She attacked *me*. I haven't done anything to her."

Okay. He was being truthful. "He's a werewolf," Elise whispered in what she hoped was the tiniest, most terrified voice in the world. "I thought he was going to eat me."

Gustave made a choking noise.

But Harrison—he stiffened. "Come near her again, and you're dead."

"I've done nothing to—"

"You've been warned." He turned away. Kept a tight hold on Elise.

She hurried to keep up with him. She stumbled. Dammit. This whole walking thing was *hard*. Especially since she'd only started walking around fairly recently. Until then, she'd used a whole other method of transport. Her feet were hurting and bruised and—

She tripped. Over nothing.

She would have gone smacking down face-first again, but Harrison caught her. He lifted her into his arms and frowned at her. The guy seemed to frown a whole lot.

"What is your deal?" Harrison demanded.

Her lips parted.

Before she could reply, his gaze dropped to her feet. Her bare feet. He stared at her wiggling toes an oddly long time as he held her and they just kind of stood in the werewolf den.

"Ahem." Elise cleared her throat, and his gaze flew back up to hers. "We were making our getaway."

"Where in the hell are your shoes?"

"Back in the alley?" She considered this. "Probably covered with vampire ash."

He cursed, but started walking again, so she considered that movement as a win. Right before they slipped out of the door, Elise looked over Harrison's ever-so-broad shoulder and gave a little wave to the werewolves who were glaring after her.

Very clearly, she saw Gustave mouth, "You're dead."

Not yet, she wasn't. In fact, not only was she not dead...

But, because she'd gotten her big, bad hunter to say the most precious words in the whole world...

We're together.

Well, she was now *married.* As per the customs of her people. With that sweet, sweet bonding, the odds of her continued survival had improved dramatically.

Unfortunately, though, her hunter didn't realize he was her husband. She'd be sure to tell him...eventually.

But first, there was the little matter of...*staying alive.*

CHAPTER TWO

"It is so sweet of you to carry me. Absolutely chivalrous, and I did not expect this. You are very much more than they say, and I think people have been incredibly wrong *and* rude when they say that you are a cold-blooded, heartless bastard of a man who doesn't care about anyone but himself and who—"

"All right. Ride's over." He plunked Elise down on her feet before she had a chance to reveal any other details about what people said about him. Not like he cared what others thought. Screw them.

She tottered on her feet. Her eyes went huge, and then her hands flew out to grab him—it looked like it was either grab him or fall.

Her upper body smashed into him as her hands clamped around his arms.

Harrison shook his head. "Seriously, are you hurt? Is it your legs? Your feet? Something I should know about?"

"Walking is…difficult."

No shit. The woman kept tripping. He knew because…maybe he'd seen her fall in the alley.

Maybe he'd gone back to check on her. Just —
hell, why had he gone back again? Harrison
wasn't sure. He'd just done it, dammit. He'd gone
back to the alley. He'd followed her as she made
her trek down the street, and he'd tailed her into
the club.

"I'm used to a different method of
transportation, but I'm all good now." She stared
up at him. All dark eyes. Sweet scent. Seductive
curves.

"You're good," he repeated.

"Um..."

"If you're good, then do you want to get off
me?"

"No. I like being on you."

His dick was already up. Being so close to
her, getting turned on had been a fast and instant
reaction, but at her words...

*Yeah, the zipper just left an impression on my
dick.* Because he was rock hard and aching for her.
So big and ready that if she glanced down, there
would be no missing his current situation. Hell,
she probably *felt* his reaction. He cleared his
throat. "Don't say things like that."

"Why not?" Elise seemed genuinely curious.
"I like you. You're strong. You're warm. And you
carried me when my feet didn't work."

Her feet. Her *bare* feet. Maybe that was why
she'd fallen — because she wasn't wearing shoes
and the pavement could be uneven?

Once more, he scooped her up. They were near his motorcycle, so he hurried forward and sat her on the seat.

She gave him a sunny smile.

He blinked. Harrison had zero clue what to do with her.

So…he knelt in front of her. He reached for her left foot.

"Oh, is this some sort of foreplay? I bet it is." Her foot did a little jiggle. "I like it."

His fingers slid over her foot. First around her ankle. Then up the sole of her foot.

She shivered.

"Are you drunk?" He didn't smell alcohol on her. But… "High?"

"No." Elise bit her lower lip. "Is it *supposed* to turn me on this much when you caress my foot? Because it does."

His nostrils flared. *Not a lie.* "Who are you?"

"Elise. I told you that." Her head cocked to the right. "Are you going to rub my other foot? I'd like that."

"I'm not rubbing your feet." He rubbed her foot. Dammit. She had *cute* feet. Dirty feet, but cute. "I'm looking for injuries." He reached for her other foot. Stroked.

Saw her sigh. No, *felt* her sigh. A blissful, pleasure-filled sigh.

The woman liked having her feet rubbed.

Stay focused. "No cuts. Your feet don't seem to have any broken bones." He let go of her and rose.

What in the hell should I do with her? "If I let you go, are you going to wind up facing off with another paranormal tonight?"

"Probably." A nod. "I told you, the paranormals are drawn to me—"

"You stabbed Gustave."

"He grabbed me." Her words tumbled out as she added, "He was a werewolf! His eyes were glowing, and he was baring his fangs. I panicked!"

"Why are the paranormals drawn to you?"

She looked around the street. Cars whizzed past. A couple made out near the bar on the right. "Could we go somewhere else and talk about this? Somewhere, that is say, not in the open?"

"I can drop you off at your hotel." Harrison made the offer grudgingly. Very, very grudgingly.

Her gaze swung back to him. "Couldn't we just go back to your place?"

His heart stopped. Then raced. Then he decided to be blunt. "I take women back to my place only if we're planning to fuck."

Harrison saw her swallow before she asked, "Is that on tonight's agenda?"

Was that on...

He backed up a step. "You're offering to sleep with me...if—what? I protect you?"

"No, I'm offering to sleep with you because you're really sexy and I like you. And...why are you staring at me like I have two heads?" She lifted up a hand and touched her *one* head. "Surely you've heard of one-night stands before? People hook up all the time. It's a thing humans do."

There was something about the way she'd just worded that statement…"*It's a thing humans do.*" Now he was curious. And on high alert. "You never answered my question before."

"You've had so many questions for me." She fiddled with one of the handlebars. "Can you be more specific?"

"*What* are you?"

Her hand dropped away from the handlebar. "I can see why you don't have a lot of one-night stand experience. You're not very charming. Women like charming men."

"I didn't say I don't have experience."

She perked up. "Great. This should be fun then. For a minute, you had me worried that the sex would be bad."

Bad? What in the —

"The werewolves are walking up behind you," Elise whispered. "Does that mean you have to kill them now?"

He spun around. He'd been so distracted by *her* and her hot level of *crazy* that he hadn't even realized the werewolves were there.

But when they saw him, the three wolves — the underlings, no sign of Gustave — lowered their heads in submission. They turned and headed the other way.

CYNTHIA EDEN 36

"So…you don't just kill paranormals at will?" Her voice was curious and a bit too loud now. "That's good to know. Because the word I'd heard was that you pretty much went after any paranormal that breathed."

He had to get her out of there. He turned toward her once more. "Scoot back."

Her lips curved down. A sexy pout. "Why can't I drive?"

Seriously? "Because you seem to be having trouble walking, much less driving, so I don't know that I trust you with my baby."

She patted the handlebar again. "This is your baby?"

"Yes." And she was a bad bitch that he adored.

"Fine. I guess you should drive since I've never actually ridden on a motorcycle before."

She'd never *ridden* on one? And hell, yes, he should be driving. "Scoot. Back."

She scooted back. He slid in front of her. "You should hold—"

Her arms locked around him. Squeezed tightly. Her body pressed to his so that he could feel oh, so much of her.

"That good?" Elise wanted to know.

Better than good. "Fabulous," Harrison growled. Just fucking fabulous. The motorcycle snarled to life, and he shot them away from the curb.

***

"This is where you live?"

The lady didn't sound overly impressed. Not surprising considering the fact that, from the outside, it looked like his house was a breath away from collapse. "Home sweet home," Harrison muttered as he kicked down the stand for the bike and killed the engine.

She hopped off the motorcycle and glanced around the garage. "I'm sure that the place is great on the inside. You know, once you get to the actual *house* part."

He climbed off the bike and lowered the garage door. "I wouldn't get my hopes up if I were you."

Her gaze swung back to him. "No?"

"Definitely, no." The place wasn't home, despite his sarcastic comment. It was just where he was currently crashing while he did his job and eliminated the supernatural killers out there. Without glancing to see if she followed him — because, come on, the woman hadn't exactly been trying to run from him so Harrison knew she'd follow — he headed for the door. He unlocked it, stepped into the small laundry room, and reset his alarm system.

"Are there spirits here?" Her voice was low and all whispery. It also came from directly behind him.

Harrison laughed. "No, they're all gone." Sure, the place *did* look like a haunted house, though. An old Victorian that had been built back in the early 1900s, the house was huge and sprawling and in total disrepair. The porch in the front was sagging and littered with holes in the floor. The columns near the entrance were broken. Windows had been covered with plywood. The yard was totally overgrown, and the vegetation was doing its best to retake the house.

The interior was no better. As he headed for the kitchen, he realized why she'd asked about the ghosts. Cobwebs covered one hell of a lot. Sheets were over what furniture remained in the house. He just hadn't gotten around to uncovering those things. He'd used the kitchen and the bed upstairs and that was pretty much it.

"Where is your staff?" She gave a quick spin as her horrified gaze took in everything. "Your servants?"

He laughed again. "You are freaking hilarious."

She rounded on him. "I am dead serious."

She looked it, too. Another laugh. He couldn't remember ever laughing so hard. When he managed to control himself, Harrison told her, "I gave them the night off."

"Call them back. Cancel the night off. You *need* them."

She hadn't gotten his joke, and he wasn't sure he got her. Harrison headed for the fridge and yanked open the door. Sure, the rest of the house might look like shit, but his fridge was well stocked. He grabbed a beer and popped the top. Harrison saluted her with the bottle. "There is no staff. There's no one else here. There's just me and there's you."

She wrapped her arms around her middle. "Why do you live this way?"

"Because I'm a hunter. Because I drift into town when I'm tracking down monsters. Hunters have a chain of safe houses that we all use. In and out, staying only as long as necessary. There *is* no home for us. There's just the job. So you don't exactly get comfortable and hang up family pictures. You sleep. You eat. You kill. Then you move the hell on." He drained the beer and slapped it down on the counter.

"That is so sad." She took a few quick steps toward him. "I had no idea. Is that the way you've always lived?"

Shit. Now the most gorgeous woman he'd ever seen was staring at him with *pity* in her eyes. Great. His night was rock star stellar. "Hunters are born to the life." He didn't need or want pity. "It is what it is."

Her eyelids flickered. "Are you sure?"

"Yeah, pretty damn sure. My dad was a hunter. His dad before him. I come from a long line of supernatural ass kickers."

Her gaze slid away. "Where is your father now?" She was peering around as if she expected him to pop up from behind one of the sheet-covered pieces of furniture.

"Last I heard, he's doing a job in Dallas. We don't work together. I prefer to work alone."

Her shoulders sagged a little. Huh. Was that relief? Sure looked like it to him. He didn't mention the fact that after the Dallas job was complete, Jason Key was supposed to be heading to Savannah. Not that Harrison cared. He didn't exactly get the warm and fuzzies where his old man was concerned.

Jason had raised him to be hard, to be brutal, and to form as few connections as possible in this world.

"So…" She rocked forward onto the balls of her bare feet. Her hands lifted and gestured toward him. "Are we going to do this?"

"This?" Now what was she talking about?

A quick, eager nod. "Yes. *This*. You said the only reason you brought a woman back to your place was to fuck."

True, he had said that.

Her hands spread wide. "I'm here."

His lips twitched. "You are."

Another rock forward. "So are we going to do it here? Or is there possibly a cleaner room that we could move to?"

She still wanted to have sex with him. The woman was walking perfection — well, except for when she kept tripping. She could bat those long lashes of hers and probably have any human male she wanted groveling at her feet. Instead, she'd picked him. She'd ridden home on his loud-ass bike, she'd come into the house that even he referred to as the "pit of hell" and she was still up for bedroom games?

Oh, yes, he wanted to take her up on the offer, but he wasn't a dumbass. He smiled, though. "Sure, let's go upstairs."

Her eyes flared. She gave a happy little jump. He could have even sworn that she hummed. Hummed, for God's sake.

Then she was rushing ahead of him and climbing the spiral staircase. He was sure that staircase had been a thing to behold back in the day, but now, it mostly resembled a death trap. And with her tripping rate...hell, he hurried up to — *literally* — catch her as she stumbled mid-way up.

His arms slid under her when her feet did a weird little shuffle. She fell right back against him.

"Got you," he rasped, his lips brushing her ear.

A shiver slid over her. Her head turned. "Thank you. I-I seem to just be having a little trouble — "

"Because you're used to a different method of transportation." Like that wasn't a giant red flag. Who did she think she was kidding? He scooped her into his arms, though, so she wouldn't break her neck on the way up those stairs. A neck that still sported dried blood. The sight of the wound on her throat made a hard anger stir in him.

Vamps were sadistic bastards. They'd rip their prey apart and laugh while their victims screamed.

So he'd killed them and laughed, too. He'd killed so many vamps over the years that he'd lost count.

"I'm not normally clumsy." Her hands wrapped around his neck. She snuggled closer, like he was some kind of friggin' teddy bear and not a bloodthirsty hunter. "But it's been a really long night. A long day. A long *week*. And I'm not myself."

Everything she said had the feel of truth. He almost hesitated and changed his plans for her.

Almost.

But he was a hunter first and foremost, and he wasn't about to be fooled by a pretty face and a hot body.

He took her into the bedroom. Lowered her next to the bed.

Correction...he wasn't going to be fooled by a *very* hot body.

Harrison stepped back. "I'm going to get something for your throat."

"That's nice of you." She smiled at him.

Another correction...Elise wasn't just pretty. She was drop-dead gorgeous. So pretty that it was almost unnatural. *Probably because her beauty is unnatural. It's a trick.*

She nodded approvingly. "This room is much better than the area downstairs. I can actually see your furniture."

Yes, it was rather hard to miss the massive, brass bed and the tousled covers in the middle of the room. Light spilled onto the bed, coming from the lamp on his nightstand. A leather chair sat to the right of the bed. A heavy, cherry dresser was to the left. A fireplace waited in the far-left corner of the room. An old, wood-burning fireplace. He'd put some wood in there earlier, and for a moment, he had a quick flash of that fire burning, crackling, and Elise naked in his bed.

His dick jerked eagerly as if to say...*Yes, wonderful plan. Let's go with that.*

But he ignored his dick, or tried to. "Make yourself comfortable." He cleared his throat because it sounded like he was growling and not talking. "I'll be right back."

Her little hum followed him, and Harrison glanced back. She was twisting around and looking at everything in the room. He *almost* smiled.

Instead, he stalked into the bathroom. Got her a wet cloth for her neck. Swiped a few other supplies from the pack he kept in there. Then he returned to her. He took two fast steps into the bedroom —

"Holy shit."

She smiled at him.

He took in the stellar view before him. "You took off your dress."

Elise blinked. "You told me to get comfortable."

That wasn't the same as saying get naked. And, luckily, she wasn't completely naked. She'd ditched the dress and now stood beside the bed wearing a black bra and matching panties. No lace for her—looked like satin or silk or one of those soft and delicate things. Her bra pushed up her breasts, doing that Victoria's Secret kind of magic and making every bit of moisture draw up in his mouth. As for her panties, they were…hell, what was the term? He'd seen a damn commercial on TV about them. Boy shorts. Hip huggers? Who the fuck knew? He couldn't remember, not right then. All he could do was stare at her. He hadn't thought those panties were sexy in the commercial. On her, though, hell, yes, they were sexy. Sexy as—

She walked toward him. "We did come here to make love, didn't we?"

"You are so blunt."

"Is that bad? Did I say something wrong?"

"No." Again, he was growling. His right hand lifted the cloth and pressed it carefully—damn, almost tenderly—to her throat. "You didn't say anything wrong."

"You're taking care of me." She seemed shocked. Her smile was sunny and quick. "Thank you."

"It doesn't mean anything. I just don't like staring at blood."

"But you're a hunter. Blood is your thing."

He tossed the cloth aside. "Blood is a *vampire's* thing. Not mine." His head cocked as he studied her. "And while we're talking about hunters, just how much do you know about me?"

"Not enough."

But he was wagering she knew a whole lot more about him than he knew about her. Which brought him to his next move... "Really sorry about this..."

"About what?"

His right hand flew up and he splashed water onto her chest and the front of her bra.

She blinked. Looked down. "Is this more foreplay? Some sort of really weird, hunter foreplay?"

"No, it's holy water."

She wiped away the droplets. "You thought I was possessed? Or like...what? A demon?" Elise shook her head. "If that's what you believed, why not just put the holy water on the cloth you were using to clean my neck? Why splash me?"

Because he'd wanted to distract her with the splash. And she *was* distracted. She was looking down, wiping away the water, not focusing on him at all and—

He slipped the iron chain around her throat.

She screamed. Yeah, he'd rather been expecting that reaction. What he *hadn't* expected? The fast and furious kick to his groin. *Sonofabitch.* She had one hell of a kick.

CHAPTER THREE

"I am *not* into this!" Elise yelled as she yanked the chain off her neck. Harrison had doubled over in front of her after she'd delivered the kick to his groin. "No. Hard no. *Hard.* So hard!" She stormed for the door. "You don't put a chain around a woman's neck. You don't do that shit. You don't just—"

"It's iron," he huffed out from behind her. "And I had to test you."

Elise froze. Her back was to him, so Harrison couldn't see her face. She'd already known the small, intricate chain was made of iron. She'd known it was a test when he put the iron against her skin. But she had to play the scene the right way. "Test?" Her voice quivered a bit. The quiver was real because she'd been afraid she wouldn't pass the test.

She had, though. Because, for the moment, anyway, she was wretchedly, weakly human.

That's why I need him. Even if he'd just seriously pissed her off. She could hold a grudge forever, so the man had better watch himself.

"Iron burns most supernaturals."

Elise shot a fast glance over her shoulder. He'd picked up the chain from the floor and was shoving it into a nightstand drawer. Her eyes narrowed on him. "Holy water, iron...what's next? Want to feed me some garlic so you can see that I'm not a vampire? Or maybe you want to stab me with a silver knife to be sure I'm not a werewolf? What else is on tonight's agenda?"

He shut the drawer. "I know you're not a werewolf."

"How do you know that?"

"I can smell the scent of the beast on werewolves. You smell like strawberries and vanilla cream. Sweet and delicious."

Oh. Okay. "What about me being a vamp? How do you know I'm not going to drink your blood?"

He turned away from the night stand. Looked at her.

She was still craning her head as she glanced back at him, so Elise decided to spin around and fully face him. She didn't move closer to him, though, because she was afraid of what Captain Crazy would try next. Her hands clenched at her sides.

"The vamp wanted to drain you in the alley." His voice was low and calm. "They were all desperate for your blood. Vamps don't get desperate for their own kind."

True enough. Vamps didn't think their own blood tasted *fresh* enough. Probably because of the whole being undead thing.

He advanced on her.

She stiffened. "You try something freaky again, and I will kick you so hard in the balls that you can taste—"

"I appreciate the warning." His lips quirked. "You've got one hell of a kick." He stopped in front of her. "I'm not planning anything freaky. I just need to make sure the iron didn't leave a mark."

Because if the iron *had* marked her, then he'd know she was a paranormal.

Her hand flew up and clamped around her neck. She didn't feel anything beneath her fingertips. "My neck has had enough attention for the night, thanks so much."

He lifted a brow. Just one. Kind of quirked it and stared at her. "You want my help with fighting off the paranormals?"

Sadly, yes, she did.

"Then show me your throat. If you're clear, then I will give you my best apology and we can start over."

She didn't drop her hand. "You're going to grovel? Going to beg for my forgiveness on bended knee?"

"Is that what you want?"

"It would be an excellent start." Elise sucked in a deep breath. Her hand fell back to her side.

"Look. Have at me." She bared her throat as she tipped back her head and offered her neck to him. "Then bow before me." *Whoops.* She'd gotten a little overly dramatic there at the end. Her bad. For a minute, she'd slipped back into her old habits.

Back when plenty of people *had* bowed before her. When she'd had a world at her feet. In other words, the good old days. She missed those days. Elise closed her eyes.

He leaned closer to her. She *felt* him lean in. Her nostrils flared as she pulled in his scent. He'd told her that she smelled delicious. He smelled...sensual. Strong. Masculine. Sandalwood. Fresh rain. Such a mix of scents...all her favorites. He smelled like her favorite things, and the more she inhaled, she even caught the scent of...

Fire?

Her lips parted and a little gasp slipped from her just as his fingertips stroked over her throat. "You okay?" His voice was a low, rough rumble.

"Y-yes. Your touch just startled me." Her eyes were still closed. Her body was so sensitive to him. His fingertips were lightly callused and ever so tender as they trailed over her neck. He leaned in even closer, so close that she could feel the light touch of his breath on her skin.

Her nipples tightened. She found herself arching closer to him.

His fingers trailed down her throat. Down over her collarbone.

Oh, right, damn, she was still in her underwear. Because she'd totally misinterpreted the situation and while she'd been thinking of fun, sexy times, he'd been thinking of burning her with iron. *Bastard.*

She licked her lips. Heard the quick inhale he gave. *Uh, huh, because you're not immune to me.* In the paranormal world, no one was ever truly immune. Weaknesses were just carefully hidden. "Am I clear?" Elise asked, voice husky.

His fingers eased down a little more. His callused fingertips skimmed the top of her cleavage.

"Clear." He was all growly and dark.

Her lashes lifted. She stared straight into his gaze. Such a bright, bright blue gaze. It was almost startling to peer into his eyes. Especially right then because that blue stare of his was burning with unmistakable desire.

Figured. Now that he didn't think she was a monster, he was all about the sexing.

She wasn't. They had other matters to attend to, first. "No marks?"

"No."

"So I'm not a monster?"

"Doesn't look that way." His fingers had dropped away from her, but he hadn't moved back. "Want to clue me in as to why the paranormals are after you? If you aren't one of their own, why did both the vamps *and* the wolves decide to make you prey tonight?"

"I'm not answering yet." She tapped her bare foot.

His eyebrows shot up. "Excuse me?"

"I think you forgot something." And her breasts were still all achy, the nipples tight. A knot was in her stomach, and his scent was making her practically light-headed. Her response to Harrison was *not* what she'd planned, but she'd adapt and she'd figure things out. *After* she took care of a few other items on her to-do list.

"What did I forget, Elise?"

Seriously? Did he have memory issues? They had *just* talked about this. "The apology. The grovel. The bowing down before me." She waved her hand regally for him. "You may commence. I am ready."

"Yeah, okay. Sorry I threw holy water at you and slid iron around your throat."

Elise waited.

He shrugged. "But if I had to do it all over again, I would. No way do I let a stranger get close without checking things out first."

She continued to wait.

He frowned at her. "You need to borrow a shirt or something? Are you getting cold? I think I see chill bumps on your skin."

Her teeth ground together. She waved again.

He simply shrugged those strong shoulders of his.

Unacceptable. "That is not a grovel."

"Uh, it's not?"

"No, this is shit. What you need to do is say something like…" She roughed her voice a bit for effect and began, "'Elise, beautiful Elise, I was terribly wrong and horribly inconsiderate. I scared you, I offended you, I damaged the delicate trust we were starting to build…' *That's* the beginning of a good grovel." She pointed to the floor. "You're also not on bended knee. I don't understand. Do you *think* what you gave me was even an apology? It wasn't."

"You know…I mean, you understand that I'm not going to bow, don't you? That was a joke before."

She didn't think it was funny. "One day, you will bow to me." That was a promise and a warning.

Only instead of being properly chastened, his gaze dropped to her body. Down, down ever so slowly, and when he got to her boy shorts — she freaking *loved* those, by the way, so comfy — his gaze brightened even more. Then he licked his lips.

"Maybe I could think of a reason or two to be on my knees before you."

Her heart jerked hard in her chest.

But he stepped back.

A lot of steps. He marched away from her and headed for the closet. A moment later, he was pushing a soft cotton t-shirt into her hands. "We need to talk, and we can't do that when you're in your underwear."

"Why not?"

"Because you're sexy as fuck and my dick is rock hard. I'm a horny bastard, and I can't take my eyes off you."

So many reasons. She pulled the shirt over her head. It carried his scent. She liked that. Elise also liked the way the soft cotton felt against her skin. It was warm. Gentle.

"Tell me why the paranormals are after you."

Her lips twisted. "I'm truly not getting a better apology?"

"I'm *sorry* that I had to test you," Harrison said as he seemingly pushed those words through clenched teeth. "It's the job, and it's who I am. Didn't realize it before? Spoiler alert, I'm a hunter. Not some sweet knight in shining armor who will bow and tell you all the tender things you want to hear. I'm a fighter. A killer. I kick ass and destroy. You want something else? Then I'm not the guy for you."

He was *exactly* the guy for her. In so many ways. "You're the man I want."

His gaze sharpened. "Why?"

"Because I need someone who can kick ass and destroy." Obviously.

"*Why* are the paranormals after you?"

Tread carefully. "Because I've been cursed."

"Who cursed you?"

"Someone bad, of course. Until the next full moon, I'm like some kind of supernatural beacon. All the baddies out there will be drawn to me. Monsters will find me...um, pretty irresistible. They'll want to either kill me, drink me dry — if they're vamps — or..." She coughed. "They'll think I'm really attractive and want to — "

"Fuck you."

"I was going to say have wild sex with me, but yes, we'll go with that." She sucked in a quick breath. "Normal attraction is heightened. It's some kind of moon magic BS. I went from being in the shadows..." *Ha! Literally!* "To being the main game in town. Since I don't want to be killed, I don't want to be drained of my blood, and I'm not in the mood to fuck psychotic monsters, I thought you could help me out."

His brow furrowed. "Yet you were ready to have sex with me..."

Sure, that would be the part he clung to. Elise sighed. "Are *you* a psychotic monster?"

His shoulders stiffened. "I'm a monster hunter. I stop the bad guys."

"And *you're* not bad?"

"I'm not good, if that's what you want to know. But I'm not someone you need to fear. You're human, you're being stalked, so then, yes..." A firm nod. "I'll keep you safe. I'll either find a way to break your curse or I'll stop the freaks coming after you. Either way, you'll be okay."

The surge of relief she felt made her dizzy.

"There is no payment involved," he added, voice a bit stilted. "Don't think there is, all right? It's my job. I protect humans. I'll protect you. Case closed."

No, the case was very much not closed.

But his expression seemed to soften as he stared at her. "This started with the last full moon?"

She nodded.

"That was a week ago. You've been hunted since then?"

She had to wet her dry lips. "The nights are the worst."

"Because monsters always come out at night."

Yes, they did.

He motioned to the bed. "They won't get to you tonight."

Since paranormals had already gotten to her — twice — that night, Elise wasn't so sure she believed him.

"You can sleep in my bed. You'll be safe there." Harrison cleared his throat. "I'll bunk downstairs on the couch. No one will get past me and my security. I swear, you'll be safe."

Safe. Such a foreign concept to her.

"You're swaying on your feet. Get some rest. We'll figure everything out tomorrow." He gave her a curt nod, then skirted around her and headed for the bedroom door.

How interesting. "You can be kind."

He paused. Stiffened a little.

"I mean, I wasn't sure at first, not when you left me in the alley, but then you came back for me. You followed me to the werewolf den, didn't you?"

He didn't look back. "I had a feeling you'd find more trouble."

"You *act* like a tough asshole, but you're not. A heartless hunter wouldn't have come for me in that terrible place. You saved me twice tonight, and now you're giving me shelter." Excitement and hope swirled in her. "Thank you."

But he spun on his heel—a sharp, military-like turn—and faced her. "You're under a misconception. I'm not kind."

"But you saved—"

"My job is to kill monsters. You just told me that you were a monster beacon until the next full moon. I figure you're saving me some effort. I don't have to go out and hunt because all of the big, bad beasts will be coming to you. As they come, I can take them out. You just made my life easier."

Damn. She blinked. "So I'm bait?" That wasn't so exciting. Or flattering.

He nodded. "The best bait I've ever had." A wink. "Get some sleep. And if you need me, scream."

Wonderful. She would scream. Very loudly.

Harrison gave her a long, lingering look before he left her. The door clicked closed behind him.

She stood in the middle of his room. She wore his shirt. She was about to climb into his bed. She had his protection. She should be absolutely thrilled with the developments but…

"Bait?" Elise fumed.

That bastard had no idea who he was dealing with. She wasn't bait. She was freaking royalty. Before she was done with him, he *would* be bowing to her. As would every paranormal in every realm. It was her destiny, after all.

She would make him bow. And she would make him beg. He'd give her the glorious grovel that she deserved.

But for the moment, she was going to crash. Because he'd been right about one thing. She was freaking exhausted. Elise climbed into his bed. A surprisingly comfortable, soft bed. Soft and massive. Easily big enough for two people and the quick flash that she had in her mind — a flash of her and Harrison wrapped up together, naked, his strong body cradling hers as he thrust so deep inside —

Breathe, Elise. Breathe. Her kind was notoriously sensual. Sex was power and strength. Being around Harrison made her a little extra twitchy. The man had resisted her advances that night. Insulting. But also challenging. She did enjoy a challenge. Some days.

Her head hit the pillow. Her eyes closed. She let out a long moan because the mattress felt like heaven after sleeping in the places she'd used for the last week. The street, abandoned houses, that piss-poor excuse for a motel —

"My lady? Is the goal achieved?"

The disembodied voice had her screaming. Then slapping a hand over her mouth. Harrison hadn't heard her cry, had he?

"Uh, my lady?" Now he was impatient.

"Shut up," she whispered. "I'm sleeping."

"No, you're not. You're talking to me. You're obviously not sleeping if you're talking to — "

"Leave me the hell alone. I told you to go get laid or something. You need to stop spying on me. It's not cool."

"I'm looking out for you!" Now he was offended. And hurt. She could hear it in his tight words. "Someone has to do it or otherwise you're going to get killed — "

The door to the bedroom flew open. "*Ahhh!*" A man's guttural roar seemed to echo around her.

She shot upright and yanked the covers to her chest.

Harrison stood in the doorway. Harrison, minus his shirt. He looked positively scrumptious. Rock-hard abs. Lickable six pack. More than a six pack really. He was muscled perfection and her over-active libido was so excited to see —

"Where is the damn threat?" Harrison demanded.

She looked to the left. To the right. "Not...here?"

"You screamed!" He stalked toward her.

Elise bit her lower lip. It was either bite her lip or bite him. Sometimes, she hated her own nature.

"You. Screamed," he gritted out when she didn't speak.

"Sorry. I'm a sleep screamer."

His eyes squeezed closed. His hand lifted, and he squeezed the bridge of his nose. "That isn't a thing."

"I'm sure it is a thing. There are people out there who scream in their sleep. I've certainly had nightmares before that made me wake up screaming. Therefore, I am a sleep screamer." She smiled. "Sorry. Did I scare you?"

His eyes opened. His expression was frustrated, his stare suspicious. "You were talking to someone."

"I was?" *I was.*

"No one is here."

"We're here. You and I. We count as someone."

He growled.

"I'm sorry I scared you."

"You *didn't* scare me. I was—" But he broke off, blinking. His frustrated expression vanished. He looked surprised. "I was worried about you."

Her smile stretched. *Progress!* "That is so sweet! I know, I know, you said you weren't sweet, but you are. That is just the sweetest —"

He pointed at her. "Don't scream again, not unless you want me to come in here and kill someone."

Elise swallowed. "Duly noted."

He marched out. *Slammed* the door this time.

Her breath expelled in a rush. She waited a moment, knowing the question would come from the dark shadows...

"Wow. That's the guy you want to mate? Are you mad?"

She settled back down on the comfy mattress. Fluffed the pillow a little bit. "I don't just *want* to mate him." She thought about those magical words he'd voiced earlier at the werewolf den...

We're together.

"I already have," Elise confided in a whisper. "Now, screw off. I'm sleepy."

***

Harrison hurried down the spiral stairs. Shit, when he'd heard Elise scream, he'd lost his head. Terror had clawed through him. He'd been desperate to get to her, ready to rip and tear apart anyone who'd dared threaten her.

His reaction had been the same in the werewolf den. When she'd stared at him, her dark eyes all wide and terrified, he'd had one response...

Destroy.

He'd wanted to destroy anyone who hurt her.

Insane. He wasn't some kind of protector. He was a hunter. He didn't get involved with anyone. There were no attachments allowed in his life. His father had taught him that lesson early on. Jason Key was one brutal teacher. Anytime Harrison had gotten attached to anything, Jason had taken it away. No toys. No pictures. No pets.

No friends.

Attachments made hunters weak. Weakness wasn't allowed.

Elise...she was tempting. Sexy. And he *would* make sure she survived until the next full moon. But it wasn't like he was going to keep her or anything. This whole setup was temporary. Not like she was—

Mine.

The whisper came from deep inside. That deep, dark place inside that he tried to ignore. A place of savagery and darkness.

Harrison shook his head. No. Elise wasn't for him. She was bait to lure monsters to him. She made his job easier. There was no way on earth that she was—

Mine!

Dammit, he needed a drink. Also, maybe a shrink because that voice hadn't been a whisper in his head that time. It had been a freaking bellow.

CHAPTER FOUR

Her eyes flew open and a gasp slid past her lips. Fear churned through her body, and Elise knew she wasn't alone. Something dangerous was with her. Something big and bad and —

A hand pressed over her mouth. A familiar, sandalwood scent teased her nose. "Don't scream," Harrison told her, his voice barely more than a breath. "We've got company coming."

Her heart slammed into her chest.

He slowly lowered his hand. He sat on the edge of the bed, his body curving over hers. She could see perfectly in the dark — at least she hadn't lost *that* trait — and Elise noted the tenseness of his handsome features. Battle-ready. That was how he looked. She swallowed. "I don't want company, thank you very much."

His lips quirked. "I'll be sure to tell the wolves to fuck off."

Oh, no. She sat up and grabbed his arm when he tried to move away. "It's the werewolves? They followed us?"

"Caught a howl outside. They're circling the place now, thinking they can close in and trap us." He smiled. "Dumbasses. If they come at me tonight, they won't survive until tomorrow."

Wonderful. The paranormal war was in full effect. "And, ah, how will you defeat them?"

"The usual way. I'll empty silver bullets into their hearts." He reached under the mattress and his hand came back up with a gun. "Thought you might want a backup."

"I was sleeping on your gun?"

"You were sleeping on my backup." He reached down again. Pulled up a small box. When he opened it — surprise, surprise — there were silver bullets inside. He loaded the gun for her. "You know how to shoot?"

She nodded. "No."

He frowned. "You nodded."

Yes, she had. She'd also told the truth, dammit. "I mean, I know you pull the trigger, but it's not like I've ever had to shoot a werewolf." There weren't any guns where she'd come from, mostly because guns didn't work there.

He caught her hand and pressed the gun against her palm. "You aim and you squeeze the trigger. If a werewolf is coming at you, you fire, got me?"

"Yes, I've quite got you. But…"

"I won't let them get you. It's just a precaution, understand?" Tension seemed to roll off him in heavy, hot waves.

Actually…was the air heating? "Is it hot in here?" Elise asked as she kicked away the covers.

His gaze immediately darted to her legs. "Christ." His stare flew back to her. "You stay in this room, okay? I don't care what you hear, you remain in my bedroom. I'll come back for you."

"After you kill the werewolves." Um, good plan. Except…She could hear howls. Like a lot of howls. "How many are out there?"

"I think Gustave sent his whole freaking pack."

"Is that about four wolves?" Elise asked hopefully.

He shook his head.

"Five?"

"Try a dozen."

Oh, crap.

He rose.

She grabbed his shirt and yanked, intending to pull him back to her.

Only the guy was an immoveable object. She'd forgotten how strong he was supposed to be. She wound up just fisting her hand in the soft material. "You can't face that many wolves alone."

He smiled down at her. "Of course, I can."

"But—*it's a dozen werewolves.*"

"I'm the best hunter in North America. Relax. They won't get to you."

He was supposed to be the best. Wasn't that why she'd sought him out? This was sort of his chance to show her how tough he could be. To see if he lived up to expectations, so to speak. Only, if he *didn't* live up to expectations…

Then he dies.

She didn't want that. "No." Now she hopped out of bed. She put the gun on the nightstand and then put her hands on him. Her palms flattened against his chest. "Let's run."

He blinked. "I'm not the running type."

"Why not? I've heard running is great for the lungs." She searched his eyes. "I don't want you getting hurt." Her mouth dropped open in surprise after that confession because…it had been the truth. The actual, real truth. She didn't want her hunter hurt.

He gave her a half-smile. "You've got a target on you. What did you think would happen when you came to me for protection?"

She hadn't thought she would *care* about him. Caring about him hadn't been part of the plan. Yes, that was cold and cruel and, well, her. *She* was cold and cruel most days. So were many of her kind.

Most days.

Not that day. Or rather, not that night. "Don't go out there."

He laughed. "Sounds like you care." He pulled away.

"Don't!" She grabbed him, yanked him back and —

Kissed him. She shoved up onto her tip-toes, pulled his head down toward hers, and planted her lips against his. His mouth was open, as if he'd been about to say something, and her parted lips met his.

Her tongue slipped inside his mouth. Just a little taste...

The explosion of lust slammed through her. She moaned into his mouth and the spontaneous kiss turned into something frantic and desperate. His arms locked around her as he lifted her up against him. He took over the kiss, claiming her, seducing her, making her whole body shudder and quake. Wow. Elise hadn't expected the intensity of her response, but she sure as heck loved it and couldn't wait to see what was going to happen next—

He dropped her on the bed.

She bounced a little and frowned when she realized he wasn't following her down onto the mattress.

"We'll finish that..." Harrison assured her as his eyes gleamed, "as soon as I get rid of the wolves."

Hold up...what?

He was heading for the door. No, he was walking through the doorway. As she watched, he *slammed* the door. He left her there.

Her.

Left. *Her.*

After a kiss. A kiss that had made her toes curl, made her sex quiver, made her *yearn*...

He'd left her.

That was just damn unacceptable. Elise huffed out a breath. By the time she was done with Harrison, that jerk would be *begging* for her kisses. First, though, before he started begging, she had to make sure that he did his job and slayed those wolves. She rather needed Harrison to stay alive.

She grabbed the gun and headed for the door.

***

Harrison watched the figures on his security monitors. Night-vision cameras let him see the wolves as they closed in. Not that the guys were exactly trying to hide their presence. Seriously, what was up with those idiots? Coming straight at a hunter? Did they want a swift trip to hell?

He sighed and grabbed his rifle. He was on the second floor of the house, in a room just down the hallway from Elise, and he turned away from the monitors as he made his way to the windows. He set up his weapon. Glanced through the scope.

He'd warned them to stay away. They should have listened.

He put his eye close to the sight and saw —
Fuck me.

Two of the wolves were in shifted form, but the other stood as a man, and he had a human shield in front of him. A woman. Though the werewolf wore the form of a man, his claws were out, and those claws were at the woman's throat.

And the bastard was smiling. After a tense moment, the werewolf shouted, "I know you see me!"

Yeah, Harrison saw him just fine. *I see a soon-to-be dead wolf.*

"I know you *hear* me! Hunters...sharp eyes...the better to see..."

"The freaking scope is helping out, too," Harrison muttered.

"Enhanced hearing...the better to hear..."

He could hear the jackass just fine. It was lucky no one else lived close by. The way the fellow was shouting, any close neighbors would have freaked out.

The werewolf's claws cut into the woman's throat, and she sobbed.

"Strong sense of smell, too, right? The better to pull in that rich scent of blood." Laughter from the werewolf. "There's gonna be a whole lot of blood. If you don't come out here, right now, I will rip this woman's throat out! I will tear her open from ear to ear!"

Harrison sighed. Then he leaned toward the window. He lifted it up. He had planned to shoot *through* the glass, but since someone was being a pain in the ass, he'd spare a few minutes to talk. "Hey, Cujo!"

The werewolf frowned up at him.

"You kill her, you're dead two seconds later. Actually, I think I might just go ahead and start shooting right—"

The werewolf bellowed, *"Burn the house!"*

More figures surged forward from the darkness. Figures holding what looked like gasoline containers as they rushed toward the house.

The woman who'd been the sobbing victim? She *laughed* and grabbed one of the containers.

Shit. She wasn't a victim. She was with the pack.

Harrison started firing. One, two, three. The bullets slammed into their targets, but the pack was swarming. Swarming and pouring gasoline all over the place.

Harrison whirled and rushed for the door. He had to get down there and stop those bastards before they ignited the whole house. But as he ran for the door, Elise appeared. Still wearing his t-shirt and now holding her gun, she stood in the doorway.

She looked at him. At the rifle he held. Then back up at his face. "I think I smell smoke."

He surged toward her and grabbed her left hand. "You do. They're trying to burn us out."

"Burn us out...or just burn us?"

"Does it matter?" He hauled her with him. "I'm getting outside and I'm—" He stopped. They were at the top of the stairs, and when he looked down—

Chaos.

Alarms were shrieking. They were shrieking because the werewolves had busted a few of the downstairs windows. Busted the windows and tossed in some kind of explosives. Explosives or Molotov cocktails or maybe even some paranormal magic to go along with the freaking gasoline they were dumping everywhere. Smoke billowed from below, and he could hear the crackle of flames.

Werewolves normally attacked with fangs and claws. Since when did they try to *burn* their enemies? His gaze darted to Elise. Since her?

She'd stiffened at the top of the stairs. Dug in her heels. "We can't go down there." She shook her head, hard. "I'll die."

The flames were getting bigger, wilder. "I think that's the plan for us both." That fire had spread fast. Far faster than it should have. Definitely a little paranormal help had been given to the flames.

Okay, so going out the first floor wasn't an option. That left…

"Come on," he growled at her, and they ran back into his bedroom. He barely glanced at the tousled covers. He hurried toward the window and yanked it open. He saw two werewolves down there. He didn't know where the others were, but he was sure they'd be showing up soon enough. "Too bad you can't fly," Harrison muttered as he climbed through the window. "That would really help us both out right now."

"I—" She gaped at him. "Sorry?"

A grunt. "Climb on my back." He was hanging onto the window's edge, with his back partially toward her. "Hurry."

"You're *not* jumping."

"We don't have an option."

The werewolves below were already screaming for backup.

"Climb on, Elise, *now*." The flames were eating up the first level. He sure hoped that when he surged downward, he could avoid the lash of the fire.

He felt her gingerly climb onto his back. She wrapped her legs around his hips. Curled one arm around his neck as he waited near the window, his body tense.

"Now what?" Her question whispered against his ear.

"Now you don't let go."

He jumped.

CHAPTER FIVE

Wind rushed around her, flames crackled, and Elise sucked in a sharp breath—

His knees didn't even buckle. Harrison just kind of slammed down into the ground and immediately took off running. She had one arm looped around his neck—basically in a stranglehold—and her legs were clamped around his hips. He raced forward and werewolves—some shifted, some not—lunged at them.

"Shoot!" Harrison snarled.

Shoot? Oh, yes. She still had the gun in her right hand. Elise aimed at a charging werewolf. She fired.

The bullet missed him. She thought it might have thudded into the ground. Or maybe hit a tree. Crap. She tried again.

Missed by a good foot.

"You have to *hit* them," Harrison threw at her.

"It's hard! You're running, they're running, and this shit is way harder than I expected it to be!"

A wolf leapt right at Harrison. She fired and at this close of a distance, she hit the guy. Finally. The werewolf fell back with a whimper as smoke rose from his body. Harrison surged forward —

Then stopped dead. Crap, they were surrounded. Elise cast a desperate glance around them and realized that the wolves had circled around them.

Oh, no.

"Slide down," Harrison ordered softly.

She unhooked her legs from his hips. Ever so slowly, she slid down. Her arm pulled away from his neck.

"Stay behind me."

She was behind him. The problem? The wolves *circled* them, so even being behind the big, bad hunter wasn't helping her out too much.

"You don't disrespect our leader," one of them blasted. "You don't ever —"

Harrison grabbed Elise's hand — the hand that held the gun. His fingers curled around hers, he aimed and said, "Fire."

She did.

He jerked her hand again, moving so quickly.

She fired again.

He pulled her hand, she fired. *Fired.* The werewolves went down and she just kept shooting until the gun only clicked.

By that point, the wolves — those who hadn't been shot — had run. The others were sprawled on the ground, and their path to freedom had been cleared.

A fast glance showed her that the flames at the house were growing and thrashing. Smoke billowed. Harrison ran toward the side of the house — heading for the garage — and she ran with him. The werewolves didn't seem particularly interested in attacking right then. They were too busy fleeing.

Harrison didn't have any close neighbors. The street had been dead quiet when they arrived earlier, but surely *someone* would notice the flames and smoke? She figured the human cops had to be coming soon. Right? Maybe? Only she didn't hear any sirens.

He hit a code on the garage wall and a few moments later, the garage door was open and he was jumping onto the bike. She hopped on right behind him and held tight. Sure, she wasn't wearing shoes, *was* wearing his shirt and no pants, but hey, what was the point in worrying about clothing? The house was burning, werewolves were on the run, and Elise knew they had to get the hell out of there.

The motorcycle growled and raced them forward. As they fled the scene, she saw a few of the wolves turn toward them. Their eyes were glowing and furious, and she mentally urged the motorcycle to go faster. *Faster.* To get them the hell out of —

Harrison hit the brakes. The bike lurched. So did she. Elise almost flew right off the bike, but he twisted and grabbed her with those lightning-like reflexes of his. Her breath heaved in and out, and Elise managed to gasp, "Why...stop?"

Harrison's head turned so that he was staring straight ahead. She followed his stare. The light from the motorcycle fell on the man who stood in the middle of the road.

Gustave. Not shifted. Simply standing there as calm as you please with his arms crossed over his chest.

Oh, sweet hell. Again... "*Why* did we stop?" They should've just driven over the alpha werewolf.

"Because if you cut off the head, you kill the snake." Then Harrison got *off* the bike.

She grabbed the handlebars. "He's not a snake," she loud whispered at Harrison. "He's a werewolf, and his pack just attacked us!"

Gustave uncrossed his arms. He lifted his hands. "No claws. I'm not here to fight."

He sure could've fooled her.

"No?" Harrison called back. "Too bad. I am." Harrison bent low and she saw him unsheathe a knife from his ankle. Handy. She hadn't even realized it was there. In the next moment, he ran forward, moving with enhanced speed as he barreled at Gustave. She could barely breathe as she waited to see what would happen.

And then, just before Harrison's knife would have plunged into Gustave's chest —

Gustave knelt in the middle of the road.

Her mouth dropped open. A sign of submission? From an alpha?

Harrison stopped, the knife gripped in his hand. "What in the hell are you doing?"

Gustave stared up at him. "They didn't attack on my order."

"No?" Obvious disbelief from Harrison. "Then who sent them?"

A siren screamed in the distance.

A shiver slid over Elise. She glanced around. That fire was sure raging. Where had the other werewolves gone?

"They came on their own. Wanted payback for what they perceived as an insult against me. I assure you, I'll deal with them."

Elise wanted to scream out, *"Don't believe him! Werewolves can't be trusted!"* But she was too busy looking for threats. Where had those werewolves gone? She didn't like the fact that they'd all seemingly vanished. Not one bit.

"Deal with them?" Harrison asked. "I hope you mean you'll kill them. The ones who survive their injuries, anyway. They came at *me*. They burned my home. That shit doesn't go unpunished."

"I will punish them. My pack. My punishments."

Her gaze jerked back to Gustave. He was rising.

Harrison hadn't stabbed him yet. What was the hunter waiting for? Christmas?

"I'd had an agreement with the hunters," Gustave continued. "We can continue as we'd been. A peace can exist between you and me."

Harrison shook his head. "You broke the peace when your wolves came after *her*."

"Not on my order, not on my —"

"I know lies when I hear them, asshole. A hunter always knows. You're *lying* to me."

Gustave's face twisted with fury. "Do you even know what you have?" Gustave demanded. "I don't think you do. I don't think you realize just how much she's worth!"

Hell. She needed to end this. Right now. Elise grabbed tight to those handlebars at the same moment she saw a flash of movement. A wolf had just lunged from the darkness and was rushing toward Harrison's back.

Oh, no, you don't. She ground her teeth together and she raced forward on the motorcycle. As the motorcycle's wheels and engine screamed, she let loose a powerful yell of her own.

The vibrations from the motorcycle shook her whole body.

Gustave let out a roar as she came barreling forward. Harrison glanced back at her, and his eyes widened. She wondered — briefly, vaguely —

if she looked as crazy as she felt as she hurtled toward him.

Then the wolf who'd been trying to attack Harrison—the jerk who'd gone in while Harrison's back was turned—whirled away and tried to run back toward the darkness. She yanked the handlebars in his direction. Unfortunately, when she yanked, Elise pulled a bit too hard. The bike lunged to the left, then to the right as she overcorrected, and she tried to pull it back, tried to control the motorcycle, but it was spinning beyond her power. The motorcycle started to career off the road, and Elise knew the crash was going to hurt. Elise tried to prepare herself for one heck of an impact.

The motorcycle lurched. Not because she'd crashed, but because someone had just landed on the thing. Landed *behind* her. Her head whipped around. Harrison. He'd *landed* on the seat and his hands were on the handlebars now as he curved his body around hers. He brought the motorcycle to a jarring halt.

The motor kept growling. Her thighs kept shaking.

"What in the hell was that?" Harrison demanded. His rough voice seemed to slide over her body.

The werewolf who'd been sneaking up for a while-your-back-is-turned attack was gone. He'd disappeared into the dark. "Um, I was trying to save you." She looked around. The pack leader was gone, too. No sign of Gustave. But there was plenty of signs indicating—

"Humans," Harrison muttered. "Coming in fast. We have to go." The motorcycle flew forward and headed straight for the firetruck, police cars, and the ambulance that were now rushing up the dark road. The shrieks of the sirens filled her ears but at the last moment, he swerved around the oncoming vehicles. Never slowed. Definitely didn't stop. He drove fast and hard and the wind whipped against her as they escaped into the night.

Wow. Talk about a near miss. Yes, she *had* been trying to save Harrison. She'd also been trying to cover her own ass. Gustave knew the truth about her. It was a truth that she couldn't afford to let Harrison discover. Not yet.

If he found out too soon, he just might kill her. Not exactly what she wanted her new husband to do.

***

"That didn't go well," Elise announced. Her body was still curled in front of Harrison's. She'd been quiet during the mad dash through the city as he headed for the one safe place he knew they could use for shelter. A safe place...A bar for hunters. Sort of.

He braked the motorcycle near their destination.

"Another alley?" She didn't sound excited. "I don't have the best of times in alleys, just so you know."

The alley was dark and dank.

"Monsters usually ambush in alleys," Elise mumbled. "At least, that's been my experience."

"You won't be ambushed here." He rose and moved away from the bike.

She didn't follow. "I'm wearing a t-shirt."

It had hiked up to show her legs. Those long, gorgeous legs.

And her bare toes.

Hell.

"I think I need clothes. Everyone seems very concerned with clothes in this town."

In this town? Try *all* towns. But she'd just spoken strangely again, giving one of those little slips that he filed away because he knew it meant trouble. "I'll take care of the clothes." He turned away. Glanced toward the brick wall on the right. Only it wasn't all brick. Right in the middle of the wall, there was an old, wooden door.

He headed for the door.

The rush of her footsteps followed him. *She* followed him. About time.

"What are you doing?" Elise almost ran into him.

Harrison lifted his hand. "Knocking." Two raps.

A small panel opened on the door, a panel that was eye level for Harrison.

"Kill the queen," he said.

Elise flinched. "What?" Her hand grabbed him. Her nails dug into him. "Why would you say that?"

The panel closed. A moment later, the door opened.

Harrison lifted a brow at Elise. Why had he said to kill the queen? "Because it's the password to get us in the speakeasy tonight."

"A speakeasy?" She blinked. Frowned at the corridor that had been revealed by the open door. Curiosity suddenly poured from her. "I don't think I've ever been to a speakeasy."

"You should probably know, this isn't your typical speakeasy. This one's guarded by magic."

Her gaze whipped up to him. "What kind of magic?" Now she was all suspicious.

"The kind of magic that keeps the bad guys out. Only hunters and humans can slip inside."

She backed up a step. "You're testing me again."

Actually, he wasn't. He was just out of options.

"First the holy water, then the iron, now this." Elise shook her head. "Is a little trust too much to ask?"

"Yes." He didn't trust anyone.

Her lips thinned. "Why not bring me here first? Before the whole iron and holy water routine? Why not just—"

"Because this place is loaded with hunters inside, and if you didn't pass the entrance test, I didn't want to watch as they killed you." Truth. Even now, he wasn't crossing over that threshold to go inside because he knew when he did...

There is something different about her. If she gets hurt in there...

She smiled. Her beautiful, innocent, charming smile. The one that made him extra nervous. "You care?" She gave that little hum that he realized meant she was happy...in her own way. "You don't want me hurt? That is so sweet."

No, she hadn't called him that, not *again*. He was many things, but he would never, ever be sweet. "Elise—"

She crossed the threshold. Kind of danced across it. Nothing happened. He realized he'd sucked in a breath and forgot to let it go. She did a quick spin and faced him again. "See? I told you. Human as can currently be."

He followed her. Shut the door. Secured it. There was no sign of the person who'd *opened* the door before, but he could hear voices up ahead. Elise advanced eagerly toward those voices, but he caught her arm. "Stay close to me."

Her body pressed to his. "This close?"

Heat slithered through him. "I think we could, uh, put in a little more space."

Her lips curled down in a pout. She backed away a little.

He immediately wanted to drag her back. Harrison didn't, though, because his self-control was holding. Mostly.

A few moments later, they were in the main part of the speakeasy. Not much to see there. A bar. Some wooden tables. And hunters. Four of them. Three men and one woman. They all turned and stared at Elise.

Elise…in his t-shirt.

Elise, looking sexy as could be when she should have been looking like she'd just survived hell.

"They're staring," Elise stage whispered to him.

Of course, they were staring. He had a hard time looking anywhere but at Elise.

Harrison recognized all four hunters. The woman's gaze was suspicious. But then, Krista Hart was suspicious of most people. Her long, curly, red hair had been pulled back into a ponytail, and her green eyes raked Elise.

As for the three male hunters…suspicion wasn't the main thing he saw in their eyes. Lust was.

Harrison stepped forward, moving to put his body a little closer to Elise's.

"I thought you wanted space." Again with her stage whisper. He knew the woman could be quiet. She just didn't want to be at that moment.

One of the hunters—a blond with too long hair and a grin that was already flashing his dimples—advanced toward them.

"Stand the hell down," Harrison snapped to Grayden Flash. Or, rather, Gray to most of the other hunters.

The other two hunters laughed at Harrison's order. "I think someone is feeling territorial," the dark-haired one on the right said. A long scar slid over his cheek. Ward Trisk had gotten that scar when he'd just been eighteen years old. Harrison had been at his side, and he'd made sure the werewolf slashing at Ward hadn't been able to do any additional damage.

The final hunter spread his tattooed hands over the bar top—Since the speakeasy was his, he'd been pulling bartender duty. Light gleamed off his bald head. Bald by choice because Razor— no last name, just Razor—liked to shave his head. Hell, that was where he'd gotten his name in the first place. He always carried razors to keep his head shiny and smooth. Razor studied Harrison and Elise in silence for a beat before drawling, "You bringing a *friend* to my place, Harrison?"

Friend? Not exactly the way he'd describe Elise but…Harrison gave a grim nod.

At that small move, some of the tension slid from the room. He'd just told everyone that Elise wasn't a threat. He hoped he hadn't lied.

Elise, meanwhile, decided to give the whole crew a friendly wave before she called out, quite cheerfully, "Who does a girl have to kill in order to get a drink around here?"

Gray and Ward smiled at her.

Harrison growled. He was gonna need more than one drink.

***

"Only one room, hmm?" Elise spared a quick glance for the small room and the sagging bed. "Guess we'll just make it work."

A knock pounded against the door. Harrison immediately tensed, but when he opened the door, Krista stood there. She held a bag in her hands. "Clothes. Shoes. Looks like your lady friend and I are roughly the same size," the female hunter said with a shrug. "Consider this my one good deed for the year." Her gaze slid over him. Lingered a little. "Good to see you again, Harrison."

He took the bag. "Thanks, Krista. I owe you."

"You absolutely do. I'll collect soon enough." She turned away.

He shut the door. Flipped the lock.

"Have you slept with her?" There was a distinct edge to Elise's voice.

He spun and frowned at her. "Come again?"

"Have you slept with her?"

Harrison laughed.

Elise's face went dark. Obviously, laughter had not been the right response. He coughed, trying to chase away the laugh, and managed, "Why?"

"Because I want to know." She advanced with fast steps. "Her voice went all soft when she said your name. So, have you had sex with her?"

"I don't think Krista ever goes soft. She's pretty much in constant kill mode." He stretched his tight shoulders. "But, no, we haven't slept together." He lifted the clothes. "By the way, you should tell her thanks the next time your paths cross. She gave you her clothing."

Elise stared at him as if he'd lost his mind. "She *wants* to have sex with you. I'm not thanking her."

"Clothes. She gave you clothes and —"

"I don't want you sleeping with her." Her hands twisted in front of her. "I think I'm jealous." Now she sounded...horrified? "What is wrong with me?" Elise asked in a hushed voice. "I'm never like this. Not ever."

But these weren't exactly normal circumstances. "I think you're exhausted. You're riding adrenaline. You're scared. You're confused. You're —"

In my arms. She'd yanked the bag out of his hands and tossed it to the floor. She grabbed him and pulled him toward her. "I liked kissing you," she confessed.

It had been the highlight of his night, too.

Seeing his place get burned? Fighting werewolves? Not for the highlight reel.

The reel was only her.

"Will you kiss me again?" Elise asked.

He wanted to do more than kiss her. That was the problem. He caught her hands in his. Pulled them away from his body. "We need to sleep." *All I want to do is fuck you. So hard and so long that you scream and scream for me as you come.* "More attacks could be coming soon, and we have to be ready." *I want you naked and beneath me. Or on top of me.* "We need to get in that bed and crash." *I want to taste every single inch of you. Did I mention that I want to fuck you? Over and over.*

Her lower lip trembled. "Right. Sleep." She turned away. Stumbled a little. Then stilled. "You're sleeping in the bed *with* me?"

"No." *Yes. Hell, yes.* "Bad idea." *Great idea.* The dark part of him was having a freaking field day in his head. Harrison gritted, "I'll sleep on the floor."

"Sleeping on the floor. Giving me the bed. Very chivalrous of you." She moved toward the bed, then hesitated. "Do you think…is there a shower I could use before I go to sleep? My feet are dirty. *I'm* dirty, and I'd really like to get clean."

Of course, he had an instant visual of her under a spray of water. Looking sexy as hell.

He closed his eyes.

"Harrison?"

He kept his eyes closed.

The floor creaked. "What are you doing?"

"Counting."

"Why?"

Because it helps me not to fuck you.

The floor creaked again. Reluctantly, his eyes opened. She was staring straight at him. She was right in front of him. He swallowed. "There's a bathroom down the hallway. Towels are inside. You can shower there and then we'll crash. Okay?"

She nodded, but then bit her lower lip. "Why don't you want me to touch you?"

He turned away from her. "Because I'm dangerous to you." In so many ways.

"I want you. I've *told* you that."

"You don't want a man like me." He yanked open the door. "Trust me."

She slid by him. "I do."

It took a moment to understand the full meaning of her words.

Elise trusts me.

She didn't look back at him as she headed for the bathroom. He trailed after her. Her scent was making him freaking dizzy and his cock was rock hard. He was —

She stopped in front of the bathroom. Glanced back at him with narrowed eyes.

Harrison cleared his throat. "I'll stand guard out here."

She looked up and down the empty hallway. "Why?"

"Because I'm not going to risk you being away from me. Not until I know just what all we're facing." He gave her a quick nod. "Shower. I'll be here."

A smile lifted her lips and lit her eyes. "Thanks for protecting me."

Sweetheart, it is my pleasure —

"Though I do really wish you'd consider making love to me."

Holy mother — she *hadn't* just said that. No. Yes. She had. She *wanted* to make him insane.

Before he could drag his thoughts together and manage to pick his jaw up off the floor, she'd shut the bathroom door. He heard the rush of water a moment later, and his hand lifted, flattening against the door.

She was naked on the other side of the door. Naked, and she wanted him to fuck her, and he was about to kiss his self-control straight to hell. He was going to go in there and worship every single inch of her delectable body —

He heard the rustle of a footstep.

Harrison whirled around.

Gray stood at the top of the stairs. He lifted his hands, palms up. "Easy. I was just going to my room. It's on this hallway, too." His gaze slid to the bathroom door. Lingered a moment. Then his stare returned to Harrison. "I'm staying the night. Getting a little lodging from Razor, same as you."

Harrison grunted. *Then keep walking, buddy. Nothing to see here.*

Gray lowered his hands. He advanced slowly. "Though I do have to ask, are you crazy? Because if she asked me to fuck her, I'd —"

Knew the sonofabitch was there listening. Gray had been hiding just out of sight. Before the guy could finish his sentence, Harrison had slammed him against the nearest wall. Harrison shoved his forearm against Gray's throat. "She's not asking you to do a damn thing."

Gray wheezed. "Like...that...huh?"

Harrison let him go. Stepped back. Sucked in a deep breath so he could calm his ass down and *not* rip the other hunter's head off. "Like what?"

"You always were possessive with your toys." Gray smirked. A smirk that was ruined by his wheeze. "Don't want anyone else...touching what's yours."

"You're damn right no one else is touching her. She's under my protection. That means I'm going to watch out for her. I'm going to keep asshole paranormals away from her *and* keep asshole hunters away, too."

Gray's eyelids flickered. "Why would the paranormals want her?"

"Elise says she's cursed and they are coming at her like she's some kind of all you can eat buffet."

"Oh, man, I would love to eat at that buffet."

Harrison's eyes turned to slits. He was going to beat the shit out of —

The bathroom door flew open. Elise stood in the doorway, her wet hair sliding over her shoulders, droplets of water on her skin, and a thin towel wrapped around her body. "Happy?" Elise demanded. "I took the fastest shower of my life in absolutely ice-cold water."

"Oh, God, I'm starving," Gray muttered. "Please, please let me go to the buffet —"

Harrison drove his fist into Gray's jaw. The guy staggered back against the wall.

Elise frowned over at him.

Harrison picked her up and hauled ass with her back to their room. Her body was wet and soft and oh, shit, his self-control was disintegrating. When she wiggled against him, he practically ran into their room. He kicked the door shut. Locked it.

Harrison spun back around and put her on her feet. He was all set to back away.

Slither. Rustle.

Her towel had just slithered off. Rustled to the floor.

She was naked. Standing in front of him with her perfect breasts thrusting toward him, her legs stretching for freaking ever, and —

Elise turned away from him. Her world class ass — *world class* — nearly brought him to his knees before she climbed into the bed. The old mattress dipped a little. She pulled the covers up. Sighed. Settled in and shifted her body against the mattress.

He had frozen. Every muscle in his body was rock hard. The image of her ass was seared into his mind. Where it would be *forever.*

"I wasn't going to jump you." Her voice was soft but flat. Annoyed. Hurt? "You need to settle down. I got it, all right? You aren't interested."

He slammed his hand against the light switch. He probably broke the damn thing, but he also succeeded in turning off the lights and plunging the room into darkness.

Harrison made his way across the room. He lowered his body on the floor, right near her side of the bed. And, of course, her scent was everywhere. He stretched out and glared straight up.

Not want her? He was practically shaking he wanted her so badly. He couldn't ever remember wanting someone so much. "You try to be the good guy," he groused. "And it bites you in the ass."

"What?"

"Nothing. Get some sleep."

But her covers were rustling about. "Did you say you were a good guy?"

"Go to sleep."

"Because I don't remember wanting good. I like bad. Just so you know."

You could be so very bad with her. That stupid voice in his head needed to shut the hell up.

Silence.

Then her voice came again. Low, soft. Worried. "Am I still bait? Are you hoping all of the monsters will come to this place so your hunter friends can take them out?"

"You're bait." *No, she's more.* The voice needed to shut the fuck up. "I'll make arrangements so that they'll keep you safe when I go out and end the werewolves." When Harrison left for his hunt, Gray had better keep his damn horny hands off her.

"But—"

"I'll end them, and then I'll come back for you. If any other paranormals come for you, I'll take them out, too. You don't need to worry."

"I'm not worried." Her voice was so husky. Such a sensual sound. "Not when I have you. You promised to keep me safe."

Had he? Even if he hadn't before, Harrison heard himself say, "I will. I swear, I'll keep you safe."

It took a while, but her breathing finally evened out, and he knew that Elise had gone to sleep. His dick was still at full, painful attention, so Harrison knew that he wouldn't be sinking into the relief of sleep anytime soon.

Instead, he stared up at the ceiling. He saw Elise in his mind. And he knew...

I am so screwed.

Because she had him, all right. Had him as her protector. As her hunter. If he wasn't careful, the woman would *have him* wrapped around her cute little pinky finger.

CHAPTER SIX

A man with a gun stood at the foot of her bed.

A man who was *not* Harrison. A man with a wicked scar on his cheek, icy eyes, and, yep, he cradled a gun with far too much confidence.

Elise lurched up in bed and grabbed for the covers. She held them tightly against her chest. "Harrison!"

The fellow winced. He was one of the hunters she'd met the night before. Not Gray. Not Razor—that had been the Vin Diesel wannabe. This one...*what was his name?*

"Calm down, lady. Harrison is out taking care of some business."

Wonderful. She shoved a lock of hair out of her eyes. "And you're standing at the foot of my bed, watching me sleep like a vampire with a super crush because...?"

His lips twitched. "Because you cried out in your sleep. I was afraid something was wrong. Sounded like you were in pain, so I rushed inside."

Oh, no. She tried to smile. "I suppose I was having a nightmare." She truly was a sleep screamer, as she'd told Harrison.

"Must've been one hell of a bad dream." His lips weren't twitching any longer. He'd cocked his head to the side so he could study her. "You were begging someone, saying over and over, *'Give them back. Please give them back.'*"

She got chatty when she slept. A good thing to know.

A hint of Texas slid beneath his words as he asked, "What did someone take from you?"

Just everything. "Um, vampires *did* recently try to take my life." Elise slid from the bed. She pulled her sheet with her. Normally, she didn't care about nudity. Shyness wasn't part of her lifestyle, but the people here—they were different. She'd noticed that. She didn't think Harrison would be wild about her prancing around naked in front of his hunter buddy. She was being *good.* Not that anyone would notice and give her bonus points.

"No. That's not what you were going on about." He shook his head. "You said 'Give *them* back.'"

She grabbed for the bag of clothes that the female hunter had brought her last night. "I can't remember. The dream's gone." She held up the bag. "Maybe it was my clothes. Maybe I wanted them back."

He didn't look convinced.

"I'm sorry, I can't remember your name," Elise blurted.

"Ward."

Just that. No last name. Okay. "Thanks for rushing in, Ward, but I'm okay and I should get dressed. I'll just hurry down to the bathroom. Brush my teeth. Comb my hair." She backed away from him. "Put on clothing so I'm not naked when strange men rush into my bedroom."

Once more, his lips seemed to twitch. "Bet he doesn't know what to do with you."

She stopped. "Who?"

"Harrison. I'm thinking he's never met anyone quite like you."

To be honest, most people hadn't come across a being quite like her before. "I'm your average, desperate-to-survive woman." Until the curse was broken. "A woman on the run from vamps and werewolves. I'm sure Harrison meets people like me all the time."

Ward shook his head. "Be careful with him. You don't want to push that man's control."

That's exactly what I want to do. Ward now held her complete and total attention. "Why don't I want to do that? Does he get all psycho crazy without his control?"

"Control keeps the monsters at bay."

She stiffened at those words.

"For us all," he added grimly like he was a dark greeting card. The kind you couldn't get at a local drugstore. "Without control, hunters can't do their jobs and stay sane."

She'd always thought sanity was a bit overrated, but Elise gave a quick nod and hurried into the hallway with her bag. She darted into the bathroom—a bathroom that was the size of a matchbox—and dressed as quickly as she could. A few moments later, she was swinging open the door, wearing her borrowed clothes and shoes that were a little loose but would do the job, with her hair combed, her teeth brushed and—

"Aah!" Elise yelled as she jumped back.

The female hunter was there. Arms crossed over her chest. One eyebrow raised.

Elise slapped a hand over her chest and her racing heartbeat. "What is it with you hunters? Do you just enjoy sneaking up and scaring people?"

"Who the hell are you?"

Elise blinked. "You loaned me the clothes." Harrison had said she should thank the woman. Though it felt alien, she added, "Thank you."

"Whatever. They were castoffs."

Well...*aren't we friendly?*

"Who the hell are you?" she demanded again.

"Elise."

The woman—Krista, Elise certainly remembered *her* name—raked her with an assessing glance. "How'd you wind up with Harrison?"

"He saved my life. Offered me protection. You know how it goes." She gave Krista a woman-to-woman smile. "He met me and wanted to be with me every single moment."

Krista's lips tightened.

"It was just typical..." Now Elise waved her hand vaguely in the air. "The usual way one meets a hunter."

"You don't strike me as some delicate flower who needs a big, bad hunter to keep her safe." A pause. "So what's the deal?"

"The deal is I'm cursed. Every supernatural around wants a bite out of me." Elise shrugged. "And thanks for saying I'm no delicate flower. That's so good of you to notice." It was getting easier to say thanks. She was even starting to warm up to Krista —

Even though Krista was frowning at her. "Cursed, huh?"

"Yes, it would seem that way. Especially since — "

An alarm cut through her words. A high-pitched, screeching alarm that hurt Elise's ears.

Krista's eyes flared wide. "No way!"

"No way — what?"

But Krista wasn't staying around to answer her question. She'd turned tail and ran and Elise gaped after her. The alarm kept blaring, and she dropped the bag and slapped her hands over her ears because that shit *hurt*. Elise stumbled forward, swearing, and she nearly smacked straight into Ward's chest.

"What's happening, Ward?" *Someone make the alarm stop.*

"Oh, not much. We're being attacked...in the freaking daylight."

That—no. That didn't make sense. "Paranormals hunt at night. The day is supposed to be safe."

He hauled her down the corridor. "Tell that to them."

She would, if she got the chance. "Harrison said paranormals couldn't get inside here. He said magic kept the monsters out."

"Yeah, they can't gain entrance." He pulled her back into the bedroom she'd used before. He peered through the window. Swore. "But they can use their human pets to do their dirty work for them."

She pressed close to the window. Saw the line of humans rushing to the building right before—

Boom.

The whole building seemed to crumble.

***

He wanted to get back to Elise.

Harrison prowled through the werewolf den. The fucking *empty* werewolf den. He'd headed there so that he could kick Gustave's ass, but the alpha was hiding.

And I want to get back to Elise.

Leaving her had been surprisingly hard. She'd been sleeping in the bed, looking like some sort of fallen angel. Her hair had been spread over her pillow, her lips parted, her face relaxed and soft.

He'd wanted to reach out to her. To hold her.

Instead, he'd decided to go out and kill for her. A guy had to have his priorities.

But every moment that he was away from her, something just felt wrong. Harrison rubbed his chest. An ache was growing there. His muscles were tight. He could've sworn that he even caught the scent of —

Harrison whirled and brought up his silver knife. He shoved it against Gustave's throat. "Did you really think you could catch me by surprise?"

Gustave's eyes were huge.

Harrison let the blade slice the werewolf's skin.

"I could smell you coming," Harrison snarled.

A tremble slid over the alpha. "I am no threat to you—"

"Bullshit," Harrison called.

"Or to your mate," Gustave added quickly. "I seek an alliance. Those wolves went rogue last night. They acted without my permission, and I saw to it that they were put *down*."

"Back the fuck up."

Gustave tried to take a step back.

Harrison jerked him closer. "I didn't mean literally, dumbass. I meant—start that explanation again."

The alpha yelled when the blade sliced him deeper.

"Oh, calm the hell down," Harrison ordered gruffly. "It was only a nick. We both know werewolves heal fast."

Gustave clamped his lips together.

"Why'd you call Elise my mate?" Hunters didn't have mates. That was a werewolf thing. A paranormal thing. A…monster thing.

"Because that's what she is."

"No. No, I'm offering her protection because she needs help, but she's not—"

"You claimed her. Right in front of me and my men. Said that you were together. I *heard* you." Gustave suddenly seemed very, very eager. "Was that a mistake? Did you not mean the words?"

"I…" He *had* said that, hadn't he?

The ache in his chest grew. Elise's image flashed through his mind. So did a bolt of solid fear. What the hell was that fear about?

"If you aren't with her, if you haven't fucked her, then it's not too late," Gustave said. He smiled. His sharp canines flashed. "It's not too late—" Gustave broke off and looked far too smug.

"Not too late for *what?*"

The werewolf's scent had thickened. Excitement. "I can take her. I can call off my men. I can—"

Call off my men?

Fuck. *That* was why the den was so quiet and empty. The bastard's henchmen were out hunting Elise. "What have you done?"

Gustave's claws flew up and sliced across Harrison's stomach.

Harrison jerked back, snarling.

"You don't know what you have!" Gustave's laughter was wild. "I'll take and take and she'll be—"

Harrison moved in a lightning-fast maneuver. The silver blade sliced over Gustave's throat. Then Harrison drove it down and plunged the blade into the alpha's heart.

Gustave's breath choked out as his claws dug into Harrison's arms.

"I know exactly what I have. Something you will *never* take," Harrison promised. He twisted the knife. "Elise is mine, and if your men have hurt her…"

Gustave was dead. His eyes stared at nothing.

"I will fucking destroy them," Harrison swore.

He dropped the alpha. Harrison ignored the blood that poured from his wounds as he ran from the den.

Elise, I'm coming for you.

***

It was like a war zone. Like something she'd seen on TV when she'd been searching for Harrison. TVs were funny things. They showed all of these shows. All of these actors. Good things happened in the shows. Bad things.

Something bad was happening now.

The building was shaking. Great booms sounded every few moments. Gunshots? Bombs? Both? Elise wasn't sure. She was attempting to get through the debris and the fire and get her ass out of there.

Ward was gone. He'd told her to stay down and then he'd left her and run away. She'd stayed down, all right. She'd crouched near the bed until the ceiling had started falling down on her. Now she was just trying to get out. Trying to make her way out of the speakeasy and to fresh air.

Escape was hard because of the dirt and dust and flames. *Everywhere.* And there were people, too. People that she had to avoid. The humans Ward had pointed to before. They were in the midst of the chaos. They wore black suits — not suits, really. Black pants. Shirts. Masks over their faces. They carried guns and were shooting like crazy.

She darted to the left, then to the right. She could see the door. So close. She was almost —

A voice shouted, "There she is! Shoot her!"

Elise stiffened as she waited to feel the bullets plunge into her back. She'd tried, but failed. Everything would crumble. She was going to die, weak and alone.

Bam, bam, bam!

The bullets didn't hit her.

But...they hit someone. She heard a groan, and Elise whirled around. Behind the bar, she saw Krista stagger, then get off two shots from her weapon.

Two of the humans in masks immediately fell.

But a third lifted his gun and aimed it at Krista.

Krista tried to fire, but her weapon didn't seem to work. Uh, oh. *Is she out of bullets?*

The standing human laughed. "You're dead."

Elise glanced at the door. At freedom.

Then she looked at Krista's face. At the sheer terror there.

Dammit.

Elise raced forward. *What in the hell am I doing?*

The bad human fired his weapon.

The bullet slammed into Elise's shoulder. It hit her because she'd just put herself between a human female — one she didn't even particularly like — and a bullet. Her breath sawed out. "You *asshole!*" Elise screamed at the gunman.

He blinked. Lifted his gun. He was going to shoot her again. Oh, no, no, he wasn't. She launched at him. They slammed into the floor. More of the ceiling fell. The damn *ceiling*. And the gun went off again as she struggled with the human. Only, when the gun fired, he stopped struggling.

Elise lifted her head. Smoke was everywhere. And the human beneath her? He was not moving. She yanked off his mask. His eyes were closed. His breath barely whispered out.

He wasn't dead, but he wasn't about to shoot again, either. A win for her. She jumped off him. Bounded for the door. She'd just done her good deed for the century. She'd saved the woman who'd loaned her clothes.

"*H-help...*"

Again...Dammit.

Elise spun around.

She didn't see Krista, but she could hear the other woman's heaving breaths.

The flames were rising. The building was collapsing. There was no sign of the other hunters. There was only Elise. And Krista. This was one of those stupid, ethical moments that she hated.

"*H-help...*"

Crap! Elise crawled through the wreckage. She glared at Krista. "You stay the hell away from my man after this, got me?"

Krista groaned.

Elise grabbed Krista's foot and started dragging the hunter out of there. She kept her eyes on the door. One precious inch at a time. They could do this. They could get out. They could —

The second story fell in on them.

***

Police were at the scene. Firefighters. Reporters. Ambulances.

Harrison leapt off his motorcycle and ran toward the remains of the speakeasy. Terror choked him. No, no, this couldn't be happening. It looked like the whole building had just erupted. He'd left Elise in that building.

"*Elise!*" Harrison roared her name as he shoved past two cops in uniform.

They tried to push him back. They failed.

Three more joined them. "You can't go in there!" One shoved Harrison and barked, "The building is collapsing, for everyone's safety — *stay back.*"

Harrison grabbed the young cop and prepared to throw him out of —

"Harrison. Let him go."

He knew the voice. Harrison turned — didn't let go of his prey, not yet — and met the hard, dark stare of Detective Shawn Taylor. The African American cop was pretty much a legend in the city and in the supernatural world. He was one of the few humans who knew the real score, and he actually tried to keep the streets safe from monsters.

"Let him go," Shawn ordered again. "Look, if you're searching for the woman, she's in the back of the ambulance." He jerked his thumb over his shoulder. "She crawled out, but she's got a bullet wound and—"

Harrison freed the uniformed cop, turned on his heel, and hauled ass for the ambulance.

"Yeah, he's sorry," Shawn called out, "my friend didn't mean to grab you, Officer Davenport, he's just worried about—"

Harrison didn't hear the rest of Shawn's words. He'd yanked open one of the ambulance's rear doors and leapt inside the vehicle. Two EMTs were hovered around the patient, and there was blood and— "You were shot?" His voice was too loud and rough.

One delicate hand pushed—shoved—away one of the hovering EMTs. "I'm fine."

He blinked. He was staring at Krista.

Krista. Not Elise.

"Caught me by surprise, that's all," she groused. "I'm not dying, so these guys..." She glared at the EMTs. "Need to chill the hell out."

He sucked in a breath. "What happened? Where's Elise?"

She licked her lips. Fear flashed in her eyes. "She's not outside? Not with that mess of cops?"

Harrison gave a hard, negative shake of his head.

The fear deepened. "She...dragged me to the door. Told me to keep going. I-I crawled forward a little and the cops grabbed me." She tried to sit up. An EMT pushed her right back down. "I thought they got her." Her voice rose. "I thought they got her out, too!"

He leapt out of that ambulance and rushed right back toward the blazing building. Another fucking fire. Twice in such a short time? He wanted to kill Gustave all over again. The sonofabitch had sent his humans to do this.

Shawn saw him coming. He threw up his hands. "Stop, you can't go in there! You can't—"

"*She's still in there.*" He didn't slow down. Just snarled those words. Cops were coming at him. Shawn was swearing. Harrison didn't care.

Elise was in that building. She could be burning. Dying. He had to get her.

So, yeah, he tossed the cops aside. He might have punched one—two?—and he forced his way inside the speakeasy. He rushed inside and smoke filled his lungs. He could taste fire and ash and he could—

He kicked something. The smoke was so thick he could barely see, but he reached down because he'd touched something soft. Well, not soft exactly...

His hand closed around an arm. A rough, hairy arm.

Harrison crouched as he peered down at his find. *Ward?* Shit. Yes, it was the hunter.

"I…" Coughing and a weak, husky voice came from nearby. "I…couldn't get him…out. Too…h-heavy…"

His head whipped around. Elise. She'd collapsed next to Ward. Her hand was still around his ankle, as if she'd been dragging him out. So close to the door, but not there. And she was coughing and choking and —

He grabbed her in his arms. Scooped her up and held her tightly against his chest with one arm. His body shuddered as he held her.

Her head nuzzled against his neck. "G-get…him…"

He grabbed for Ward with his other hand. Then he got them the fuck out of there. Fire was everywhere. Chunks of wall. Ceiling? Hell, he didn't know what was in his way. He didn't care, either. All that mattered was getting out with Elise. But he couldn't get back out via the main entrance, so Harrison kicked at the closest wall until the thing gave way, and he got out. He kicked and kicked until that bitch collapsed, then he carried out Elise and Ward. Okay, he mostly dragged Ward out, and he kept a death grip on Elise — *but I got them out.*

And as soon as he cleared the building…

"Get EMTs over here!" Shawn yelled.

The chaos outside was even worse. More cops. More firefighters. Civilians who were filming with their phones.

Harrison let go of Ward. The hunter was unconscious and blood trickled from his forehead. EMTs grabbed him and went to work on Ward immediately. But when they reached for Elise—

"Keep your fucking hands away from her." The low warning tore from him.

They jerked their fucking hands back.

Shawn hurriedly closed in. He stared at Harrison's face and winced. "Everyone, give the man some space!" He pointed to the left. "Harrison, another ambulance just arrived. Why don't you take your, ah, friend, there for some privacy? We need to make sure she's..." A pause. "Alive."

"She's damn well alive," he snarled. He didn't ease his hold on her, though, and he realized that he was holding her so tightly that the others probably couldn't tell much about her. He wanted her away from the crowd, so he stalked toward the waiting ambulance. He jumped inside.

A female EMT was in the back. She stared at him with wide eyes. "Uh, are you—"

He put Elise on the stretcher. Spread her out gently.

She had ash on her cheek. A small burn on her wrist. He inspected her carefully. Was that *blood* on her shoulder?

Looked like a bullet hole in her shirt. Hell. "She's shot," he snapped at the EMT.

Shawn stood at the back of the ambulance and peered nervously inside.

"We need to see if the bullet is still in her." Harrison ripped the sleeve off Elise's shirt.

The EMT scrambled toward him.

"I'm not shot." Elise's eyes were closed. She coughed. "Just…choking."

"She needs oxygen." The EMT gave a firm nod. "Let me take care of her. Move back."

He didn't want to move back. He wanted to stay right there, holding her. He inspected her shoulder — dried blood was on her delicate skin, but he didn't see any bullet wound.

She coughed again.

Shit. He backed away. "Give her oxygen. Give her whatever she needs." He looked down and realized his hands were shaking. What in the hell? He balled his hands into fists.

"Harrison."

He turned his head. Locked his gaze with Shawn.

"We need to talk." Shawn peered over his shoulder at the chaos. "Now. Your lady is out, she's safe. You can spare me a few minutes."

His lady?

Harrison swung his stare back to Elise. An oxygen mask had been placed over her face. The color was already starting to return to her cheeks. If he'd been a little bit later...a few minutes... "Talk in here. I'm not leaving her."

Shawn cursed, but then asked, "Is anyone else inside the building?"

Harrison's breath caught. Shit, he didn't know. Where was Razor? And Gray?

Elise pulled away the mask. "Only...d-dead..."

Harrison leaned down and put that mask back on her. "You breathe. You don't answer questions right now. You get stronger, understand me?"

She nodded. Her gaze met his. A tear slipped from her left eye. Slid down her cheek.

He wanted to *destroy*. This was on Gustave. That sonofabitch. He'd done this.

"Uh, I need to know what happened here." Shawn's voice was hesitant. Careful. Probably because the EMT was darting nervous glances at them all. "I've gotten reports of several explosions from witnesses who were in the area. They reported seeing men with guns. Hell, looks like some kind of mob hit to me..."

Harrison didn't take his eyes off Elise. She looked stronger already. Her gaze was brighter. She was sitting up —

"*Harrison,*" Shawn prompted, voice tight. "This is a freaking nightmare out here, what happened?"

"If it looks a mob hit, then I'm sure that's what it was. And innocent people got caught in the crossfire. Maybe check out Gustave Etienne's place. Something tells me he might be connected to this mess. I've heard plenty of rumors that the guy has underworld ties."

"Gustave?" Shawn repeated. Yeah, he knew exactly what Gustave was. "Shit." He spun away. Harrison heard Shawn shout out orders to the cops.

Elise pushed the mask back toward the EMT. "Thank you."

The EMT frowned at her. "Let me examine you. Let me—"

Elise shook her head. "I'm okay. I just…" She focused on Harrison. "I want to get out of here."

He wanted to take her out of there. Fast. But first… "Baby, you need to get checked out."

Her eyelids flickered. A little furrow appeared between her eyebrows.

God, he wanted to hold her. Odd since he typically never wanted to hold anyone. Harrison cleared his throat. "I'm not taking you anywhere, not until I'm sure you're all right."

Elise's gaze drifted over him. "You're okay."

He was battling a fast and hot rage, that was what he was doing. *Okay* didn't cover things—

"The smoke didn't bother you?" Elise asked as her head tilted to the right. "The fire?"

He'd barely felt the heat. Harrison waved his hand over her body. "Check her," he told the EMT. "If anything is wrong, *fix* her."

Elise's lips quirked. "Look, I told you, I'm fine." Her stare was on him. "Don't need fixing right now, but thanks."

He wasn't leaving the ambulance until she'd been cleared.

When the EMT bent toward her, Elise batted the woman's hands away. "Where is Ward? Is he all right?"

"I got him out." He looked over his shoulder and saw that Ward had been loaded into the ambulance with Krista.

"But is he *okay*?" Elise demanded. "The place was caving in. He got hit — hell, I don't even know what hit him. Please, *please*, make sure he's all right."

That would mean he had to leave her. Harrison shook his head. "You were targeted. You're at risk. You—"

"Take me with you. I don't need checking out. I'm all right."

Was she? Because when he'd been in that burning building, he'd nearly lost control because he'd feared she might be hurt. Might be dead. She still wasn't safe. He didn't know who was a threat to her and who wasn't.

He reached for her. Elise's fingers curled with his. "Stay at my side," he told her.

"Funny. That's exactly where I planned to be." She gave him a weak smile.

He wanted to kiss her. Hard and fast. Deep and slow. Every way.

Instead, he carefully took her out of the ambulance, ignoring the EMT's protests. They made their way to the other vehicle and Ward — hell, yes, he was conscious. Conscious and already shoving his way out of the ambulance.

"I don't need help!" Ward blasted to whoever was trying to help him.

"Jesus," Shawn muttered from behind Harrison. "You guys are such ungrateful messes."

Ward sported a big bandage on his cheek.

"You know hunters heal fast," Harrison told Shawn.

"Yeah, well, what's her excuse?" Shawn pointed to Elise. "You a hunter, too?"

She shook her head. Edged closer to Harrison.

His hold tightened on her hand. "She's mine. You don't need to know anything else about her." He leveled a hard stare at the detective. "When we leave, forget you saw her."

Shawn frowned. "Gonna be hard to convince *all* these folks they didn't see her — or you. Hard to forget a man kicking down a wall — "

"The building was collapsing, you said so yourself. I didn't kick anything down, it fell."

Ward was weaving toward him. Seriously, weaving. The guy needed to sit his ass down.

Ward's eyes narrowed on Elise. "Where are they?"

Elise glanced around. "Who is he looking for?" Her voice was low. Curious.

Ward lurched forward. *"Where are they?"*

A siren screamed from somewhere around them.

"No one else made it out," Elise said. Her voice sounded normal when moments before she'd been choking on smoke. She had made a quick recovery. Too quick?

Harrison's gaze swept over her.

And then Ward attacked. He *grabbed* Elise and yanked her against him.

Elise screamed.

Harrison basically lost his shit. He grabbed Ward — a hunter he'd known for most of his life, the closest thing to a friend he had — and he drove his fist into Ward's jaw. Ward crashed onto the ground, falling hard on his ass. He gaped up at Harrison.

"Don't fucking touch her like that ever again!" Harrison barely recognized his own voice. It was deep and low and cold.

Deadly.

Ward frowned groggily at him. Seemed confused. "Where's...her wings?"

What?

Ward let out a groan and collapsed on the ground.

Harrison turned his head very slowly and gazed at Elise. She stared at him, eyes all wide and innocent. As if she had no clue what was happening.

"That poor man," she cooed as she batted her long lashes. "He must have really taken a hard hit to his head." She bent over Ward and gave his cheek a gentle pat.

And that was when Harrison noticed that her shirt had holes in the back of it. Not holes, exactly, but more like two long slashes...right over her shoulder blades.

As if something had cut through her shirt.

Something like...

Fucking wings?

CHAPTER SEVEN

She liked this safe house. Provided it could be, really and truly...*safe*.

Only, technically, it wasn't a safe house. It was a luxury suite. Elise strolled through the high-end bedroom and noted the rose petals on the bed. Rose petals that had been carefully sprinkled in a heart shape. She gave the petals an admiring nod before heading back toward the den. Or sitting area. Or whatever those places were called. Soft, romantic music filled the air as Elise strolled over the lush carpet.

This wasn't just a luxury suite. It was the *honeymoon* suite in the swanky hotel. One that had a killer view of the city and had come stocked with chilled champagne. Win, win. Now this, this was more her style. The style that she hadn't encountered since her rather unfortunate curse situation had started.

Elise reached for the champagne. No sense letting it go to waste. When they'd checked in, she'd learned that the couple who *should* have stayed there, well, their wedding had been called off. Something about the bride running off with the best man. *Very* unfortunate. For the groom.

Not so much for me. She popped the cork. Champagne dribbled onto her fingers and a wide smile curved her lips as—

"You seem to be in a good mood. For a woman who is being hunted."

She grabbed a champagne flute. Poured in some bubbly. "I didn't die today." She plunked the champagne bottle back in the ice bucket, and Elise saluted Harrison with her glass. "That is definitely cause for a celebration." She sipped the champagne. Felt the ever-so-delicious bubbles on her tongue. Lovely. "Ward didn't die. Krista didn't die. Wins all around." Another sip. The champagne was *awesome.* But she had to be careful. She didn't get to drink often due to a very specific reason.

Alcoholic beverages tended to hype up her base instincts.

Hype up as in...*I lose control.* But she'd be careful. Very careful. It had been one hell of a day and she needed a little relaxation, so she took another sip.

"Others died today." Harrison's voice was all grim and dark. Buzz kill.

The bubbles stopped feeling quite so good. She lowered the glass. He stalked toward her. The honeymoon suite was huge, and she was standing in front of a fire place. Flames flickered behind her, and she was reminded of what it had been like in that speakeasy. Trapped. So much smoke choking her.

"Gustave sent the humans after you. I found one of their bodies before we left the scene."

Yes, she'd seen him nosing around with his cop buddy.

"The guy had a wolf bite mark on his neck. Figure the humans who attacked were wannabes who thought that if they did Gustave's bidding, they'd be transformed."

She forced herself to take another sip. The sip gave her time to think of a proper response. She'd realized the men had been bitten because she'd smelled the wolf on them. "Humans will do just about anything for a little more power."

"Um." His head tilted. He was right in front of her now. All big, bad, strong and sexy. He'd rushed into that fire like he had no fear. He hadn't burned. Hadn't so much as coughed when all of the smoke surrounded him.

That just made her nearly...giddy.

Or maybe it was the champagne making her giddy. Usually it took more than a few sips to do that but...

But so much about me has changed recently. And keeps changing.

"Why did you save Ward and Krista?" Harrison wanted to know.

Oh, she had an answer for this one. Elise gave a determined nod. "Because they needed saving."

"You could've died saving them."

Yes, true. She drained the glass. Just to be done with it and *not* because he was making her nervous. She dropped the flute near the ice bucket and considered flopping down on one of the nearby designer couches. For the moment, she resisted the urge and remained standing. "I was the only one there who could do anything. If I hadn't helped them, they would've burned or died from smoke inhalation or..." A long sigh. "They wouldn't have gotten out. You would have lost your friends." *Truth.* "I didn't want your friends dying because of me."

He watched her with those eyes that Elise was starting to think could see in her very soul.

"I'm selfish." Shit. The champagne had made her chatty. Or maybe his bright blues had done the job. "I know that. One of my big flaws. I look out for myself because that's the way it has always been. Survival of the fittest. My mom died when I was born, and my dad? Let's just say he was a straight-up demon and be done with it." *Oh, damn, damn, damn. Please let him just think 'straight-up demon' was an expression and not a confession.*

Harrison's eyes flickered.

"You can relate, huh?" A quick distraction, but one that she needed. "You have some family issues you want to talk about? You can, you know. You can talk about anything with me."

"Never knew my mom," he said flatly as if it didn't matter. "She cut out right after I was born. Didn't want to be saddled with a kid."

Her lips parted. "That's not—"

"My dad, yes, sure, there are plenty of people who say he's a bastard. And that I'm exactly like him."

Elise pressed her lips together. Before he'd dropped that line about his mom, she'd been about to tell him... *That's not what I heard.* He was being all tough and stoic. Typical hunter. But she could see through his mask. He hurt.

She didn't have the heart to hurt him more. In fact, she wanted to take away some of his pain. *What in the hell? Am I sick? Did I catch a human cold or something?*

"Elise? You okay?"

"I don't think you're a bastard." Truth. Maybe she had when they'd first met but...no, he wasn't. "I think you're a good guy who has done the best he could do with a hard life."

"Every hunter knows the life is hard. We don't have a choice about facing the monsters out there."

Her gaze lowered. "And you hate monsters?"

"I hate evil. I hate the freaks who get off on killing and torturing. Someone has to stop them, and it's my job. Been my family's job forever."

She glanced over at the fire. "Speaking of...is your dear old dad still out of town?"

"I got word that he's coming back to Savannah."

Her shoulders stiffened. "Oh, that's..." *Horrible.* "Will you be meeting up with him soon?"

"No." Clipped. "We don't see eye to eye. Like I told you, people think I'm just like him but..." His words trailed away.

Her gaze swung back to him.

"But I don't want to be."

Her heart hurt for him. "You don't have to be like him. We don't have to be a damn thing like our family members. We are our own people. We make our own choices. We create our own paths in this world."

"You and your father...you have your own paths?"

"Definitely. It's much easier now that he's dead."

"I'm...sorry."

Elise had to laugh. "Don't be. He wasn't a nice man." There had not been a whole lot of *nice* growing up with him.

"Are you alone then? No other family?"

"I have another relation. Though he isn't exactly a fan."

"Then he's a fool."

She rocked forward and gave a little hum.

He smiled. "You hum when you're happy."

"It's an old habit. One I've been told over and over again that I have to break."

His hand lifted and his knuckles stroked her cheek. "I like it."

I like you. Her eyes widened. She caught herself before she let those telling words slip out. "I, um, I'm not good at letting a lot of people get close to me." She was sharing so much with him when her intent had been to get him to open up to her. But Elise found she couldn't stop. "You can put up walls to protect yourself from the world out there, but, after a while, you realize all those walls can make you cold."

"You don't seem cold to me." His hand slid down her neck.

She shivered. "You seem really hot to me," Elise mumbled. It was the truth. The man's touch was scorching her. But, honestly, that should be something that made her happy. She knew what his growing warmth meant and it was good. Part of her big master plan. Yet when she thought of the plan, Elise could have sworn she felt a strange hollowness inside of herself. She stepped back, sliding away from his touch. Time to distance herself—physically and mentally. "You killed Gustave?" She hadn't been able to ask that question when the human cops were around.

"He wanted to take you from me. That wasn't going to happen. Since he threatened you, since he wanted me out of the way, the bastard had to die."

Not like she'd mourn him. Elise angled to stare at the flames, giving Harrison her back. "One more threat gone."

She *felt* him advance on her. The air heated. Thickened. Then his fingers were sliding over her shoulders. He was touching her on one of the most delicate, sensitive parts of her body, and she had to bite her lower lip to hold back her moan.

"I'll stop all the threats to you. I promised I would, didn't I?" Harrison's breath blew over her ear. "You told me the truth, that you were desperate and cursed, and I gave my word to help you."

"Y-your word is important to you." He was still lightly running his fingers over her shoulder blades and her whole body was pulsing. Her nipples were tight. Her sex was aching. She wanted to arch against him and demand more of his touch. So much for the idea of more distance between them. She wanted to spin around and jump him.

"It's very important." His index finger traced her left shoulder blade. "You changed clothes."

"I—" What? What had he said? Clothes? Elise cleared her throat. "You ripped my shirt when I was in the ambulance. And there was blood and ash on it, so I just grabbed some different things from the downstairs gift shop. Boutique. Whatever it was. I billed all of the stuff to the room." She'd picked up lots of items—gone a little wild, in fact. Elise currently wore a silky, sleeveless top. Soft, black pants. Black heels. Everything was expensive. Stupid expensive, but she liked the clothes.

She liked his touch more.

"Gustave said something right before I had to kill the bastard...something that I can't forget."

Her eyes squeezed closed. "Seems to me like Gustave was a crazy-ass werewolf. I mean, he sent a hit squad after me. Don't think you should go believing anything that nut-job had to say." *Don't believe him. Don't!*

"Werewolves don't usually mistake things like this."

She had to think of a way out of this mess. If old Gussy boy had spilled the beans and said —

"He called you my mate."

Okay, I can work with this. Her eyes opened. She turned, easing her body so that she faced him. So that she was wicked close to him. Elise gazed into his eyes. "That's how werewolves think, isn't it? They think in terms of mates. Not boyfriends or girlfriends, not lovers, it's all about — "

"He said I'd claimed you in front of him and his men. Then I remembered that he was right. I *told* him that we were together. You used those words, and I repeated them."

"Hmmm." She blinked. Hoped she looked innocent. "Maybe it's like...handfasting? Is that the term?" She damn well knew it was. "People join hands and declare their commitment to each other. Witnesses are present." Elise tapped her chin. "I guess it's sort of like what happened at the werewolf den, and werewolves do have a rep for being very old school." She nodded enthusiastically. "That's probably what he meant."

"I don't think so."

Hell. She'd thought she sounded so —

"Because he asked if I'd fucked you."

Oh, my. *Gussy, you're a jerk and I'm glad you're dead.*

"Said if I hadn't, then it wasn't too late. That he could still take you." His eyes glinted on that last bit. "Then Gustave died because I wasn't in the mood to have anyone take you from me."

Her body leaned toward him. She was *pulled* to him.

"You're hiding secrets from me."

Elise nervously wet her lips. "How could I be? You're a hunter. You know when someone lies."

He smiled. A sensual and dangerous smile. "I do."

Her stomach knotted.

"*Mate.*" He seemed to taste the word.

She was afraid to breathe.

"If I fuck you, does that mean there's no going back? Because I think that's what Gustave meant. Whatever is between us will get set in stone the minute I sink into that gorgeous body of yours."

Elise didn't say a word. She couldn't.

"Talk to me, Elise."

Her name seemed like an endearment. So strange when his gaze was blazing, but his voice had turned tender on her name.

"Talk to me." A pause. "Or are you afraid that I'll discover your lies?"

No. "I'm not afraid of you." She wasn't. She was drawn to him. She wanted him. She needed him. Fear didn't enter the equation for her. "If we make love, then there's no going back. Not for you. Not for me. Because I don't think it's just going to be some big one-and-done business that we forget the next day. I think it will change us both." She'd managed to tell him the truth. Because she could *only* tell the truth. He didn't understand that about her yet. Eventually, he would.

"I don't make love, baby." He stepped back. "I'm not looking for some happily-ever-after ending. That's not what hunters do." Now he paced around her and moved toward the fire. "We fuck. We give our partners so much pleasure they scream." He glanced back over his shoulder. "Hunters have incredible stamina."

"I do not doubt that." She shrugged and tried to look careless. "But I believe there is more involved than just fucking. Or at least, I think there will be more for us." She held his gaze. "Like I said, I think when we make love, it will change things."

He peered back into the fire.

She exhaled. Shook her head. Blew out another breath.

"Mate."

Elise stiffened.

"A mate is forever in a werewolf's world."

"Good thing you're not a werewolf." *You're something so much better.*

"Hunters don't mate. We live for the job. We kill. We move on."

She couldn't stop herself. "Have you ever thought there might be more to you than just being a hunter?"

His laughter was low and bitter. "My father was a hunter. His father was a hunter. It's been that way for centuries. We hunt the monsters. We put them down."

He was looking into the fire. He missed her flinch.

"By the time I was six, my father was teaching me how to track werewolves. How to find demons. Other kids were playing with toy trucks or going to little league practice. I was sharpening my knives and learning how to melt silver in order to make bullets that would kill werewolves."

Her arms wrapped around her stomach.

"I made my first kill when I was fifteen. A vamp came for my father. I stopped him. And, shit, you know the thing about vamps? How they always look the same, no matter how old they are? The vamp I killed...he looked like me was

my age. That...stayed with me. He just—" But
Harrison broke off. "Screw it. You don't need to
hear about my shit." He whirled away from the
fire. Focused that electric gaze of his on her. "I
want to know about you."

"I like hearing about your past." What she
didn't like? "But I am so sorry you had to grow
up that way."

"Running from town to town? Fighting?
Killing?" A roll of his shoulders, as if the matter
didn't merit any concern. "Someone has to do the
dirty work and keep the world safe from
monsters."

The knot in her gut grew worse. "And that
someone is you? You're so sure about that?"

"It's the only life I've ever known."

Yes, it was.

"But what about your life, Elise? I want to
know more about you. You told me about your
folks, yet I have the feeling that's just the tip of the
iceberg. I want more. I want everything."

If she gave him everything, he'd destroy her.

"So far, I know that you say you were
cursed."

"I didn't just *say* it. I am cursed."

He took a step toward her.

She backed up.

His jaw hardened. "I thought you weren't
afraid of me."

"I'm not."

His look was doubting.

"When you touch me, I tend to not think as well as I should. And I've been drinking." She could still taste the champagne on her tongue. She wanted to taste him. "I'm trying to be good." Hah. A truer statement had never been spoken.

His lips quirked. "But *are* you good?" Another step toward her.

She wanted to back away. Instead, she stiffened her spine.

"Tell me the truth. Are you good, sweetheart? What was your life like before the curse? What secrets are you keeping from me?"

She didn't speak.

"Who are you?" Harrison rasped the words.

"I'm basically the queen of the universe," Elise announced flatly. "And my heart is as dark as they come. So don't worry about happy endings with me. That isn't in the cards. Instead, I'll make you love me. I'll make you need me. When I have you completely wrapped up and lost in me, then I'll use you to do my most wicked bidding and you will be helpless to resist."

He stared at her. Just stared.

Fucking champagne. She needed to take back all of those words. She was in such serious shit right then and —

Harrison threw back his head and laughed.

Laughed hard and loud and, oh, but he was completely adorable.

She smiled at him.

He was so freaking cute as that deep, bellowing laughter echoed around her. He was cute because...he thought she was being sarcastic. Precious. She smiled at him.

His laughter slowed. His gaze seemed to soften as he stared at her. Then he was lifting his hand and cupping her cheek. "There's one thing you should know about me."

There were dozens of things she wanted to know about him.

"I'm never helpless, baby. Never." Then his head lowered and his mouth crashed onto hers.

***

"I'm telling the friggin' truth," Ward huffed. He stood outside of the hospital, the setting sun hitting him as Gray waited by the open door of a black truck, a doubtful expression on his face. "The woman had wings."

"And *you* had a concussion," Gray cheerfully reminded him. "So while the building was collapsing around you and fire was raging, maybe you imagined things."

Ward didn't budge from the sidewalk. Gray had come to pick him up, and he owed the other hunter for that solid, but Ward wasn't crazy. "The wings covered us. The place was collapsing and we would've been buried alive, but her wings flew out and took the brunt of the impact."

Gray tapped his fingers along the open passenger door. "So you're saying she saved you."

"Yes, of course, Elise saved me. She saved me, she saved Krista —" Krista had cut out and left the hospital without him, and he had no idea where she'd gone. Like a few bullets flying and a collapsing building would keep her down for long.

"Uh, huh." Gray nodded and pursed his lips. "You see the problem here, don't you?"

"I see a jackass who won't believe me. A jackass who is supposed to be my friend."

Gray smiled. "If Elise has wings, she's a monster."

"I —" He stopped.

"Fallen angels have wings. Demons have wings. Don't really know of anything else that does. Fallen angels and demons? Bad. They are *very* bad."

Ward didn't know what to say.

"Why would something like that save a hunter?" Gray pushed.

He didn't speak. *I don't know.*

"Right." Again, Gray nodded. "A monster wouldn't save a hunter. That shit isn't done."

Ward climbed into the truck. Maybe he was wrong. He *had* blacked out for a while.

Gray slammed the door shut and took his time strolling around the front of the truck. He hopped inside and, a moment later, he had the engine purring. "How about we give the woman the benefit of the doubt? She saved your ass and Krista's, so let's not get the hunters to swarm in and kill her, sound good?"

"I don't want anyone to kill her." He rubbed his aching eyes. "Maybe I was wrong."

"I'm *sure* you were wrong." Gray tapped his fingers on the steering wheel. "Did you tell anyone else about this nonsense with the wings?"

"Yeah." He winced. "I told Harrison."

Gray swore.

"It's okay, man. He's her protector. Not like he'd hurt her."

Gray's jaw dropped as he gaped at Ward. "When it comes to monsters, we both know Harrison never hesitates. He's more the kill first and ask questions later type of guy."

"He...he wouldn't do that with her."

"If she's a monster, he sure as hell will. If she's a monster, the woman is screwed."

CHAPTER EIGHT

"I want you," Harrison growled against her lips. Her mouth—God, her mouth was making him insane. Those full, pouting, red lips. She tasted so sweet and she made him want to sin in a thousand different ways. He kissed her again. Harder. Deeper. His hand slid to sink into the thickness of her hair as he tipped her head back and just *took*.

Her hands rose. Curled around his arms. He felt the bite of her nails through his shirt, and he loved that little sting. She was sexy and tempting, and he wasn't going to walk away again. Not ever again.

He wanted her naked. He wanted *in* her.

But then her hands slid to his chest. She pushed against him. "Stop."

Fucking hell. He sucked in a breath and lifted his head. Her eyes—those *incredible*, unforgettable eyes – searched his.

"What's happening here?" Elise asked him.

Despite the dark lust thundering through his body, Harrison's lips quirked. "I'm trying to have sex with you."

"You're trying to fuck me."

Moments before, she'd talked of making love. He didn't make love. He fucked. Love wasn't part of his life, never would be. Sweet and tender times weren't in the cards for hunters. "This isn't about mating. I don't care what bullshit the werewolf spouted. Sex is sex."

"Fucking is fucking?" Elise whispered. "Not with me. Not with us. I told you, we cross this line—"

"Everything changes. I was warned." The problem? He didn't give a shit about the warning. He wanted her. His control had broken and there was no holding back or playing it safe. She'd nearly died in the speakeasy. She could have been crushed beneath the debris, could have died from smoke inhalation, could have *burned*...

And then what the hell would he have done?

When he'd seen the wreckage, he'd been desperate to get to her. Ready to destroy anyone in his path. He'd never reacted that way before.

He didn't have to worry about crossing a line. It was far too late for that. He'd already stepped over the damn line. He'd run past it. Now, it was just about them. "Not forever."

She licked her lower lip.

"This isn't forever." He wanted her mouth again. He leaned down. Nipped her lower lip. Enjoyed her soft moan. "This is sex. This is need. This is a hot, dark lust that makes me want to strip you and fuck you right here. It makes me want to take you against the nearest wall. I want to be in you so deep that you think I'm part of you. Then I want to make you come harder than you've ever climaxed in your life."

Her breath hitched. "That, um, sounds like a lovely plan."

How the hell could she keep making him want to smile when the desire he felt for her was so savage that he wanted to roar his need? His whole body was too hot. Too hot, too tense. A haze of red had started to cover his vision, and he wanted her more than he wanted breath.

But she'd said stop. That one word pierced straight through him.

Her right hand was still over his chest. Over the heart that raced too fast for her.

"You were the one who turned away before." Elise leaned toward him. "What changed for you?"

Everything changed when you were trapped in hell, and I couldn't get to you. He couldn't tell her that. So he'd give her another truth. "I realized what a great shame it would be if I never had the chance to fuck you."

Her hand dropped. "I'm amazing so it would be a shame." Elise gave a hard, negative shake of her head. She eased back. "But there's more to it. There has to be. I don't get to lie to you. So you can't lie to me. Tell me why you've changed your mind. The real reason. Tell me why you were pushing me away and now —"

He locked his hands around her hips and lifted her into the air. Her hands flew out and curled around his shoulders. "Why I'm pulling you as close as I can get you?"

"Yes." A breath.

"Because you're not dying," he promised her grimly. *Not on my watch.* "I'm not going to lose you. I haven't ever wanted anyone the way I want you. It's not rational or normal and I know that." He stared into her eyes. "I just don't give a damn. I make my own rules. I want you, so I'm taking you."

Her body trembled. "Hunters are supposed to always have control. Yet you don't seem to have much control right now."

"It's hanging on by a thread." It was hanging in place for her. "You said you wanted me before."

"I did."

"Do you still? Do you want *us*? Not forever, that's not what I'm offering you. I'm offering you sex. Dirty, rough, and so good you'll scream. This isn't mating. This isn't love." The last words felt brutal, but he didn't want her to misunderstand. He wasn't meant to mate or love anyone. That wasn't for a hunter. Hell, most people believed hunters *couldn't* love. He'd sure never loved anyone in his life.

There wasn't softness in a hunter's life. No tender moments. He'd never known his mother.

And his father had trained him with a fierce and cold discipline. No attachments, no —

"You can love." She leaned down and pressed a kiss to his cheek as he still held her before him. "You might not know how, but you can."

No, no, this wasn't about love. "Sex," he rumbled at her. "Choose. If I can't give you what you want —"

"I want you. Only you. You are exactly what I want." She smiled. "I choose you. And you —"

"*You're mine.*" The possessive words tore from him. He'd never been possessive about anyone or anything before, but Elise was different. He was different with her. His mouth took hers once more as he carried her out of that room and into the bedroom. Her legs wrapped around his hips and her arms looped around his neck. Her body pressed against him, her full breasts and tight nipples easy to feel through their clothes. But he wanted those damn clothes gone. He wanted her naked. He wanted her moaning. He wanted her climaxing.

Harrison kicked the door shut in the bedroom. He pulled his mouth from hers long enough to glance at the bed — and all the rose petals. The room smelled sweet and the bed was massive. Perfect for them. He headed straight for the bed and put her in the middle of those rose petals.

She shook back her hair and gazed up at him. "I have a request."

He yanked his shirt over his head. Dropped it.

"Can you...turn on all the lights in the room? I mean, I know there's light in here, but the sun is setting. It's just going to get darker and darker. I'd love all the lights on."

His hands were on the snap of his jeans.

Her stare was on his chest. Then it dropped to his abs. She bit her lower lip even as her cheeks flushed.

"Baby, I wasn't planning to do it in the dark. I want to see every inch of you." See her, touch her, taste her, and fuck her. Yep, that was his to-do list.

But he backed away from the bed. Made sure all of the lamps were on in addition to the overhead light. When he turned back around to her...

Elise was naked and on her knees on the middle of the bed.

He stilled. For a moment, he just drank her in. Full, pink-tipped breasts. Sensual, flaring hips — perfect for holding while he held tightly to her. And her sex — bare. Gorgeous.

His skin felt even hotter. His breath heaved as he stripped and stalked toward her. Her eyes widened as she stared up at him, and for just a moment, he could have sworn that he almost saw a flicker of fear in her eyes.

No. Elise couldn't be afraid. Not with him.

She backed up, though, as he advanced on the bed. His hand flew out and curled around her ankle. Carefully, gently, he pulled her leg toward him. Pulled her and positioned her until she was spread on the bed, with the rose petals crushed beneath her. "You don't need to be afraid of me. I would never hurt you."

"Promise?"

"Hell, yes." Hurting her was the last thing on his mind. Worshipping her perfect body? Sinking balls deep into her? *Yes, yes, again.* "You're not going to know pain with me. Only pleasure."

He angled his body between her thighs.

See her. Touch her. Taste her.

Take her.

His gaze dipped over her body. His muscles were so tense he ached, and he had never seen anyone more beautiful in his life.

His hand lifted and his fingers touched her breast.

She gasped at the contact. "You...you're so warm."

He was burning up for her.

"I like it."

His fingers curled around her nipple. Stroked and teased and she arched up against him. Her breath came faster as she moaned his name.

See her. Touch her. Taste her.

His mouth took the place of his hand. Sucking and licking and she trembled beneath him. Her taste was everything he craved, and he could've sworn that he was getting a little drunk from her. It was crazy, but the more he tasted her, the wilder he became. The more he needed and wanted. The more he knew he would —

Take.

His hand slid down her body. Memorized every inch of her. Down, down he went with his fingers even while his mouth still worked her sweet nipple. Her sex was soft, so silky, and wet for him. He pushed his fingers between her delicate folds, pushed his index finger up into her —

"Harrison!"

She was tight. He was going to go insane once he got his dick in her.

He withdrew his finger. Stroked her clit.

"You're so warm and, sweet hell," she choked out, *"your touch feels so good! Yes, there, there!"*

He strummed her clit then slid two fingers inside of her as he tried to stretch her and get her ready for him. He twisted his fingers, he thrust, and he had her hips frantically surging toward him. Yes, yes, that was good.

It was about to get even better.

He kissed a path down her body. Her stomach trembled beneath his mouth and her hands grabbed his shoulders.

"I want you inside of me!" She was fierce with her need.

That was exactly where he wanted to be. But first...

Taste.

He intended to mark her with his touch, with his mouth, then —

"Harrison!"

He blew lightly over her exposed sex before he used his hands to push her thighs even farther apart. He stared at her, and all he could think —

Mine.

The thought was so savage and primitive, and it didn't even seem to be his own. The darkness filling him obliterated everything else. Everything but the need to taste what was his.

Harrison put his mouth on her. He drove his tongue into her. Licked and sucked and feasted as the hunger he felt for her grew and grew. She was all he knew. All he wanted.

All he'd ever wanted.

He couldn't get enough of her taste. Couldn't get enough of her. His dick was swollen and aching, and he knew she'd feel like heaven when he slammed into her, but first...

She screamed, crying out as her whole body arched with the force of her release. He lapped up her pleasure, greedy for more of her taste. Greedy for everything that she had.

He kept tasting and taking, feral in his need. He'd never been so far gone with anyone. Never had such a primal, consuming drive to claim someone.

She arched against him again and moaned with another release. His tongue kept working her mercilessly because he was so hungry for her pleasure. Hungry for *her*.

Her hands sank into his hair. "*Harrison!*" She pulled at him.

Another lick, and then his head lifted.

Her eyes widened as she stared at him. Again, he could have sworn—"You will *not* fear me." Harrison barely recognized his own voice.

He pushed her legs apart even more. Caught her hands. Threaded her fingers with his and pinned her hands back against the pillow.

She looked into his eyes. "I don't fear what you are." Her words were husky. So sensual. "I just want you. All of you."

He drove into her. Sank as deep as he could go and her legs clamped eagerly around his hips. There was no holding back. There was no restraint. There was only madness. Hard, heaving thrusts as he plunged into her. He drove deep, took and took because he was with the woman who finally belonged to him.

Savagery roared from within him. She was his. She'd been born for him, and somewhere, in a deep, dark place inside of him, Harrison knew that. Every thrust destroyed his control. Every soft moan from her chipped away at a wall he hadn't known was there. A wall that had been sealing away a part of himself. The wall kept weakening...

Until…

"*Harrison!*" She called out his name again in pleasure. Screaming for him, as he'd told her she would.

But while she was screaming, something had broken in him. Heat lanced his skin. No, no, the heat came from *within* him. A strong, sweeping force. His grip on Elise turned even harder, and he pounded into her again and again. His mouth went to her neck. Kissing. Licking. Down…the curve of her shoulder. Right there.

Right *there.*

His mouth opened. His teeth pressed against her skin.

"Do it." Her whisper. Tempting.

He bit her and seemed to erupt and the pleasure was so consuming that he bellowed her name. Bellowed and held her tighter as the release splintered through every cell of his body. He poured into her. His hands freed hers, and he grabbed for the sheets. His fingers dug into them because he was afraid if he held her, he'd hurt her—the pleasure was too intense. Nothing had ever been like this before. Nothing ever would be again. No other lover would compare.

No other lover would ever be Elise.

Mine.

Harrison's head lifted as his breath heaved out. He stared into her eyes. "Mine."

CHAPTER NINE

The flames of hell stared back at her from her lover's eyes. Elise tried to pull in a breath, but Harrison was crushing her. Crushing her and gazing at her with eyes that burned with fire.

Fear trickled through her once more even as her sex still trembled with pleasure. She'd known what hid inside of Harrison. Known that it would need to escape soon, but being face to face with the beast he secretly held...

Holy hellfire.

"Don't." Harrison's voice. And yet it wasn't. It was deeper and rougher. A rumble of a beast from the mouth of a man.

His body was like a furnace on top of hers. Way hotter than he'd been when they'd stood in front of the fireplace. Not like she was gonna lie, though, that heat of his felt good. When he'd stroked her with his warm fingertips on her breasts and between her legs...

How many times had she come for him?

Now she licked lips that were dry — probably from screaming his name and all the panting she'd been doing—and managed to ask, "Don't...what?"

"Be afraid," he said in the voice that seemed to roll through her with its dark power. "I wouldn't hurt *you*."

He'd bit her on the curve of her shoulder. The bite hadn't been intended to give pain, she knew that. It had been a mating bite. Did *he* know that?

All along, her plan had been to wake the beast who lived inside of Harrison. A hunter? Oh, hell, no, there was so much more to him. He'd just needed to let go of his control so the real Harrison could come out and play.

He had let go. With her.

He was still thick and heavy inside of her, and his eyes—his eyes swirled with flames. A hunter's eyes didn't do that. A hunter's eyes *couldn't* do that. The beast was doing that. She was staring right at the beast he'd secretly carried all his life.

When she'd discovered the truth about him, following a legend from a voodoo priestess who owed her a long-ago unpaid favor, Elise had been thrilled. The beast—if he truly existed—could save the day for her. He would be a game changer in the battle she fought. She'd planned to use him. To do anything necessary to wake the sleeping beast. But as the beast stared down at her with his burning eyes...

I want the man.

Her hands flew up and cupped his cheeks. Rough stubble pressed against her palms. She pulled Harrison's face toward her. Kissed him. Deep and frantic.

Harrison shuddered above her. And then his hands curled around her wrists. He kissed her back. Not with the wild need of moments before, but with a tenderness she hadn't expected. For an instant, tears stung her eyes.

She didn't let them fall.

He slowly lifted his head and looked down at her. The flames were gone from his eyes. The familiar blue had returned. Harrison didn't speak and that was probably a good thing. She was trying to gather her thoughts and pull together her pretty much shattered heart and body and figure out just what the hell she was supposed to do next.

She'd had this grand plan in place. Find Harrison Key. Seduce Harrison. Bring forth his beast. *Use* him.

Only now...

Harrison slowly withdrew from her. She flinched.

"Elise, are you okay?"

No, not really. Once again, her world had imploded. "I liked having you inside me." It was easier to just give him another truth instead of answering the question he'd asked.

"I liked being in you." A pause. "I didn't use a rubber, but, baby, you're safe—and that's not just some bullshit line. Hunters don't get diseases. There's nothing I can spread to you. And as far as pregnancy is concerned—"

"I'm not worried." She wasn't. As far as pregnancy was concerned...her body, her control. She controlled when she would get with child and when she didn't. That was the way it had always been for her kind, and even the unfortunate curse she'd encountered wouldn't change that—she'd checked with her voodoo priestess informant to make sure of that detail. "There is no chance of a child now, so you don't need to worry. Birth control is taken care of." Though she did have a quick flash of a little girl with his bright eyes. Wouldn't the child be—

Stop. Do not go there. Not now.

He slipped from the bed.

She stretched. And missed him. But he was only gone a few moments before he was back and—scooping her up?

Elise let out a startled cry as she threw an arm around his neck.

He gave a warm chuckle. "Relax. I just thought you might like a hot soak." He carried her into the bathroom. More rose petals were in there—rose petals and even a giant, heart-shaped tub. He'd turned on the tub—a Jacuzzi tub—and bubbles danced on the surface.

He lowered her into the tub, and the water was heaven. Elise tipped back her head and closed her eyes as the water jetted over her body.

Harrison slid into the water with her. Her head had lowered to rest on the side of the tub, and his body brushed against her. She didn't open her eyes to look at him. She was afraid he'd ask questions, and she just felt too hollowed out to answer him.

She hadn't expected the intensity of her reaction to him. Sure, she'd wanted him. She'd figured the sex would be good, but Elise hadn't expected it to be mind-blowing. Life-changing.

Absolutely addictive.

I already want him again.

A thousand warning signs were flashing in her head.

His knuckles brushed down her neck, then slid over to the tender spot he'd nipped during sex. "I left a mark on you."

That was the way mating worked. For certain paranormals. Shifters. Not for hunters. *Put the pieces together, Harrison. I don't want to be the one to shatter your world.*

Oh, damn. Her breath caught. Her eyes flew open as she gaped at him. When had she started caring about whether or not she shattered his world?

His eyes were on the little mark. A mark she didn't even feel. "I'm sorry." He sounded it. "You must think I'm the biggest bastard on earth. I'm saying I won't hurt you even while I'm leaving a mark on your beautiful body." He leaned forward and brushed his lips over her skin. "I'm sorry. It won't happen again." Another kiss. He pulled back.

She touched his cheek. "You didn't hurt me. I liked it."

A faint furrow appeared between his eyebrows.

"You promised me dirty and rough. That's just what I like. So you got a little carried away and left a mark or two on me." She shrugged. The water teased her breasts. "You'd better do a body check because I'm pretty sure my nails tore apart the skin on your back and shoulders."

He held her gaze a moment longer. The water was so warm and the jets kept—

Harrison smiled at her. "You screamed for me."

Yes, well… "I'm pretty sure you screamed for me, too."

"I think I bellowed. Roared. Not screamed."

"Semantics."

His head cocked. Beneath the water, his left hand slid to her thigh.

She sucked in a breath.

He gave a low, sexy laugh. "Just making sure you're not too sore…"

Her legs parted. "Better do a thorough check. Like, super insanely thorough."

He laughed again and kissed her neck and for a moment, she forgot who she was.

What she was.

His fingers dipped between her legs. The water jetted over her as his fingers stroked her. His long, strong fingers dipped in and out of her, and she found herself pushing against him. Wanting more. Deeper.

"Not too sore?"

"If you think of stopping," she threatened, "I will hurt you."

More laughter. She liked his laughter, but she liked what his fingers were doing even more. His thumb pushed over her clit, strumming her beneath the water. Two fingers were inside of her, and he worked a third into her even as he kept pushing against her clit. The climax hit her hard, pulsing through her whole body. Elise turned her head toward him and she bit him, locking her teeth right over his shoulder and trying to muffle the cry that burst from her lips.

It took a moment for the aftershocks to ease. He stroked — no, soothed her — with his touch, and then his hand slowly withdrew.

She pulled away from him. Looked up into his eyes and felt completely lost.

He wasn't smiling. Fire didn't burn from his eyes. It was just Harrison, staring back at her.

"I…" *Think of something to say, Elise.* "It was my turn to bite. Hope you didn't mind."

"Trust me, I don't mind a damn thing that you do."

She wanted to smile. Because she wanted it so badly, she didn't. Elise looked away and realized that rose petals were floating in the bath tub with them. The honeymoon suite. He probably had no clue just how perfect that was. Harrison didn't realize that they'd sealed the deal, so to speak. As far as her people were concerned, she was married. A marriage that they had just well and truly consummated.

Her gaze drifted around the immense bathroom and she saw the shadows lurking in the corners. Such heavy, thick shadows. There was only faint, sort of...mood light in the bathroom. That soft light that fancy hotels favored. A light that created too many shadows.

Shadows.

She grabbed for Harrison. "Let's go back to the bedroom."

"Of course." He rose. Water poured down his body.

His body...oh, wow. The man had abs for days and a cock that was long and thick enough to make a woman drool. He'd touched her everywhere. Stroked her. Tasted her. But she'd barely gotten to touch him. During sex, he'd caught her hands and pinned them on the bed.

That wasn't going to do. She wanted to learn every inch of his body.

He brought a towel back to her. When she stepped out of the tub, he dried her off. It was odd, having him take care of her. "You don't seem like the big, bad hunter right now."

He dropped the towel. It fell near her feet. "I am. Don't ever forget that." His jaw hardened.

She stood on her toes and kissed his jaw. "Then it's a good thing I think you being all big and bad is sexy." She walked away from him, giving him a nice view of her ass. She hoped he enjoyed the show. She hoped—

"What...in the *hell*?"

Elise stilled.

His steps rushed toward her. His hand flew out—

And touched her back.

Her breath shuddered out. He'd touched her left shoulder blade, and the area was so incredibly tender.

Sensitive. She bit her lip to hold back her moan.

"Elise..." His voice was rough. Dark.

"Y-yes?"

"You have wings on your back."

Her eyes closed. "T-tattoos..." She knew what they looked like. She'd stared at them in mirrors often enough since her curse. "Don't they look like beautiful tattoos?" He was lightly tracing the designs on her shoulders and her sex quivered in response.

"Tattoos..." His voice was thick. Unreadable. And he was still tracing the markings on her skin. Markings that she knew looked like small wings on her shoulders. Delicate, blue and gold, almost like butterfly wings on her shoulder blades.

She opened her eyes and glanced back at him. "Don't you like ink?"

"You're sexy as fuck. *They* are sexy as fuck." But a furrow was between his eyes. "I saw your back before — when we were at my place — and I didn't notice them."

"Um, you were probably distracted by my stellar ass."

"It is stellar but...I swear, I think the tattoos were just glowing."

Oh, shit. She laughed. "You know what that could have been? Maybe it was a trick of the light." She hurried into the bedroom, mostly so she could get away from his touch before he gave her an orgasm just from touching the design of her wings. Explaining that one wouldn't be easy. She dove under the covers and made sure her back was away from him. Elise looked up —

He filled the bathroom doorway. His shoulders were so huge they brushed the wood on either side of him. He was naked and gorgeous and he made her mouth water.

But Harrison stalked all determinedly toward her. "I have questions I need to ask you."

Questions? She'd rather get back to the mind-numbing sex, thank you very much.

He neared the bed. "There's something that Ward told me. Guy had to be confused, but..." He stopped.

Uh, oh. What was it now? "Harrison?"

He touched the side of the bed. Lifted the sheets. "What did this?"

She glanced down. Felt her eyes widen. They were slices in the sheets. In the mattress. She'd been so distracted that she hadn't noticed them. "I—"

"Claws. *Claws* did this."

Elise gulped. The man wasn't wrong. Yes, claws had made those marks.

He grabbed her hand. Rubbed his fingers over her short nails.

"I don't have claws," Elise told him.

And it took all of her strength, all of her control not to say...*But you do.*

***

Gray pulled into the swanky hotel's parking garage. He needed to see Harrison, right the hell then, and he didn't care if he interrupted the guy's beauty-freaking-sleep.

They had to talk about Elise. They were going to clear the air. But his phone rang as he rushed toward the elevator, and he glanced down, just for a moment.

His ex-wife's number flashed on the screen. Shit. He stilled. They weren't on good terms. Mostly because she knew what an asshole he was. He'd screwed up with her far too many times, and he hated it every single time. If she was calling, then it was important. He turned away from the elevator and put the phone to his ear. "Look, Cassie, this is not a good time—"

"It's not fucking Cassie," a low voice snarled back at him.

Gray's body swayed. No, *no.*

"Found your secret, hunter. Thought you could have a wife? A kid? Thought you could hide them from the monsters?"

He'd damn well tried.

"That's not the way this shit works. You get *none* of this."

Gray eased out a low breath. "I want to talk to Cassie."

A scream echoed around the parking garage. He whirled—and there was Cassie. Standing near a black van. Some bastard had a knife to her throat. A bastard who wasn't alone. Three other guys were with him. All were tall, muscled, and blond. Their hair was long and braided on the sides. They kind of looked like old school Vikings as they stood there. Soon to be *dead* Vikings.

The asshole holding Cassie dropped the phone he'd held in his left hand. His right hand tightened on the knife. "She's alive. I could've killed her and brought you her body, hunter."

Tears streamed down Cassie's cheeks. "What's happening?"

He'd never told her the truth about himself. There were some secrets that were better off not shared. "It's going to be okay, Cassie."

"Yes," the man with the knife hissed at her. "You'll be okay. Because I'm going to let you go. A gesture of good will." He lifted the knife.

Gray lunged forward even as he yanked out his gun. He was packing silver that night, and he didn't know what those guys were, but silver could hurt pretty much any mother out—

"I have your daughter."

Gray froze.

"Shoot me, hurt me in any way, and my men will kill her. You'll find her broken body and all you'll be able to do is mourn at her grave."

Cassie's tears came harder. "He has her. He took her from me!"

Gray grabbed Cassie and yanked her behind him. "What the hell do you want?"

The man smiled. His eyes were pitch black. His lips a pale pink. "I want a trade."

"I don't even know you, asshole. I don't have anything to give you."

"We have…friends…in common." A shrug. "Friends, enemies. Sometimes, they can be the same thing."

The men around the leader were silent as death.

"Elise Aine is upstairs." The SOB pointed up with his index finger. "I want her. Bring her to me—alive or dead, really makes no difference— and I'll give you back your child." He stepped forward. A cold wind seemed to sweep from him.

"But if you don't do my bidding, the child will die screaming."

Gray smiled at him. *"You're* dead."

"No. Not even close." The stranger lifted his chin. "Meet me in the Colonial Park Cemetery in an hour. Have Elise with you. If you don't, then you'll find only your daughter's grave waiting."

A ragged scream tore from Cassie. She lunged forward and ripped the gun from Gray's fingers. *"I want my daughter!"* She fired the gun.

But the bullets didn't hit anything because the men in the black—the fucking dead-looking Vikings with their braids and their black eyes—were gone. They'd just vanished.

Cassie's breath sobbed out. "Gray?" She grabbed his arm and swung him toward her. "What in the hell is happening?"

He stared into her golden eyes and didn't know what to say. He saw pain and horror and confusion. And fear. So much fucking fear.

"We'll get her back?" Cassie whispered. "Tell me that we'll get her back!"

"Yes." He'd do whatever was necessary, but he'd get his daughter back. "We will. I swear it."

CHAPTER TEN

A pounding at the door had Harrison's shoulders stiffening.

"Oh, please," Elise muttered as she let out a dramatic sigh and stretched in the bed. "Don't let that be someone else who wants to kill me."

His eyes glittered. "No one is killing you. Not on my watch."

That was exceptionally good to know.

"Stay here."

In the bedroom? Sure, why not?

He dressed then rushed away, all dramatic and strong-like, and Elise blew out a breath. Her fingers went to the torn — correction, *slashed* — sheets. She had made some definite progress in her campaign that night. Not like she'd be forgetting what it looked like when Harrison's eyes burned any time soon. His beast was close to breaking free from his chains. She should have been thrilled.

So why did her stomach feel all hollow and empty?

"Maybe I'm hungry." She toyed with the sheets. *Or maybe it's something else.*

Her eyes squeezed closed.

"Ahem."

She'd known the voice would come, sooner or later. Night had fallen and even with the lamps on in that bedroom, shadows persisted. He'd always been good at spying from the shadows.

The familiar voice poked at her as he added, rather proudly, "You've made progress!"

She kept her eyes closed. "Not now. I can't talk about this now." Harrison was just in the other room.

"I *saw* you with him! He couldn't keep his hands off you, he couldn't—"

Her eyes opened. She glared at the big, heavy shadow to her right. "You are such a voyeur. Don't *watch* me all the time, stalker." Elise climbed from the bed, fumbled around the room, and yanked on a t-shirt. It was huge, had to be one of Harrison's. It completely swallowed her.

"I'm not a stalker!" Now he was acting all offended. Like she bought that. "I am a loyal follower. A sworn protector! I want to help you. I want to see you returned to your rightful place. I want—"

"To get on my last nerve? Because you're close. Really close." Now that she had on a shirt that smelled nicely like Harrison, Elise climbed back into the bed. She settled comfortably beneath the covers.

"You're the one who taught me to be a voyeur."

Her lips twitched. He was right on that score. Looking through the veil at the human world had provided them with countless hours of entertainment, and they'd learned so much about technology. Not like they had TV where she was from. Technology didn't work in her homeland. Magic ruled there. When she was bored, instead of flipping on a TV, she'd peeked into the lives of humans. That was how she'd known so much about the modern human world when she'd found herself stumbling along the streets and searching for Harrison.

But… "I didn't watch people have sex. I gave them privacy." Elise sniffed.

"I didn't watch that part! I just — look, I know you mated him. Mission complete! You've got him, and he can cross over with you now. Bring him back and sic him on your enemies!"

She had to unclench her back teeth. "He's not a pet. Not an attack dog. I'm not going to *sic* him on anyone."

Silence. Then… "This was *your* plan, my queen."

Like she needed the reminder. But…*my queen.* The title felt foreign to her. Wrong. "I'm not a queen."

"Fine. *Prince-ass.*"

Oh, he'd done that deliberately. He did that all the time. Stretched it out so it wasn't princess so much as prince-ass. "Not funny."

"Nothing about the situation is funny! You're there, I'm here, and I can only see you when I use all my power to focus through the shadows. I can barely slip in to you, and when I do, you won't let me help!"

"Because you're not supposed to show your allegiance to me!" Her voice was low but angry. *Worried.* Sure, he could drive her crazy, but she didn't want anything happening to him. "If the wrong people find out that you're trying to help me, you know what they'll do to you. I told you to stay away. I told you to act like you'd turned your back on me. You have to look after yourself. Not me."

"But..." So quiet. Almost lost. "But you've always looked after me."

She had. She'd tried, anyway. But if her plan didn't work, she wouldn't be there any longer. He'd have to learn to fight without her. "Put yourself first. Forget about me."

"You are my princess."

Princess. Not prince-ass. She had to swallow.

"I will not forget you."

And I will never forget you.

Silence a moment, then, "Bring him to our world. I'm here waiting for you, I'm —"

The bedroom door flew open. It slammed back into the wall with a hard bang, and Elise jumped even as she gave a wild, startled cry. But no attacker — no vamp or werewolf or any other angry beast — stood in the doorway.

It was just Harrison.

His breath heaved in and out, making his chest rise and fall. His hair was wild and his eyes so intense. His fierce gaze swept over the room. "Who's here?"

She moved to her knees as she knelt in the middle of the bed. "Me?"

His gaze flew back to her. "I heard voices."

"My voice." Elise tried a laugh. "Just me and the shadows — that's all — "

He blinked. "You don't like the shadows."

"Ah, well, it's not that I don't like them. It's that — "

"You wanted the lights on earlier. You didn't want shadows." In a flash, he'd crossed the room. He turned on even more lights — lights she hadn't even known were there. *Why hadn't he turned those on earlier?* The new shadows disappeared as all the illumination flooded in —

A fat, black spider shot from the dying shadows. He raced across the room and hurtled right toward Elise.

Harrison grabbed for the spider.

"Don't!" She threw out her hand and the spider jumped onto her palm. He was shaking. She felt the tremors in his body. The spider shimmed up her arm, rushing to her shoulder, and then rubbing against her neck.

Harrison gaped at her. "What in the hell?"

"I, um, like spiders." She did. The poor guy was still shaking. She hadn't realized that he'd managed to take form and sneak through the veil to her. She'd thought that he'd just been spying. He must have been very worried about her to take such a huge risk. "Calm down," she whispered. "You know I would never let anyone hurt you."

"Elise, you have no idea what's fucking happening right now outside of this suite. Trust me, I *won't* be calming down." His eyes were on the spider. "Is that a black widow?"

"No, he doesn't have an hour glass. He's just a harmless spider." At the moment.

"Is it *rubbing* against you?"

Yes. "Does it look like he is?"

She saw a muscle flex along Harrison's jaw. "Put the spider down and come with me."

"I will, if you promise you won't kill him."

The spider's legs did a happy tap against her skin. He really liked that request.

Harrison rolled his eyes. "I won't kill your weird new friend."

Excellent. The spider's trembles stopped. He crawled back down her arm and disappeared under the covers.

"Fuck." Harrison shook his head.

She slid from the bed. "Who was at the door?"

"Gray. Get dressed. We have to move. *Now.*"

"Why? What's the rush?"

"*I'm* the rush." At that angry, rough voice, Elise's head whipped up. Gray stood in the doorway, and he was aiming his gun right at her.

Harrison swore and immediately stepped in front of her. "Gray, I told you, I can handle this."

She peeked around him.

Gray hadn't lowered his weapon. The guy didn't look nearly as cocky and put together as he'd appeared the last time their paths had crossed. In fact, she'd say his expression appeared to be quite desperate. And desperate was bad. Desperate people did desperate things. She knew because she was one of those desperate people doing some extremely shady and desperate things.

"I don't have a choice." Gray was sweating. "It's Holly. My Holly."

She had no idea who Holly was.

"I can't let her die," Gray cried out.

Okay, so Holly was someone who was in danger. Maybe dying.

"The trade is simple. I get Holly back if I turn over Elise." Gray swallowed. His gaze found hers. "I'm sorry, but she's my world."

He was going to shoot her. Elise was sure of it. "Please—"

Harrison shoved her behind him again. "You don't beg anyone for anything." His voice was a snarl.

Something brushed against her bare foot. She looked down. Saw a spider. Not the big, plump spider she'd put under the covers.

A small, black spider. One. Two. Three…

Uh, oh. A whole *lot* of spiders.

Someone's power must have gotten stronger. Someone had been practicing while she'd been gone. She was both proud...and afraid.

"You are not taking Elise."

Her head whipped up at that dangerous rumble. Harrison was a giant, angry wall in front of her. Was the air heating up? She rather thought it was. His shoulders were stiff and his back ramrod straight as he added, "I'll help you get Holly back, I swear it, but you aren't putting Elise at risk."

"Get out of the way, Harrison! I don't want to shoot you!"

"And I don't want to have to beat your ass, but if you try to take Elise from me, that's exactly what will happen."

His words made her feel all warm and tingly. Harrison wanted to protect her, and that was awesome except for —

"You won't shoot Harrison!" Elise heard herself yell as a wild fury blasted inside of her. She didn't even realize she'd moved her hand in the fast motion to signal an attack until the spiders swarmed. They rushed around Harrison and went straight for their target. Not just a few spiders. Hundreds of them.

"What in the hell?" Yes, Harrison sounded shocked.

Gray was busy yelling and swiping at the spiders.

"Stop it!" Harrison ordered. "You'll have all the humans in the hotel rushing up here! Dammit, these walls had better be thick." He lunged forward.

When he moved, she saw that the spiders were rushing up Gray's body. He'd dropped his gun and was swatting at the spiders with his hands. "Stop, stop, stop!" Gray yelled at them. "My daughter, I have to get my —"

Daughter? Curious, Elise raised her hand and spread out her fingers. "Stop."

The spiders immediately retreated. They raced back across the room, searching desperately for shadows. She backed up, turned off a lamp, and let them go.

Gray's gun was near his foot. Harrison scooped it up and aimed the weapon at his friend.

"What just happened here?" Gray's eyes were huge. "Where the hell did those spiders come from?"

You don't want to know. "This hotel obviously has a spider problem." Elise cocked her head as she studied him. "Someone should complain to the manager. Personally, I think I'd like a new room."

A low, rumbling growl broke from Harrison. It was the only warning she had before he attacked. One second, he was growling, and in the next instant, he'd shoved Gray against the nearby wall. Shoved him so hard that she was pretty sure Gray's head had dented the sheetrock.

Harrison lodged one forearm under Gray's chin, pressing hard to his neck, and with his other hand, he put the gun to Gray's head.

Hold up. He was going to *kill* the other hunter? "Uh, Harrison," she began.

"He would have shot you. He was going to *shoot* you."

"It's...m-my d-daughter..." Gray gasped. His face was purpling. "H-have t-to save..."

"You didn't care about Elise's life." Harrison's fury filled the suite. "I had already told you that I'd help you to get your girl back. We've handled monsters before, we can handle whoever the hell has your kid."

A kid. Her heart did a funny flip. "How old is this girl, this Holly?"

"S-seven..." Gray barely managed to say.

All right. That particular shade of purple was not flattering on anyone. She hurried forward and reached out a hand to tentatively touch Harrison's shoulder. *Wow.* He was so hot he was practically burning her. She snatched her hand back. "Let him go, Harrison."

He didn't let Gray go.

She cleared her throat and tried tapping his shoulder again. "Let the not-so-nice hunter go, Harrison."

Still no change. She was pretty sure that if she didn't stop Harrison, Gray would lose consciousness soon.

So Elise slipped between their bodies. Not a whole lot of room there, but she managed to wiggle up between them. Her back pressed to Gray's chest while her front slid against Harrison's rock-hard body. He'd forgotten to put on a shirt. Yum. Well, normally yum. For the moment, though... "Hi, there." She smiled at him.

His gaze flickered over her face. No flames were in his eyes, just ice-cold, deadly rage.

Elise kept her voice gentle as she informed him, in case he didn't realize it, "You're killing your hunter friend."

"He was going to kill *you*." A low, savage declaration. "No one hurts you."

She smiled at him. "I love this protectiveness. It's the sexiest thing I've seen in ages, but we all need to take a breath here." Elise heard gurgles behind her. "Like, really, I think Gray needs a breath or he's going to pass out and die."

Harrison's gaze dropped to her mouth. "Why are you defending him?"

Why the hell was she defending him? If Harrison snapped and killed the other hunter, wasn't that good for her? Another point for team bring-out-his-wicked-ways? Only...Elise stared into his eyes and tried to figure out what she really wanted, and she realized it *wasn't* for Harrison to lose himself to the darkness he carried inside. "He's your friend."

Harrison's eyes flickered.

"And he needs you." Actually… "He needs us. Someone took his little girl. One of those jerks who's been after me. Gray is desperate and he's scared and when people feel that way, they can make bad choices."

"He was going to shoot you. That's not a bad choice. That's asking for death."

"It's his *daughter*. He loves her. He wants to keep her safe. Don't you understand how he feels? Haven't you ever loved anyone?" No, no, she had not meant to ask that.

"No, I've never loved anyone, and I don't think I fucking ever will."

Huh. Wasn't that a cold blade to her heart?

But at least Harrison stepped back. He let Gray breathe. And he even dropped the weapon onto the bed. Lots of wins.

"Th-thank you," a hoarse whisper from Gray.

She spun to stare at him. "I don't like you."

He flinched.

"Normally, I'd want you dead at my feet." Total truth. "But there is more to you than I thought. Your daughter is out there, and you need me to get her back."

A weak nod. "Need you…" He sucked in a breath. "Alive or dead. Doesn't m-matter which."

A deep, angry snarl came from Harrison. Low and deadly enough to have goosebumps rising on her arms. For the moment, she ignored him. She didn't exactly want to face Mr. I'll Never Love You. Not like she loved him, either. But still.

Still.

Elise tried to consider the situation. "I'm guessing whoever took your daughter gave you a place for the exchange?"

Another one of those weak, bobbing nods. "Colonial Park Cemetery."

She had no idea where that place was, but Elise figured finding it wouldn't be that hard. Not with all the helpful technology humans had at their fingertips. She'd grab a phone and have the address in seconds. "Who took her? Vamps? More werewolves?"

He didn't nod this time. He gave a slow, rolling shake of his head. "L-looked like Vikings."

"Say that again?" Had he been denied too much oxygen?

"Tall. Blond. Wearing all black." He motioned to the side of his head. "Wore long braids right here." A shudder. "And their eyes were pitch black."

Oh, crap. Crap, crap. "How long do you have to deliver me?"

"An hour."

She lunged away and started grabbing clothes. "We need to move. *Now.* If we're even a minute late, your daughter is dead."

"Y-you know who they are." Gray's voice was stronger.

She didn't bother replying. Mostly because, yes, unfortunately, she did know who they were, and this was so bad. A million times bad. But she could handle this. She could save the girl.

Hopefully. Maybe.

"Get the hell out of here," Harrison suddenly bellowed.

Her head whipped around just as he threw Gray out of the bedroom. Then he slammed the door and flipped the lock.

Gray pounded against the door. "My daughter!"

Harrison had focused his stare on Elise. What a very, very angry stare it was.

"We'll get your daughter!" Elise called out. "Give us a minute!"

Harrison stood right in front of her. He seemed to suck all of the light from the room. So many shadows dipped and swirled around him. She shivered even before he said —

"You've lied to me."

Elise shook her head. "Never. Not once."

He smiled, and it was chilling. She almost backed up. Almost. Then she remembered who she was and that she should retreat from no one. Her chin lifted as she held his gaze.

His eyes were so cold as he told her, "You will not die for Gray."

"I'm not planning on dying. I just want to help the hunter's daughter." Words she'd never expected to say. Not in a million years.

"Why?"

Her mind went blank and it took her a moment to say... "Because she needs me."

His eyes narrowed.

"She was taken because of me. She had no control. No choice in this matter." Elise wet lips that felt too dry. "Children shouldn't be hurt."

His hand lifted.

She flinched.

And something happened—his face hardened with such fury...

Oh, no. What did I —

"You flinch at my touch?"

"I—"

"You flinch as if you expect me to hit you?"

She didn't say a word, but her eyes must have given her away.

"Someone fucking hit you."

Elise forced down the lump in her throat. "It was a long time ago."

"I will kill him."

"Too late. He's already dead."

"Good."

She couldn't look away from his gaze. She also couldn't speak.

"I *will* not hurt you. How many times do I have to make that promise?"

He didn't know the truth she was keeping from him. When he did, would he still want to protect her? Or would she become just another one of the monsters he wanted to destroy?

His knuckles slid over her cheek. "I'll break your curse, and I'll kill any beast who comes for you."

Of course. Beasts. Monsters. He thought he had to kill them. She would not let her tears fall. "Let's go get the girl. If we're late, she's dead." She backed away from him. Searched for clothes. *There.* She could wear—

"We will talk about the spiders."

She didn't look at him. "I don't see any spiders."

"We'll talk about them and everything else you don't want me to know. We *will* talk, my Elise."

Sure. "After we get the girl." She glanced over her shoulder.

He nodded. "After, and then, every secret you have will be mine."

He stormed out.

She released the breath she'd been holding. A big, fat spider ran across the floor. "I am so screwed."

***

Gray stood in front of the fireplace. His shoulders were hunched and his head bowed forward. Harrison marched toward him. Gray heard him coming and spun around. "Harrison, look, I—"

Harrison drove his fist into Gray's jaw. Gray staggered back. Harrison grabbed Gray's shirt and fisted his hand in the material as he jerked Gray toward him. "If you *ever* aim a gun at her again, you're dead."

Gray's Adam's apple bobbed. "It's...my daughter. I didn't have a choice."

"Yeah, you did. I had already told you that I'd get Holly back. But you went in there after Elise. You aimed your gun at her. You were going to shoot."

Gray didn't speak.

"We get your daughter back and I don't ever see you again." Rage burned so hotly that Harrison swore he could taste ash on his tongue.

Gray's face blanched with terror.

Harrison let him go.

"What are you?" Gray's expression was stunned.

Harrison frowned at the dumbass. "I'm the man you just made into an enemy. I'm also the man who is going to save your daughter. For the record, you're fucking welcome."

Gray blinked. Appeared confused. "Your eyes...I thought..."

The suite's bedroom door opened. Elise had changed—she wasn't wearing his t-shirt any longer. She'd put on some of the fresh clothes she'd bought earlier, down in the hotel's boutique. Designer jeans that fit her like a second skin, black boots that hit just below her knees, and a filmy, blue top that dipped low to reveal the swell of her perfect breasts. Her thick, golden hair slid over her shoulders. Her dark eyes held a thousand secrets, and her blood-red lips curved in a smile. "I'm ready."

He wasn't. Harrison stalked toward her. The bastards holding little Holly only cared about one thing. He stared into Elise's eyes. "You don't die."

Her head tilted as she studied him. "Be careful, or you're going to make me think you care."

He...

"Don't worry," Elise continued breezily, as if they weren't off to confront who the hell knew what. "I don't plan on dying. We'll get the girl, save the day, and vanquish the bad guys. I mean, isn't that what hunters do?"

"You're not a hunter."

"And neither are—" She stopped. Cleared her throat.

What had she been about to say? His stomach twisted, and deep inside, a voice whispered... *You know.*

"The things we're after..." Elise nodded. "I've seen them before. They like shadows. Dark places."

Gray bounded forward. "That's where I saw them. In the shadows. They were waiting in the hotel's parking garage. And Cassie told me they grabbed her when she was walking home through the park with Holly. The trees are thick, and there are plenty of shadows. She never saw them coming."

"Who's Cassie?" Elise asked, voice soft.

"My wife." Gray shook his head. "*Ex*-wife. After those freaks vanished — like, the SOBs literally vanished in front of me — I sent her home, called Razor and told him to guard her until I was back at her side." A determined nod. "Back with Holly."

Elise seemed to consider his words. "It's good that she's not here. I would hate for Cassie to die in the crossfire."

Gray's mouth dropped. After a moment, he snapped his lips closed. He paled and finally said, "Yeah, we'd all hate that."

Elise walked toward him. She lifted her hands.

Gray's nervous gaze darted over her. "Are you about to punch me, too?"

"I did notice the bruises you're sporting." Her stare darted to Harrison.

He shrugged. "He aimed a gun at you. He's lucky I didn't break every bone in his body."

"It's hot when you get all protective." She winked at him, then faced Gray once more. She still had her hands up, and Elise wiggled her fingers at him. "You're going to need to cuff me. Or tie my hands together. Or, you know, do some kind of bondage thing." A shrug. "Then you can take me to the cemetery and they won't suspect that you're betraying them. You give them me, you get your daughter, then you run with her."

Harrison didn't like where this was going. Suspicion settled heavily around him. "Seems like you already have a plan in place."

She slanted him a quick glance. All confidence. "I do."

He waited. She didn't share more. Of course, she didn't share more. She never did what he expected. He tapped his foot. Sighed.

Her head angled toward him as her smile bloomed. "You're my plan."

Harrison lifted one eyebrow.

"You promised to protect me."

He had. He would.

"So when the bad guys get their hands on me, let's just see how protective you can be." Her smile slipped away. "These bastards — if they are who I *think* they are — like I said, I've encountered them before. Iron won't work against them, so don't even try it."

Gray ran a hand through his hair. "What does work? Holy water? Are they some kind of demon?"

She shook her head. "No, holy water doesn't work, either."

Iron hadn't worked on Elise. Neither had holy water. He'd tested her again and again, and she'd passed those tests.

Harrison still held Gray's gun. "What about silver? Will silver bullets stop them?"

"Silver will sting, and it can slow them down. That slow down helps. Silver can wound them but to kill them, you'll need to take their hearts."

"*Take* their hearts?" Gray repeated.

"Yes, take them. As in, cut those bitches out. You take the hearts, and they stop." She headed for the door. "Oh, one other thing. Don't let them get near any shadows. If they're on the run and they slip into the shadows, they're gone."

Gray rushed to keep up with her. "How the hell do we keep them away from shadows...in a graveyard...at night?"

"I'd suggest using a light. A very, very bright light." She exhaled and squared her shoulders. "Okay, let's do this."

No. Not yet. Harrison strode to her. There was one thing he wanted to do, all right. He grabbed her. Spun her to face him. His mouth crashed down on hers. And her mouth—it greedily opened and met his with a wild, fierce passion.

After a moment, he pulled back. "You don't die."

"Not planning on it."

"They don't get you."

Her lips curved in a slow smile. "How could they? I have you watching my ass."

CHAPTER ELEVEN

"I didn't realize you were fucking her," Gray said as his hands tightened around the vehicle's steering wheel. They were in his massive truck, a beast Gray had always ridiculously loved. "I mean, sure, you two were sharing the suite, but I didn't know you were, um, together, not until I saw her wearing your shirt in that bedroom and the bed was wrecked and — — "

"I'm in the rear seat, not a million miles away," Elise announced, voice vaguely amused. "I can hear you."

Gray took a hard right. "No wonder you were ready to rip my head off when I aimed the gun at her. You're involved."

"What we are...it's none of your damned business," Harrison snapped back. He wasn't going to be forgetting what Gray had done anytime soon. The hunter had crossed a line, and there would be no going back.

I'd told him that I would help his daughter. I swore I'd get her back, yet he still went after Elise.

"I'm sorry," Gray sounded miserable as he braked the vehicle. "Sorry this shit happened, sorry—"

"Save your apologies," Elise ordered him. "Could you just tie me up already? The longer this takes, the longer those jerks will get twitchy." She shoved her hands into the front seat.

Harrison pulled out a rope and twined it around her delicate wrists. Not too tight. He didn't want to hurt her. He made sure to use a special knot, one that looked secure but really wasn't. "To get out, just jerk the rope back toward you."

"Got it."

He turned to stare at her. "I'll have my eyes on you the whole time."

He caught her smile. "That's because you just can't take your eyes off me."

Harrison knew she was trying to lighten the mood. But did *she* know...she was right?

They exited the vehicle. Gray immediately pulled Elise toward him and jabbed a gun in her side. Yes, that shit was for show, but Harrison didn't like it. He stepped forward, moving toe-to-toe with the other hunter. "You get a twitchy finger around her, and I'll put a bullet in your brain."

Gray's mouth dropped. "But...but—"

"But nothing. You've been warned."

Elise sighed. "You're kind of being a hard-ass, Harrison. I do love that vibe with you, find it sexy as all get out, but take a breath. His daughter's life is on the line. He's desperate."

There was no *kind of* about it. He was a hard-ass and Harrison knew it. "I'm not exactly the forgiving and forgetting type."

"What is it? What's your code?" Her head tilted. "Betray you once and it's over?"

"Yes."

She backed up. Bumped into Gray. Harrison could have sworn that fear flashed on her face. Her tongue swiped over her lower lip before she said, "Things aren't black and white. There's lots of gray in this world."

He just waited. His enhanced vision let him see her and their surroundings perfectly.

Elise looked worried. On edge. "Harrison, he was aiming the gun at me. He was ready to shoot me. I've moved on."

He hadn't. Harrison made sure all of his weapons were in place. Guns, knives, a few surprises. Weapons were all over his body, and he was ready to kick ass. But before they went into that cemetery, he swept his gaze over Elise. "You sure there's nothing else you need to tell us about these guys?"

Her lashes fluttered. Her bound hands twisted. "What do you mean? I thought I was great at sharing. I told you lots on the way here."

"If you're holding back something we need to know, tell us."

Her delicate face tightened. "I'm not holding back anything that would put a child's life at risk."

"Time's up," Gray announced as he nervously glanced at his watch. "We're going in, *now.*"

She nodded. Squared her shoulders. Then… "Wait."

If she'd changed her mind, he was getting her the hell out of that place right —

"Kiss me, Harrison. Once more."

"Are you freaking kidding me?" Gray demanded.

Harrison ignored the bastard. He yanked Elise into his arms and kissed her. Fast. Deep.

"Thank you," she whispered against his mouth. Her bound hands had been between their bodies, but her hands dipped down as she backed away. "You gave me just what I needed."

I'm starting to think you are everything I need, Elise.

Harrison had to watch as she was led away, with a gun at her side and her hands tied with thick rope. She looked small and fragile, and his chest burned as she entered the cemetery gates.

***

"I'm…sorry about this."

Gray was still spouting his apologies. Elise let out a frustrated sigh. "If you would do something over again in a heartbeat, you shouldn't waste a breath on apologies." She didn't look at the headstones or the graves. Just kept her gaze straight ahead. Gray was glancing to the left and the right, she could feel the nerves pouring off him. He was distracted because his emotions were involved. Emotions were dangerous beasts. Sometimes, they could help. Other times, they were your greatest weakness.

Gray was weak then.

"Where the hell are they?" he muttered.

"They're watching us from the shadows."

"How do you know that?"

Because she could feel them. "Just stop here." She stopped and he had to follow her lead. "Call out to them. Tell them you want your daughter."

He sucked in a breath. "I brought her!" Gray yelled. "Now bring Holly to me."

The trees rustled and swayed. The shadows seemed to stretch out.

Four figures stepped from the darkness. Four men in black, with hair so very blond. Too long. She'd always thought they needed to trim their hair, but they hadn't listened to her. They should have listened. She gave excellent life advice.

One of the figures carried a young girl. She appeared to be sleeping. Sleeping or —

"Oh, God," Gray cried out as he surged forward and grabbed for his daughter. "Holly, no, don't be — "

"She's not dead," the leader of those black-clothed figures announced. *Soloman.* Some people whispered his name in fear. Elise typically muttered it in disgust. Soloman had never been what she'd call a fan. More of a hater.

"She's under a sleeping spell," Elise said, her voice carrying easily in the night. "Get her out of here. When she's away from them, she'll wake up."

He yanked Holly into his arms. He still held his gun, but he wasn't aiming it at anyone. He was too busy holding tight to his daughter.

"Get out of here," Soloman ordered him. "Or we'll kill you, too."

Gray's eyes flew to Elise.

She shrugged. "It's been fun. Thanks for an unforgettable night."

"Elise—"

"*Go,*" she snapped at him. Did the guy not remember his one job? Get the kid out of there. She'd handle everything else. With a little help from her hunter.

Gray turned and ran, cradling his daughter's small form in his arms.

Soloman and his crew circled Elise.

Soloman braced his legs apart and his dark stare locked on her. She gave him a smile just to bait the guy. "Why have you always chosen the wrong side? Is it a deep-rooted character defect?"

"I serve the ruler. You know that."

"Hmmm. If that's truly the case, you should be down on bended knee before me. Begging for my forgiveness." She didn't think Harrison was close enough to overhear her words. Sure, his hearing was good, but she didn't believe it was *that* good. Especially since she was speaking so softly. "Instead, I hear you want me dead or alive. Hardly the way to serve the rightful ruler."

Soloman's expression didn't change.

"It's your last chance," Elise told him as she kept her chin up. She didn't bother looking at his flunkies. They always followed his lead. "Give me your allegiance…"

"Or what?" Soloman demanded. A chilling, cold wind swept from him.

"Or you will die." Damn. She'd been all dramatic right then. She almost scared herself.

He…laughed at her.

Oh, that sonofabitch.

He'd just laughed right in her face.

Then he got *in* her face as he surged forward. "You were always weak. Nothing but a pretty face and a useless *second.* You were not meant to rule. You were not meant to command, you were not meant —"

She yanked her hands back, freeing them from the rope, and as the rope fell to the ground, she was grabbing for the knife she'd slipped out of Harrison's coat. He'd been kissing her, she'd been enjoying the hell out of kissing him, but she'd been busy being a little grabby fingers, too.

She'd taken the silver knife because this shit was personal. Solomon was *her* kill. She hadn't intended to leave that cemetery without taking his life. Before he could say another jerk-off word, she'd driven her stolen silver knife right into his cold, cold heart.

The others surged at her, trying to grab her and kill her —

Bam, bam, bam. Three shots. Three bastards who fell around her. She heard the thud of footsteps running toward her, and she knew Harrison was coming to finish his kills. She didn't waste time looking at the others. She knelt over Soloman. He was trying to yank out the knife from his chest.

She shoved it in even deeper. "I am second to no one," Elise snarled at him.

His eyes widened. "Wicked...queen..."

"Hell, yes, I am. Glad you know exactly who you're facing." She took his heart.

***

"I can't thank you enough." Gray's voice was thick. "I don't...I don't know how those bastards even found Holly. I try to keep her and Cassie away from our world. God, it's the whole reason I left Cassie. I knew what we did was too dangerous. I knew I was bringing hell to her by staying with her, so I left. It fucking ripped out my heart, but I left—"

Elise had heard enough. "Stop your bullshit." They were inside the home of Gray's wife. Cassie Elliott was on the couch and currently holding tight to her daughter. But at Elise's words, Cassie glanced up.

Elise glared at Gray. "It's been a bitch of a night, and I am not in the mood for any bull."

"But I—"

"You don't walk away from the people you care about. You stay beside them. You fight for them. You don't leave because you somehow think that is best. That's crap. A convenient lie you tell yourself because you don't want to admit to being a giant coward."

He swallowed. Harrison remained silent.

Elise swept a disgusted glance over Gray. "You want to protect your family? Then keep your dumbass in their lives. *Be* there. Huh? How about try that?" She needed to walk away before she did something bad...like cut out *his* heart. Some habits were sure hard to break, and she'd crossed over into some seriously dark territory that night, but she'd needed to send a message to her enemies.

Message sent.

She whirled away from Gray. Marched toward the little girl. The girl who hadn't spoken much, and she stared at Elise with giant, haunted eyes. Elise offered a hand to the child. "It's time for you to sleep."

The girl—Holly—shuddered. Elise winced. Obviously, she'd used the wrong choice of words considering the child had been put under a sleeping spell. "Just bedtime," Elise added quickly. "I'll tell you a story." Elise figured the mom needed some moments alone with Gray so distracting the kid seemed like the type of thing a good person might do. Elise's stare lifted to Cassie. "I'll take care of her," she promised. "You go rip your ex a new one."

Cassie nodded. Holly's small fingers wrapped around Elise's hand.

***

Harrison crept toward the bedroom. Cassie was outside with Gray, and his gaze swept along the hallway as he followed the sound of Elise's voice. He saw smiling pictures of Cassie with Holly. A framed photo of Holly in a pink tutu as she struck a ballerina pose. Another framed photo of Holly wearing a baseball cap, holding tightly to her bat, and smiling from ear to ear—she was missing her front tooth in that picture. He paused in front of the image, oddly charmed.

When Gray had fallen for Cassie, Harrison had warned the hunter to be careful. Gray hadn't listened to him. Gray had thought he could have both worlds.

His mistake.

Hunters don't get happy endings.

Hunters...they got monsters. They got lies. They got betrayal. They got death.

Hadn't Harrison's own father taught him that brutal truth over and over again? Their job was to protect everyone else so that normal kids could go to dance recitals or hit home runs on a baseball field. Happiness wasn't in the cards for hunters.

It sure wasn't in the cards for him.

Harrison turned away from the photo and marched for the bedroom. He needed to get Elise and leave. He wanted more details on the bastards who'd been in the cemetery, men who'd turned to stone once their hearts had been removed. Harrison didn't think he'd ever come across supernaturals who looked like them before.

Elise knew more than she was saying, he was sure of it.

"I want to hear another story." The bedroom door was ajar and Harrison easily picked up Holly's low words. Her voice was slurred, as if she was fighting sleep. "Please."

"What do you want to hear about?"

"I...like princesses."

Elise gave a soft chuckle. "Don't we all?"

"My favorite is Belle. She's so nice, and she reads a lot." A yawn. "So do I. I read just like Belle."

"Well, I don't know this Belle that you're talking about, but I know another princess." Elise

SLAY ALL DAY 195

cleared her throat. "Though she's not necessarily very nice."

"Why not?" A soft, innocent question.

They'd determined that the girl didn't remember much about her abduction, a good thing. She'd been put under the sleep spell in the park, and she'd woken up in her father's arms. She knew something had happened, but the actual details were gone from her mind.

"Why wasn't she nice?" Holly pushed, voice slurring more.

"Because she never had a reason to be, I suppose."

A weak laugh from Holly. "Everyone should be nice. Mom...mom says so."

"Well, this princess grew up in a different place. Being nice got you killed in her world. Strength, viciousness — that's what gave you power."

Maybe he should stop her storytelling before Elise gave Holly nightmares? The kid had already been through enough.

"*Tell me more.*" Suddenly, Holly didn't sound so sleepy. She sounded fascinated.

Elise gave a soft chuckle. It slid right over Harrison's skin and had him leaning forward.

"The princess lived in a castle that was made of glass. She had to be very careful or the glass would shatter and everything in her world would fall apart."

Harrison was barely breathing.

"Was she very pretty?" Holly asked.

"She was," Elise sounded rather dismissive of that. "That hardly mattered. This princess was known for being particularly bloodthirsty. She never backed down from a battle and friends and foes feared her equally."

"Wow."

"Yes, indeed. Wow." Elise's voice turned a bit somber as she continued, "She grew up knowing that she wasn't the one who was meant to rule this magical land. Because in her kingdom, power is always passed down to the firstborn child. She wasn't the first. At least, not according to everything she'd been told her entire life. She had a twin, you see. A twin brother. *He* was born one minute before her. He arrived, then she came into the world. The princess came into the world and killed her own mother."

"Her mom died?" Now Holly's voice was sad.

He should stop the damn story.

"Do you want me to stop?" Elise asked. She seemed confused. A little lost. "I'm not...familiar with children. I was trying to make you feel better, but instead you look like you're about to cry."

"Don't you have kids?"

"No."

A sniff. "I want to know what happened to the princess."

"Fine, but if you cry, I'm stopping."

"I won't cry."

He peeked into the bedroom. Elise perched near the foot of the bed.

"Your near crying episode made me forget where I was." Elise tapped her fingers on the covers.

"The princess wasn't supposed to rule..."

"Oh, right. She wasn't. She was told she wasn't the firstborn, so she always let her brother have his way. It was a rather dark and twisted way most days, but he was the power and she was just the princess."

"Was she very sad?" Holly's lips turned down.

"Sad?" Elise seemed to taste that word. "I don't think so. She was surrounded by servants. She had every luxury imaginable. She just...had to follow her brother's orders."

Holly's little brow scrunched. "What did he order her to do?"

Elise's fingers stopped tapping. "Once, he ordered her to destroy a whole village because he didn't think the village was paying him the right tributes."

"Did she?" A very tiny voice.

"What do you think?"

"I don't think she did." He saw Holly's firm nod. "I think she told her evil brother to stuff it."

"Hmmm. Did I tell you that this kingdom was full of magic?"

Harrison's shoulders stiffened.

"I love magic." Holly seemed fascinated. Considering her night, Harrison thought she should've been horrified.

"The princess controlled a great deal of magic, and she could strike her enemies down..." Elise snapped her fingers. "Just like that."

"She is so cool."

"The brother didn't think so. He had powers, too, and those powers were supposed to become even stronger once he ascended to the throne. The ascension was coming, and that was the problem, you see."

"I, um, I don't see."

"He *wasn't* really the firstborn." Elise confided this in a quick rush. "Everyone had lied to the princess. She was the one who was born first. She was the one who should rule."

Holly gasped.

"Her brother started to grow afraid. In this land of magic, the crown will only sit on the head of the rightful ruler, you see, and he feared that if the crown was put on his head — while his sister lived — the truth of his birth would be shown to everyone."

"I don't get it. Why did everyone think the brother was older? I mean, why'd they all believe that?"

"They all believed the story because that's what the father of the twins told everyone. He was there for the birth, so he swore the son was the firstborn."

"He is so bad."

"Yes, yes, he was. Quite bad. But it's not like folks realized that. The truly evil often hide what they are. You hear what I'm telling you? This is important. You can't always see evil. Look beneath the surface, got me?"

"I got you."

"Good. Back to my story. Their father wasn't the ruler, the queen was. He was her consort and when she died in childbirth, he took over. Like I told you, he was evil. Straight to his core. He groomed his son to take his place. He ignored the daughter. He was a real shit."

Harrison's lips parted.

"I don't think you're supposed to say that word to me," Holly mumbled.

"No? Why not?"

"It's bad."

"Huh. Didn't realize that. Should I apologize?"

A negative shake of Holly's head. "What happened to the dad?"

"Oh, the princess killed him. They had a fight about something or other and whoosh...the dad was gone. Remember, I told you she had a great deal of power within her. So one day..." Elise snapped her fingers.

Holy hell.

Holly tried to snap her own fingers.

"Anyway, the evil father is gone, and it's just the brother and his sister." Elise brushed back a lock of her hair. "It's sad because the princess actually thought that her brother cared about her. In his own way, of course. But then the ascension grew close and any pretense of caring fell away."

Silence.

"What does pretense mean?"

"It means he was only pretending to care. That it was make believe."

"Oh. I don't like that."

"I don't like it either."

Harrison's hands flexed and clenched into fists.

Elise released a low breath. "Her brother stripped her of her magic. He attacked the princess while she was at her weakest. He banished her from her home so that she'd be alone and helpless."

"*No!*"

"Yes. He sent her far away, and then he made sure that every wicked creature would hunt for her. He wanted her dead, but he didn't have the balls to do the deed with his own hands."

"That's...I think that's something else you shouldn't say."

"What?"

"Balls?"

"That's bad, too?"

"Yes."

Elise gave yet another sigh. "I'm just going to stop this story —"

The floor creaked behind Harrison. He turned and saw Cassie. He'd known she was behind him. He'd caught her scent. Her eyes were puffy and swollen, and a frown pulled at her eyebrows.

She'd obviously caught the "balls" part of Elise's story. She started to push past him.

Harrison put a hand on her shoulder. He needed to hear what happened next.

"Don't stop. *Please.*" Holly's voice trembled. "I want to hear a happy ending."

"A happy ending?" Elise seemed confused. "Is that required in these stories?"

"I... I want one."

"Fine. I suppose, after your night, that you deserve one. Fair enough...well, let's see..."

"Did you forget where you were again?"

"Maybe."

Holly laughed. It was a sweet sound. "The princess had the bad guys closing in..."

"They were closing in, yes," Elise picked up the story. "She was weak and scared and they thought she'd be easy prey. But guess what?"

"What?"

"They were wrong."

Cassie slipped a little closer to the bedroom door. Probably so she could hear better.

"They were wrong because the princess was clever, and though she didn't have her magic, she had her mind. She came up with a plan. She was going to make herself an army. The strongest fighting force ever, and she was going to use that army to destroy her brother."

Silence.

"What?" Elise demanded, sounding a bit put out. "Why are you frowning like that at me, child? I'm trying to give you a happy ending here."

"Well, I don't understand where the princess is gonna get her army. I mean, how many people is she really gonna — "

"Sometimes, you just need an army of one. A very, very strong *one*. The princess knew where a beast of legend waited. A being who was stronger than any other force on this world or any other. He was sleeping, you see, and he needed the princess to come and wake him up."

"Like I was sleeping earlier before daddy woke me up?" Holly asked and he saw the bed give a little happy bounce.

"I suppose you could think of it that way." Elise rose and moved closer to the child. She leaned over and stroked back the girl's hair. "Someone had played a cruel trick on this beast. The princess decided she would help him. She would wake him up."

"That's nice of her."

Her hand dropped, and Elise straightened her spine. "I'm afraid she's not terribly nice. I warned you about that earlier."

"But, I think — "

"She's going to use this beast. Once she wakes him up, she'll get him to do her bidding.

She'll get him to stand at her side. She'll get him to fight her enemies. She'll claim her crown, and they will burn everyone who gets in their way."

Cassie's jaw dropped.

Harrison winced. Right. That *probably* wasn't the bedtime story she wanted her daughter to hear after being abducted by monsters.

But little Holly said, "She's going to be the beast's best friend."

"What?" Elise seemed to strangle. "No, I think you are missing the point of my story. My princess is going to bind this beast to her. He will be forced to do her evil bidding and —"

"She's going to wake him up. Sounds like the way the prince woke up Snow White."

"Who the hell is Snow White?" Elise demanded. "And why is she in my story?"

"She was asleep. Everyone thought she was dead."

"Was she asleep or dead? You need to pick one because she can't be both."

Holly laughed. *Laughed* after what she'd been through that night. "They *thought* she was dead. But the prince kissed her, and she woke up."

"Okay, sweetness, I hate to be the one to burst your bubble, but if the man is going around kissing would-be dead women, he's got a whole lot of issues, and I think your Snow White needs to stay far away from him."

More laughter. Giggles.

Cassie smiled. Some of the shadows left her eyes.

"Is your princess going to kiss her beast?" Holly wanted to know.

"Oh, she already has," Elise replied breezily. "She discovered that the beast can kiss like no one's business."

More giggles erupted from the girl.

A tear slid down Cassie's cheek.

"So she woke him up?" Holly pressed when she managed to stop her giggles.

"Not yet. The story is still in progress. She *will* wake him up. He'll go to her side, he'll fight her enemies with her, and then they will —"

"Be best friends forever!" Holly called out, excited.

"Ah, yes, again, I think you're misunderstanding my story."

"I don't think I am. I think the beast is going to be her best friend, and she'll be his, and they will rule that land of magic together forever. The end."

"The end? That's your ending for me?"

"Yes. It's a happy ending." Holly reached for Elise's hand. "I like you."

"Well, okay, I suppose you should. I did help to save you tonight. I was willing to sacrifice myself which is a very big deal."

"Thank you."

"You're welcome." Elise turned away from the bed and when she looked up, her eyes met

Harrison's. She paled and her body seemed to tremble.

Behind her, the little girl sank beneath the covers. "What kind?"

Elise glanced back at her. "What kind — what?"

"What kind of beast was the princess's best friend?"

"A dragon."

"*Oooh...*" Absolute delight. "So what did he do to her enemies?"

Elise opened her lips to reply, but Cassie burst inside the bedroom. A good thing because Harrison had a general idea of how Elise's story would have ended. He could almost hear her say, in that easy and smooth voice of hers...*He turned them all to ash.*

Or, hell, maybe she would have said the dragon ate her enemies. Either way, the little girl had probably heard enough of that particular story for the night.

Elise headed for the door.

Cassie caught her wrist. "Thank you."

Elise's head turned as she stared at the other woman.

"You saved my little girl. I will be forever grateful to you."

Elise blinked. "I don't want or need your gratitude."

"You have it anyway." Cassie let her go.

Elise stood there. She shifted forward a bit, then stopped. She bit her lower lip and peered back at the little girl.

Holly smiled at her.

"Monsters can't hurt you," Elise suddenly said. "You don't need to worry about them coming back. If any try, tell them you're under the princess's protection."

Holly's smile stretched.

"The princess always protects what is hers." Elise gave a nod and hurried toward Harrison. Her body brushed against his.

Her scent slid around him. Sweet, sensual. His arm curled around her waist. When she'd been at the cemetery, surrounded by those bastards, he'd found himself admiring her strength. She'd been so brave, absolutely fearless, and he'd wanted to kill *everyone* who'd threatened her.

He bent his head and pressed a kiss against her cheek. She seemed to soften against him.

He liked having her against him. He…liked her.

Even though he knew she'd been lying her ass off to him.

Unfortunate.

"We should go," Elise said. "If I stay, I'm worried I'll draw more paranormals in. They just can't seem to get enough of me."

"Neither can I." The words were pulled from him.

She looked up and it seemed like she wanted to say something so very badly, but instead, her lips pressed together.

I'm going to learn all those secrets, sweetheart. "Come on. My motorcycle is waiting outside. Let's go."

"Back to the honeymoon suite? Because I liked that—"

Razor appeared at the end of the hallway. He didn't look happy. Then again, he never did. He was big and tattooed and his bald head gleamed. His eyes swept over them, and he noted Harrison's arm around Elise's waist. He stiffened and his glower grew worse.

Harrison narrowed his eyes on the guy. He didn't like Razor's posture and angry expression, but the hunter's speakeasy *had* been obliterated to the ground, so he'd give the man a pass on the attitude, for now. Harrison inclined his head and said, "Thanks for keeping an eye on Cassie." Razor had stayed with Cassie while Harrison and Gray went to the cemetery with Elise.

"Hunters stick together." Razor's gaze narrowed on Elise. "You come after one of us, you come after us all."

Elise nodded. "Wonderful to know."

Harrison kept his arm around her and urged her forward. He wanted to get her away from there, and *he* needed to get away from Gray before Harrison decided to punch the jerk again, just on principle.

Razor backed up so they could pass, but when Harrison and Elise headed outside, Razor followed. Gray was still there, lingering near the motorcycle with his shoulders hunched. And...

Ward was waiting out there, too.

Harrison tensed.

Ward *and* Krista. They were standing near Gray.

"Huh." Harrison pulled Elise closer to him because he did not like where this might be going. "The gang's all here." Wasn't that convenient?

"Like I said," Razor rumbled in that deep, gravel-rough voice of his, "hunters stick together. I called Ward and Krista when I learned the score and had them come over."

Elise pointed at Krista. "Shouldn't you still be in the hospital?"

Krista's body swayed a little, but she said, "I'm a fast healer." A pause. "You must be, too, since I hear you've already healed from your bullet wound."

"Bullet wound?" Elise's voice rose to make her words into a question. "What bullet wound?"

"The bullet I saw you take to the shoulder when you were saving my ass."

Elise laughed. "There was a whole lot going on in that speakeasy. It would have been simple for you to get confused and imagine things happening."

No one else laughed.

In fact, they all seemed to close in.

Harrison pulled Elise behind him.

Razor shook his head. "Now why are you doing that? Why are you acting like you're going to protect her from us?"

"Because I am." A flat response. "You're closing in like you're hunting prey, and that shit needs to stop. Elise has helped us, she risked her life for Gray's kid, and you're all damn well gonna back off."

Razor's bushy eyebrows climbed. "Helped? Really? That what you think she did?"

"Don't try my fucking patience tonight. You got something to say, spit it out."

Elise pressed her fingers against Harrison's waist. "Let's not hear what he has to say. Let's just leave."

"I'm sure you'd like that, bitch. But it's not going to happen."

Harrison stiffened. "What in the hell did you just say, Razor?"

"I said I'm sure she'd like that—"

Harrison drove his fist into Razor's jaw. So hard the hunter flew back and landed on his ass.

"Here we go," Elise mumbled.

Harrison stood over the man he'd considered to be a mentor, both of his hands clenched as he fought not to pound the guy again. "Don't call her a bitch. Not ever again, understand me? And don't you pull out some hunter circle around her." He looked up, his angry gaze flying over the people who should have been on *his* side. "She dragged your ass out of that nightmare, Krista. You survived because of her." His gaze whipped to an uncomfortable-looking Ward. "And you...when I found you and Elise, the world was turning to hell around you and she was still fighting to get you out. She could've saved herself and left you to die. She didn't. Elise *helped* you."

Razor spat out blood. "Or that's what she wanted you to think."

"What she wanted...?" He could only shake his head in confusion. "What is wrong with you? That's what I *saw*. I saw it with my own eyes. It's what happened."

Razor rose to his feet. His hand gingerly pulled his jaw to the left and the right. "Her kind do that. They deceive. They trick. She shows you only what she wants you to see. She controls what you think and what you do."

"Uh, her kind?"

Gray stepped forward. "She saved my daughter tonight. I'm not going along with this plan, Razor. I'm not." He marched to stand beside Harrison. Harrison and Gray were now in front of Elise, shielding her from the others.

Elise wasn't speaking behind them, but Harrison could practically feel her fear vibrating in the air around them.

He didn't like for Elise to be afraid. Didn't like it one damn bit. A snarl wanted to tear from his lips.

Disgust flashed on Razor's face. "She's the one who put your daughter in danger, Gray. Those wraiths who came for her only took Holly because they wanted Harrison's new pet."

"Pet?" Elise gasped. "Oh, the hell, no, you didn't say that to me." She tried to hurtle past Harrison and Gray.

Harrison caught her and wrapped his arms around her, pulling her back against his body. "Baby, settle down."

Razor's eyes bulged. "*Baby?*"

"Fuck off."

Razor took a quick lunge forward. "You fucked her."

"I'm about to fuck you up," Harrison promised.

"Look, just settle down. Give her up and we can—"

Harrison saw red. Actually felt his vision bleed to red as fury overwhelmed him. "*I will not give her up.*"

Razor gaped at him. "You'd fight me for someone like her?"

Had the guy missed the fist to the jaw? But it wasn't just about fighting. "I'd kill to keep her safe." He gave the others who faced him a cold glare. "Want to test me and find out if I'm telling the truth? Come at me. Try to take her." His smile felt evil. "And I will wreck you."

CHAPTER TWELVE

Oh, no. Had Harrison just threatened to kill the other hunters? If he went all dark and started offing hunters, that sure wasn't going to earn Elise any brownie points.

Time to take control of the situation. "Ahem. I think we should all just take a breath."

"She put a spell on you." The accusation erupted from Razor.

Elise sucked in a sharp breath and would have jumped at the guy, but Harrison currently had his arms wrapped tightly around her. Too tightly. So instead of attacking, she snarled back, "I have not!" She couldn't work spells. Did she look like some kind of freaking witch? Not likely.

"She worked a spell, and you can't smell her lies."

Yeah, she suspected someone had worked a spell like that on Harrison a long time ago, but it hadn't been—

"You fucked her and you went blind."

Razor was an asshole, obviously.

And behind her...Harrison was seriously starting to, um, heat up. She could feel the waves of heat pouring from his skin. "Don't kill him," she whispered.

Harrison gave no indication that he'd heard her.

She twisted and heaved against him, not to get free but to turn — *ah, there we go* — so that she could face Harrison. Elise peered up at his savage expression. "We need to go. Let's just get out of here."

"We know about the spiders." Now Krista was talking. Jeez.

"Spiders?" Elise had known they would come back to bite her in the ass. Dammit. The spiders had merely been trying to scare Gray. They hadn't hurt him. *They were only trying to protect me.*

Harrison didn't look down at her. His focus remained on the hunters who seemed to be having a semi-revolt against him. And her. Definitely against her.

"Gray told us about them." Krista's voice was taut with anger. "You sent them to attack — "

"When he pulled a gun on me." She was still looking up at Harrison. Had the blue of his gaze just flickered with a touch of flame? "Look, that whole scene happened really fast. I'm sure lots of things occurred then that no one had intended."

Gray cleared his throat. "Sorry I told."

Yes, you should be.

Harrison was like a stone statue in front of her. His lethal stare was on the others. Elise knew something was going to have to give very, very soon.

"If it's a spell, it can be broken." Krista was all confident now. Annoyingly so. "If he's acting all obsessed because of a spell, we can fix things. It's not too late."

Chill bumps rose on Elise's arms. "Are you obsessed with me?" Elise asked Harrison. Her voice was barely a breath of sound.

His gaze dropped to her.

She could see flames flickering to life in his eyes. If the others saw those flames...

They might attack him.

No, she couldn't have that. She grabbed the back of his neck and yanked his head down toward her. Her mouth slammed onto his and she kissed him with a wild, desperate intensity. She wanted to bank his rage. Needed to get him focused on something else besides fury.

"Is *that* the way she casts a spell?" Ward's voice was amused. Not pissed. "Because I like it."

She tore her mouth from Harrison's. Her breath heaved as she peered at him. His gaze was — shit, still flickering with fire. Where were a pair of sunglasses when she needed them?

"Pull back," she urged him. "Pull it in, *now.*" She kissed him again. Only this time, she made the kiss softer. Gentle. Elise tried to soothe as best she could. She let the kiss linger. Held it tenderly and...

A throat cleared.

Ward.

Harrison lifted his head. His eyes were back to normal. The beast had been soothed, for the moment. "No spell." His words were deep and rumbling.

"Uh, then how do you explain the spiders?" Krista wanted to know. "Now that you've stopped making out with the monster how about—"

He growled.

Elise's chill bumps got worse.

"*Don't* call her that."

Elise whirled around and pointed her finger at Krista. "I saved your ass. Way to be ungrateful."

"Ward said you had wings. When he mentioned them, I had a flash of seeing them, too. Blue and gold, shooting from your back." Her lips thinned. "You're not human."

Razor had a knife in his hand. "She knew those were wraiths in the park, Harrison. Wraiths took Gray's kid, and your new friend here understood what they were immediately. Wraiths aren't thick on the ground. They don't even belong in this world. They stay far away and only do the bidding of the wicked fey."

Oh, shit. He was a fountain of information. This scene was about to get very, very bad.

She needed to get the hell out of there.

"Wicked fey?" Harrison laughed. She felt the rumble in his body. "There's no such thing as fey. Fairies aren't real."

Yes, we are. You made love to one of us, and it was awesome.

"Angels have wings. Demons have wings. No other creature." Krista was adamant.

She was also wrong. Elise could think of several other beings with wings, she just wasn't going to share that information at the moment. Didn't seem like the right time.

Gray was still beside her and Harrison. She wondered how much longer that would last. Razor gripped his knife. Krista glared. And Ward just looked uncomfortable.

Wonderful.

"Fairies are real." Razor nodded. "They are evil straight to their core."

Someone was being extra judgmental. From where she stood, he wasn't exactly winning any nice awards, either.

"They were banished from this realm a long time ago because they got off too much on screwing with the lives of humans."

You play a few tricks and certain people in power got all mad. Not that she'd name names…

Razor's eyes were tight, angry slits as he kept oversharing. "Because there are so few of the fey in this realm, other paranormals are drawn to them like moths to a flame. It's her scent, her body, her essence…*that's* why she's fighting off werewolves and vampires. Not because of a curse, but because she's fey."

Well, wasn't Razor the well informed one, and she had to wonder just where he'd discovered all of his knowledge. She cast a suspicious glance his way. When she'd first met him at the speakeasy, he'd seemed harmless enough. He didn't strike her as harmless any longer.

"Tell him the truth," Razor barked at her.

The truth? Fine. "I was cursed."

His hold tightened on the knife. "You're fey!"

She hadn't denied being fey. Just because she was fey, it didn't mean that she couldn't also be cursed.

"It's a fey trick. Fey deceive." Disgust tightened his face. "That's why you're here. To cause chaos and confusion. To destroy a good hunter!"

Fey trick. Fey deceive. He was right on both counts, and that just made her extra suspicious. "Who have you been talking to?" Elise made a tut-tut sound. "It would appear someone has been filling your head with all kinds of wicked thoughts."

He lunged.

She screamed.

Harrison went wild. A bellow broke from him, one loud and thunderous enough that she could have sworn it actually shook the street. One moment, Razor leapt at her with his knife. In the next, the knife had been tossed on the ground, where it rested right next to Razor's unconscious body. Harrison stood over Razor, his hands fisted, shoulders heaving, and for a moment, she thought he was going to take that knife and plunge it into Razor's heart.

That would be it. The final line he needs to cross. Her big, bad plan finally coming to fruition. Only...

Elise rushed toward him. Her fingers swept over one of Harrison's clenched fists. "Harrison, stop. Take some breaths. I think someone played with Razor's head. Don't do something now that you will regret later."

Harrison lifted his gaze to her. She could see the fire in his stare. Oh, the beast was close. This should have been her moment. Instead...

She was wimping out.

Maybe her brother had been right. Maybe she was the weak one. If she hadn't been weak, she would've been whispering in Harrison's ear, telling him to take that knife. To plunge it into the heart of his friend. It was an act like that...an act like that would turn a good man into a savage beast.

Her lower lip trembled. She glanced around. Gray stared with stunned eyes. Krista appeared both frightened and furious. As for Ward...

"My God, man," he gasped out as he gaped at Harrison. "What happened to your eyes?"

The flames burned in his eyes. His true nature was being revealed to everyone.

They would turn on him. If they learned the full truth about Harrison, they would attack him. They would try to hurt him.

All because of her. She'd done this. She had tried to turn a good man into a beast.

Elise tenderly trailed her fingers over his clenched hand once more. Then she leaned in close and hugged him. "I'm sorry." Elise swept back. Moved away from him. Edged toward the motorcycle. "It's a spell."

They turned toward her. Well, everyone but Razor. She doubted he'd be waking any time soon. "Harrison is under a spell." Just not *her* spell. "When I'm gone, he'll go back to normal. He'll be a big, bad hunter again."

And I'll be his prey.

In that instant, she desperately wished that she could call up her wings. She couldn't. The damn things had just sort of popped out when she'd been at the speakeasy. Probably because she'd been so desperate. She didn't feel desperate as she stood there. She just felt sad.

"Elise…" Harrison shook his head. *"Don't."*

"I never do what I'm told." *Princesses don't.* "This was a mistake. People are getting pulled in…" Like that cute Holly kid. Elise shook her head. "Don't kill a friend for me. I'm not worth it." She pointed to Razor. "I think a fey got to him.

He knows more than he should. Better tell him to stay away from shadows for a while."

"*OhmyGod.*" Krista had pulled out her knife, too. Wasn't everyone blade happy that night? "It's all true?"

"No. It's not *all* true." What was true... Her eyes locked on Harrison. A very enraged Harrison. "You are so much more than you realize. But there's a price for everything, and I don't think you should pay for me."

"She's a monster," Krista breathed.

Elise flipped her off. "I'm your guardian angel, sweetheart. You're welcome for the fact that you're still breathing." She had to go. Why wasn't she *leaving?* Because she wanted to look at Harrison forever.

She'd gotten caught in her own trap. She'd wanted him to mate with her. Wanted him to get tied to her. But all she'd done...

A fey fell for her beast. Elise climbed onto the motorcycle. She'd taken the liberty of lifting the keys from Harrison during that last hug. The fey all had nimble fingers.

And cold, cold hearts. Turned out, though, a beast like Harrison had been able to melt the ice that surrounded her heart.

"Get off the motorcycle, Elise." Harrison's order was low and hard.

She shook her head.

"Elise..."

"Good-bye." She revved the motorcycle and shot forward.

"Elise!" His roar followed her.

She didn't look back. She'd always been good at doing that. *Never look back. Never waste time on regrets.* Pretty much her mantra. Looking back was a waste of time. There was no point in it. There was —

Shit. She was crying.

CHAPTER THIRTEEN

"Someone tell me what just happened." Ward shook his head. "Yo, uh, Harrison? Enlighten me?"

Harrison stood in the middle of the road and watched as the motorcycle raced away. "Elise stole my bike."

Krista coughed. "I think she did a whole lot more than that."

Every instinct he possessed screamed for Harrison to chase after her. *And I will.* He whirled away, ready to steal someone's ride and—

Gray blocked his path. "Let her go."

"Get the fuck out of my way."

"I saw your eyes a minute ago. They were *burning.*"

"What?" Harrison shoved him to the side. He'd told the guy to move, hadn't he? Gray deserved a shove. He deserved a whole lot more than that.

But Gray grabbed his arm and spun Harrison back around. "Your eyes were burning. Like they were on fire. We both know that shit's not normal. It has to be because of her. She's a monster."

"Don't."

"She was working some kind of magic on you." Gray's hold tightened. "You know it. Look at yourself! You're freaking obsessed with her! She probably did some kind of sex mojo on you. Once you had her, you craved her even more. I don't know what she was planning, but you need to consider yourself lucky that she ran away."

Lucky? He didn't feel lucky.

I feel like someone drove a knife into my chest. She'd lied to him? Tricked him? Used him?

No. Hell, no. She didn't just get to ride off into the night. She didn't get to betray him and run away.

"Calm down," Gray urged him. "Take a breath and—"

"Get your damn hand off me or I'll cut it off." Gray whipped his hand back.

"Give me the keys to your ride."

Gray shook his head. "No—"

Harrison took the keys. Fast. Maybe with a punch or two. He was seeing red. Feeling as if his whole body was about to explode, and all that kept going through his head...*She betrayed me. Lied to me. Used me.*

No one used him.

He bounded toward Gray's truck.

"You knew the truth, didn't you?" Ward's question froze him.

Ward...he'd been standing back. Been quiet while Elise fled. His head tilted to the side as he studied Harrison. "Nothing slips past you," Ward added, voice careful as he tried to figure things out. "You're the best hunter I know. If a monster was in your bed, you'd know it."

Harrison rolled back his shoulders. "Don't call her a monster again. The next person who calls her that…" He trailed off. But they knew. He could see it. They all stiffened.

"You're still defending her?" Krista was aghast. Her eyes doubled in size. "How long until this spell wears off?"

It didn't feel like a spell. It felt like…

Mate. The one word slithered through his mind. His heart pounded too fast. The werewolf alpha had used that word. Had he been trying to warn Harrison? *At least you haven't fucked her.* Yes, Gustave had said something like that. If Harrison hadn't fucked her, then Gustave had been trying to say it wasn't too late. *Too late for what?*

"You knew." Ward shook his head. "But you didn't…what? Care? You knew and you didn't care?"

Harrison's fingers tightened around the keys.

"Don't go after her," Krista begged. "I'm worried. I don't know anything about the fey. She could be more powerful than we know. She could be—"

"She tried to trick me. She doesn't get away with that." Harrison's words were lethal and cold.

Razor roused, groaning.

"I will track her, and I will make her pay. I will learn every secret that she has." Each breath tasted of rage and ash. *"She will not get away from me."*

He left them. Drove away in Gray's truck with a scream of tires and a roar of the engine.

A monster hunter's job was to hunt and stop paranormals. To kill them when necessary.

And Elise...

She is my prey.

***

She'd gone back to the honeymoon suite. Maybe not the best move, but she'd been pretty much running blind. Elise hoped that the hunters wouldn't think to look for her there. After all, they probably thought she was high-tailing it out of the area as fast as she could.

Going right back to the luxury suite? Surely, they wouldn't suspect that move.

It hadn't exactly been like she had a ton of destination options. Besides, she'd left clothes in the luxury suite. She figured she'd get the clothes and swipe a few other necessities from the suite, then be on her merry way.

But when she entered the suite...

It smelled like Harrison.

She wanted to sob. Instead, she kicked the door shut. She marched through the suite, straight back to the bedroom, and she crushed red rose petals beneath her feet.

He would hunt her. She knew it. He'd been pissed and betrayed and he'd be after her in a flash.

She had to slow down and think and figure out a way to hide—

"Are we successful, my princess?"

The voice came from the shadows on the other side of the bedroom. Dawn hadn't come, not yet, so there were still plenty of dark spaces. Perfect for her kind.

She flopped on the bed. *I should be running. Not flopping.* "We are definitely not successful." She closed her eyes.

"But he mated with you. He is yours to command."

If only. "Turns out, things don't quite work that way on this side of the veil." Elise sighed. "They don't even kind of work that way."

"You have your weapon. Come back."

Her eyes opened, and she glared at the ceiling. "First, I don't have my weapon. My weapon is somewhere out there hunting for me, and he's very pissed off."

"But you *mated* him!"

"Yes, well, I have a pissed off mate who probably wants to kill me. Joy." Elise sucked in a deep breath. "And second, even if I wanted to come home now..." Which she absolutely did. The mortal realm sucked. Why had her kind hated their banishment from this realm? They should have celebrated leaving a place filled with so much pain. "Even if I wanted to, I can't come home. The curse, remember? It stripped me of my powers. Took away my wings. It left my ass stranded here until the next full moon." Elise suspected her brother had presumed she'd be dead by that point. Right before he'd kicked her ass out of their realm, he'd told her she'd be powerless until the next full moon. He'd even laughed as he told her...

"Good luck staying alive, sweet sister."

This all sucked so much. "I failed. I don't have an army. I've got a hunter who wants me dead." A couple of hunters who wanted her dead. A whole team. "I can't get back. I'm pretty much freaking helpless." She was about to have one major pity party.

"I disagree."

She jerked up in bed and glared at the shadows. "Get your ass out here."

The fat, thick spider scuttled toward her. "You disagree with me? Since when?" That was just...unsettling. He'd never, not once, disagreed with her. He was her most trusted confidant, her advisor, her loyal sidekick. He never said anything against —

"Your wings came back." The spider didn't talk. His voice just kind of filled the air. All disembodied and spooky.

It figured he knew about the brief reappearance of her wings. He'd probably been spying. "Yes, so? They popped out once when I was all desperate at the speakeasy..." Elise flexed her shoulders and harrumphed. "Can't get them to appear again."

"Maybe if you tried hard enough, you could."

Oh, no, he had *not*. He was saying she wasn't *trying?* "Spiders are easy to squish."

He scuttled away.

"You think I'm not trying? Seriously? I am. I want out of this place so badly I can't stand it. Harrison *hates* me —"

"Why on earth do you care how he feels? You never care how anyone feels."

Back in her realm, no, she hadn't. But... "Things are different here." She rubbed her chest.

"Or maybe...you're different."

Her eyes turned to slits as she glowered at the spider.

He retreated a little more. "Maybe your brother didn't fully understand the curse he put on you. Maybe you didn't understand it. Or maybe you've just broken it yourself."

"He was pretty damn clear as he cackled at me." Elise rubbed her chilled arms. "He said I could no longer be what I once was. And bam, my wings were gone, my magic was gone, and I was booted over here." Booted out to land in a freaking garbage bin. Her brother and his sick sense of humor.

"Maybe *you* changed while on the mortal side. Maybe you don't have to wait for the curse to break because you've already broken it."

She rolled her shoulders. Nope, no wings.

"Try," he urged her.

"Beaux, you are *not* helping—"

"Break a mirror and try to come back home, my princess." A pause. "What do you have to lose?"

She rose from the bed. Headed toward the closet. A long mirror covered the door. Her reflection stared back at her. When had she become so pale? And were those tear tracks on her cheeks? Elise swiped her hands over her cheeks. The woman in the mirror continued to look pale and far too...weak.

Her brother had always said she was the weak one. She had to do his bidding. Had to stay in his shadow. All her life, she'd only known the shadows. She'd grown used to the darkness.

"Even if I come back," she whispered, "he'll be stronger than me." So much for getting her big, bad, surprise attack. Harrison wasn't on her side.

If anything, he wanted her dead.

"And if you stay there..." Beaux's voice dipped with sadness. "You'll just die. Enemies will keep closing in on you."

Yes, she was in a lose, lose situation. Lucky her. She always seemed to have the very best of times. Angry, no *furious*, her hands curled into fists. She stared at her reflection.

Weak.

Unworthy.

Cursed.

Elise drove her fist into the mirror. It cracked under the force of her blow, and the cracks seemed to take on a life of their own as they flew over the surface of the mirror. Flew and flew until—

"Elise!"

Uh, oh. That thundering shout had come from *inside* the suite. Footsteps rushed toward the bedroom.

The spider raced across the floor and disappeared into the shadows. *Way to desert me.*

"Elise!"

She flinched. She knew that roar. Hard to mistake Harrison's bellow.

She peered into the cracked mirror. The mirror was broken, all right, and other than getting herself seven years of bad luck, she hadn't done anything else. No magic gateway had opened. No mystical light shot out at her. Her blood just trickled from her cut knuckles, and Harrison was rushing toward her. She could hear him getting closer and closer and—

He was there. She saw his reflection behind her in the broken mirror. The cracks twisted his face. Made him look even more dangerous and...

Evil.

"You lied to me, Elise." Angry. Low. Scary.

"No." She lowered her hand from the glass. Her blood smeared across the surface of the broken mirror. "I never lied." She turned toward him. "I can't."

"Bullshit. You aren't human. You aren't cursed."

"You made assumptions about me. You shouldn't do that. And I am cursed. My brother took my powers away and cast me out. He thought I'd die quickly in this wretched realm." She laughed. The sound held no humor. "Bet he had no idea I'd die by your hands."

Harrison blinked. "You think I'm going to kill you?"

Lift your chin. You're a fey princess. Bow to no one. Not ever again. "I'm a monster. You kill monsters."

He surged toward her. His hands closed around her shoulders. His nostrils flared. "Why do I smell your blood?"

Elise laughed. "Are you serious? You come in here all big and bad and you want to know why you smell my blood?" She yanked away from him and pointed to the broken mirror. "I was trying to get home. Trying to get away from you. If I broke the glass, if the curse was gone, I could go back."

He shook his head. "No. You *won't* get away from me."

"I *have* to get away. I'm not just going to stand here meekly and let you kill me."

He grabbed her again and yanked her against him. "I...*wouldn't.*"

Her breath chilled her lungs. "Harrison?" She searched his eyes. "How did you find me?"

"*I can find you anywhere.*"

That was both scary and oddly reassuring. Then he ruined things by saying —

"What did you do to me? A spell?"

"Any spell on you didn't come from me. I'm not a witch." She'd told him that before.

"*What did you do?*" His hold tightened. "Why do I want you, even now, even knowing what you are?"

Wait. *Wait.* She shoved against him. He let go. Harrison staggered back as if caught off-guard by her strength. But her supernatural strength was gone...wasn't it? "You act so shocked," she sneered at him as she edged away a few steps. He was angry. So was she. She'd lost *everything.* "So shocked that you could dare to desire a creature like me." Her shoulders straightened. "Get the hell in line."

His jaw dropped.

Her chin arched up. "You seem all surprised that you could want? Want *me?*" She wasn't screaming. Her voice had grown deadly soft. Beaux always ran when she went soft. He knew softness from her meant her darkest fury was building. "I am a fey princess. I am a blood-born fey. I am a freaking prize, you get me? Men fall at my feet. They kill for my smiles and my favor. Sex with me is mind blowing. I am amazing, I am powerful, and I am not some random *thing* for you to disparage."

"Elise…"

"But then you already know this, don't you?" Her lips twisted. "Because I'm pretty sure you were the one going all crazy and having sex with me like I was your fantasy come to life. So drop that better-than-me bullshit because you are dead wrong."

A muscle flexed along his jaw. "Is it my turn?"

She wanted to run. He was blocking the door. Sure, there was a window in the suite — actually, she thought that might be a balcony, not a window — but since they were on the top floor of the hotel, leaving that route wasn't an option. Not without wings.

And her wings weren't popping out of her back.

"I'll take your silence as a yes," he muttered.

It wasn't a yes. She was thinking. Plotting.

"First…fey princess, huh? Blood-born and a prize?"

She crossed her arms over her chest. "Yes."

"So much for being human. I think we need to talk about what a lie means."

Asshole. "Fey can't lie. So we twist the truth sometimes. It's not my fault if you misunderstand things."

"I misunderstood?"

"When I was cursed by my brother and his lackeys, for all intents and purposes, I became human. No magic. No wings. No fey power."

"So you're helpless."

She did not like where this was going. Elise raked him with her gaze. "That lead wraith found out just how *helpless* I was when I took his heart in the cemetery."

"Yes, the wraiths...let's talk about them."

He was talking. Not attacking. Was that good or bad? Maybe Harrison wanted all of his questions answered before he tried to kill her.

But he'd said he wouldn't kill her. The problem was that, unlike her, he could lie.

For the moment, though, she didn't have a lot of options. "My brother sent the wraiths. They were his enforcers, I guess you could say. Certain creatures choose to swear their allegiance to various fey. They picked my brother's side." She rolled her shoulders in a shrug. "I suspect Ardon wanted to make sure I wasn't plotting his destruction and coming up with an attack plan, so my brother sent them to this realm in order to finish me off."

"You *were* plotting his destruction."

"Of course, I was."

"That story you told Holly..."

Her eyes narrowed. "Were you eavesdropping on me? That is extremely rude. You shouldn't listen to other people's conversations."

His lips twisted as he advanced on her. Shit. There was nowhere to go. She'd retreated until the broken mirror was literally pressed to her back. It felt cold against her. The mirror was cold and icy behind her, and he was all dangerous heat before her. *Lose, lose.*

"You know what's worse than eavesdropping? Tricking someone. Betraying the person." His voice rumbled at her. So angry. Yes, she could see his fury in the tightness of his face and in the hardness of his eyes. "What did you think, Elise? That I would lead you to some big, bad paranormal powerhouse on one of my hunts? That you could use me to find you secret weapon? Your *pet?*" Then he laughed at her. "Hate to break it to you, your *highness...*"

He had *not* just mockingly called her —

"But dragons aren't real. You could've seduced me over and over again, you could've followed me on every hunt I completed, but you never would've found your new best friend."

"You're mocking me. It's extremely unattractive."

The muscle jerked in his jaw again. Yes, he was most certainly pissed. Good, so was she.

"I'm not mocking you, baby. You're in a battle for your life. You're desperate. You used me —"

She — yes, she had. Guilty.

"You deluded yourself. Dragons aren't real, and there sure as hell isn't one roaming the earth who will fight your battles for you."

Elise sucked in a painful breath. "I didn't want him fighting my battles *for* me. I wanted him at my side. I wanted to be together with him." Didn't he get it? "I was going to mate with him. I was going to give him half of my kingdom."

Harrison's whole body stiffened. "You were going to do *what?*"

"Give him half of my —"

Once more, his hands closed around her shoulders. Wow — they were warm. Not burning. But doing that little sizzle that she secretly enjoyed so much.

A deep, gravelly growl broke from him. Savage. Guttural.

She shivered. Why the hell did she find his growls sexy? She was so wrong on the inside.

"You were going to mate with the jackass?" Harrison bellowed.

"Yes, he is such a jackass," she threw back at him. His scent was winding all around her, and she was starting to suspect that when his beast was close, he emitted some kind of pheromone that turned her on. Made sense — she was a paranormal and she'd react more to another paranormal and —

"You will not mate with anyone else." His hold was almost painful. Almost. "I thought we were fucking handfasted."

What?

"You joined with me. I gave you my vow to protect you —"

Her lower lip trembled. "That was before you found out what I am. Now you hate me. You and your band of hunters are planning to kill me, and the sight of me seems to be driving you into a rage." And she was miserable. Because...

Because her plans had changed.

Because she'd changed?

Because she wanted to grab tight to her hunter and never let go.

What a sorry, sorry state she was in. "Give me five minutes to mope. I'll be better soon," she muttered. "Just give me —"

"*You will not mate with another!*'

Someone was sure hung up on that part. Better reveal that *he* was the dragon she'd —

Harrison's lips crashed down on hers. The kiss was possessive and ferocious and so incredibly hungry that —

"No!" Elise shoved against him with all of her strength.

He stepped back.

"You don't kiss me, then kill me. That shit doesn't work. You don't jerk around my emotions. You don't act like I'm not worthy of you when *I* am the princess. You don't..." Oh, no. *No.* Her hand swiped over her cheek. "You don't make me cry," she fired. "You definitely don't do that crap to me!"

His eyes widened. The rage was gone, and she could've sworn that she saw fear flash in his stare.

Her breath sobbed out. *Sobbed.* No, she had not cried when she lost her wings. She had not cried when she woke up in that stupid garbage bin in New Orleans. She had not cried when the stalking and the attacks began as the supernaturals hunted her.

But she'd cried...because of him.

"Damn you," she whispered. "I hate you right now."

"*Don't.*"

"Stop watching me cry!"

But he didn't stop. His stare was on her, and he looked horrified. "You don't need to be afraid of me. I would never kill you. I *told* you that." He reached out to her.

Elise shook her head. "Stay back. Don't touch me. When you touch me, everything just gets even more confused. I still want you, I need you, and you think I'm a freak."

"You're not a freak. You're the most beautiful woman I've ever seen. I want you more than I've ever wanted anyone or anything."

"Too bad I'm a supernatural, huh? Could've been your dream girl instead of your worst nightmare." She swiped at her cheek again.

"I don't fucking care that you're a supernatural!"

Her hand stilled. "What?"

"I don't care what you are. It's *who* you are that matters to me. You're Elise. *My* Elise." Definitely a possessive edge in his voice. "And no, I'm not plotting your end with my hunter buddies. If they come after you, they'll have to go through me."

He was...really?

Hope started to stir. So faint. So...bright. She could feel the glow in her chest.

"I'm pissed as hell at you, baby, don't get me wrong. You don't lie—"

"I didn't—"

"You don't twist the freaking truth, not with me. You tell it to me straight, I tell it to you straight, and we go the fuck from there." He nodded curtly. "Forget the dragon. You don't need him. You've got me, and I'm going to keep you safe."

Her lips curled. Hope made her dizzy. "Harrison—

Something grabbed her. A hard, fierce yank from behind. She was stunned because no one was behind her. Just the broken mirror. She'd been pressed up against it and—

Elise looked down in dawning horror. Hands were wrapped around her stomach. Hands that had grabbed her from behind and were dragging her into the mirror. Only it wasn't a mirror any longer. The broken shards had vanished and bright light spilled into the suite. The light swept all around her and she screamed, "*Harrison!*"

The hands around her stomach were yanking her away from him. He'd just said that he wanted her. That he was going to stand with her. She wanted to stay with Harrison. "You're the one," Elise yelled, desperate. "You're my —"

The mirror sealed up. She saw the glass fly back into place. Dozens of jagged pieces of glass reformed the broken mirror.

"Elise!" Harrison roared. He tried to grab her, but it was too late. Everything happened far too fast. His fist slammed into the mirror, but it didn't break. The glass was glowing, still pulsing from fey power.

Elise had been ripped from the mortal realm and hauled back into the place that had once been her home. She was being pulled farther and farther away from Harrison, and it felt as if she'd had her heart ripped right from her chest.

No, it feels as if my heart stayed in the mortal realm.

"Welcome back, sister," a low voice whispered into her ear. She was reminded of a snake, hissing. "Welcome home."

CHAPTER FOURTEEN

"*Elise!*" Harrison drove his fist into the mirror. She'd been there one moment, then she'd been torn away from him in the next instant. Torn away and fear had covered her beautiful face. She'd been crying out for him. Been so desperate for him and then she'd just been...

Gone.

He pounded at the mirror again, and the glass shattered. It rained down in hundreds of small, broken pieces. His knuckles were bleeding, and he didn't care.

Elise had vanished.

He'd said he would protect her. But she was *gone.*

Something was happening to him. A fiery rage and fear twisted inside of him. Burning so hot and bright, seeming to destroy the man he'd been and leave only a dark, unholy beast inside to —

"*Go after her.*"

Harrison spun around. He didn't see anyone else. His gaze darted to the left and the right even as he yanked out his knife.

"Hurry or she's dead."

No, Elise would not die. If she did…

No.

"Show yourself," Harrison thundered.

A fat, black spider scurried across the floor.

Harrison sharpened his gaze on the spider.

"I can see him in you." A disembodied voice seemed to fill the suite. "If you want to cross over, now is your only chance. Find a mirror. I'll pull you through."

Was the spider freaking *talking* to him? He looked around to make sure no one—or nothing—else was there.

"Yeah, big guy. It's me. I mean, do you see anyone else here?"

Harrison's eyebrows climbed. "Do you want me to squash you?"

"I want you to get your fool-ass to a mirror before you lose the spark I can see. If it's gone, you'll be too human to get through the portal. So…Move. That. Ass. Find a mirror. Break the glass."

"Yeah, I just did. In case you missed it."

"Once a portal has been used once, it's no good. Find another one. Hurry. Unless, of course, you want her to die?"

"Elise isn't dying!"

"Then get to a mirror. Drive that giant hand of yours at it. Break the glass. Smear your blood—and go get her!"

This was insane. Ridiculous. He was listening to a damn spider. He hated spiders. But Harrison still found himself running to the bathroom. Driving his fist into the mirror that stretched above the sink. Smearing his blood across it.

And nothing happened.

"You're shitting me," he muttered in disgust. His head turned. Where the hell had that spider gone? He was going to find him, kill him and —

"*Let's go.*" Hands shot through what had been the mirror and hauled him forward. Harrison hurtled forward and fell, seeming to tumble endlessly as he…shit, as he left one world…

And entered another.

"Wonderful. I expected you to be all big and bold and action-oriented, and instead, you're flat on the ground and you're gaping at nothing." A head leaned over Harrison. A guy with olive skin, pitch black hair, and bright green eyes frowned down at him. The guy snapped his fingers. "Wakey, wakey. You have a job to do."

Harrison grabbed those snapping fingers as he leapt to his feet. In a flash, he'd rammed his knife against the guy's throat.

"Oh, that was hot." The stranger smiled at him. "Like, literally, your touch is way warmer than I expected, and you do have that whole I'm-A-Badass vibe going on that is delectable. I can see why Elise was so charmed by you. I see it now, truly I do. I thought she was crazy initially when I realized she was starting to moon over you. Not the first time someone in her family has gone mad, FYI, but I'd sworn my allegiance to her, so I just had to buckle up and get ready to go along for the ride so—"

"Stop," Harrison snapped. His temples were throbbing. His stomach swirling. For the first time in years, he worried he might vomit.

"Oh." Green eyes widened. "You're probably adjusting to things here. It's a little different. Air quality. Physics. Lots of other boring stuff. No matter. You've got a strong beast, and he'll handle it. If you want, you can just look deeply into my eyes and take comfort from me and this will all be over before you—"

"You talk a lot."

"I like the sound of my own voice. I find it beautiful. Don't you?"

"Where the fuck is Elise?"

"If she's not dead, then she's probably in a dungeon. Chained up. Tied up. If her wings are back, they're about to be cut away while she screams. No doubt, crying out pitifully for you because she thought you would be her endgame. She believed that you'd fall desperately in love with her and you'd be willing to do anything to keep her—"

"I have a knife to your throat," Harrison reminded him as the throbbing *finally* lessened in his temples. "And you still won't shut the hell up?"

"Elise likes it when I talk." He sniffed. "You need to know that I'm Elise's confidant. I am the only one she completely trusts in this realm."

He wasn't sure he bought all that the guy was selling, but the fellow had managed to get him there. Only...*where am I?* "Is this the fey world?" It was filled with darkness and shadows.

"Yes." A wide smile.

"Why does it look like hell? Like a morose and dark demon dimension? I thought the fey were all about shiny things. Glitter and gold and everything fancy."

"Normally..." Another sniff. "Back in the day, the beauty here would have made you sob in pure joy."

Uh, doubtful.

"But since the rightful ruler was cast out, the realm mourned. The mourning meant it deteriorated even more."

"The realm did what now? Mourned?"

"Ardon thought he was so very clever. He thought he could kick Elise out of the kingdom, and no one would know what he'd done. He thought no one would realize he wasn't the true leader, but the magic knew. The kingdom knew. As soon as Elise was banished, the realm began to wither. It turned dark as it grieved for her. The grieving wouldn't stop until she came back..." His lips pursed. "Or she died, I guess...because in that case, Ardon would become the rightful leader and the place would stop grieving. Only

Elise wasn't dying the way he'd thought she would. She fought off the vampires and the werewolves...and, oh, by the way you did a wonderful job in that alley the first time you met Elise." An approving nod. "Very fierce. Gave me a flutter the first time I saw you in action."

"Are you trying to piss me off?"

The talkative stranger's lips curled a little more. "Perhaps I am. I can't say that I've always approved of the way you've treated Elise."

Harrison was trying to follow along. "Are you the fucking spider?"

His eyelids flickered. "Are you the fucking dragon?"

The question so surprised Harrison that he let the fellow go.

He straightened his thin shoulders. Glowered.

Harrison shook his head. "I'm not a dragon."

"*Denial.*"

"Yes, I denied being a freaking dragon because I'm not one!"

"No, I mean, you're in denial. As in, you don't want to admit the truth to yourself. As in, you've grown up, swallowing all the bold-ass lies your so-called father gave you. So much for being able to smell lies. Guess your sniffer was broken when it came to him, probably because he had a spell put on you. Spoiler alert, he wasn't your dad. He *killed* your real dad. And your real mom. Your mom didn't desert you. From what I've gathered — okay, from the intel Elise gathered — your mom fought viciously for you. But then your fake dad shoved a knife into her heart and killed her. A knife like the one you're still gripping, by the way."

Harrison stared blankly at the knife.

"Your mother was human, so a knife to the heart killed her. And when he saw your mother fallen, well, your real father lost his mind." He raked Harrison with a considering glance. "Got to watch out for that. It's a weakness of dragons. When they love, they love completely. Obsessively. That can be a strength, sure, I get that, but —"

He wasn't sure the stranger got *anything*.

" —that obsessive and total love *can* be used against dragons. Your old man lost his sanity and the hunters closed in on him. He couldn't fight rationally. He was all beast and rage, and they used that against him. They slayed him and they took you and, damn, but those tricky sonofabitches even got you to work on their side." A whistle. "That is some full-blown balls. I mean, I can see how they did it. Dragons and hunters have many of the same gifts. Enhanced vision and speed. Super strength. Even that whole lie smelling thing. Though, seriously, bro, you must have a spell on you that stops you from scenting lies from hunters —"

"You're lying."

"Fey don't lie. We can't. We can only —"

"You can twist the truth. Elise told me that. You're twisting the truth right now, and I'm not going to listen to another word that you have to say. I came here for Elise. I'm going to find her and then I'm going to take her far away from you and this whole insane realm." He whirled away. Screw that little bastard. He'd find Elise on his own.

"You can't take her away. If you do, the realm will keep grieving. If she lives but she is not in this realm, then this world will die. Elise won't let that happen. She can't. She's the rightful ruler of the fey. She is the one who will bring back our glory and—"

"Your name," Harrison gritted as he looked over his shoulder.

A blink. "She doesn't need to bring back my name. It never left me."

"What the hell is your name, asshole?"

"Beaux."

"And what are you to Elise?"

"I already told you, I'm her confidant. I am her loyal follower. The chief of her guards."

"The chief of her guards, huh? Well, looks like you're doing a bang-up job on that end, *Beaux*."

Beaux sucked in a sharp and offended breath. "Do *not* mock my name. Elise gave me that name when I became her chief."

"Yeah, and when did you take that role?"

"When I was nine years old. That is when she stopped the others from killing me. That is when she stopped the others and she said they were wrong. That I was not some hideous monster. That I was beautiful." He smiled and pride shone on his face. "She said I would be called Beaux, and I would always stand with her."

And...his image flickered. One side of his face remained perfectly symmetrical. It showed only flawless skin. The other side wasn't perfect. It was twisted. Savaged. But when Harrison blinked...

The damaged visage was gone.

"Fey magic?" Harrison asked quietly as he turned fully toward Beaux.

"Elise said I needed no magic. She said I was beautiful just as I was." Beaux's chin lifted. "Elise said beauty is found in the things that are different. That perfection is a lie. Elise believes it is the greatest deceit out there."

Harrison frowned. "But you still use magic..."

"I am beautiful," Beaux said flatly. "No matter what form I use. But only those I trust may have the privilege of seeing all that I am."

Wait... "You trust me?"

"I trust Elise. I trust my princess with my life. If she believed in you, then I will, too, dragon. I will put my lot in with you, and I shall take you to her. We will fight the guards and the wraiths and anyone who dares to challenge us—"

Harrison held up a hand. He was realizing that if you didn't stop the guy once he got going, he'd ramble for a bit. For a long bit. "I'm not a dragon."

Beaux stared at him. "Not right now, you're not." He leaned forward, as if imparting a deep, dark secret. "But the more the magic here seeps into your skin, the harder it will be for you to keep the beast chained up. Can't you hear him already? Calling to you? Calling out, so eager to be set free?"

It was total bullshit. Harrison knew he wasn't a dragon but...hell, deep inside, he could almost hear that stupid voice...the voice that slithered through his mind every now and then, the voice that promised...

Soon, we'll both be free.

Harrison shook his head. "Take me to Elise. *Now.*"

"And you'll kill anyone who gets in our way?"

"I'll fucking slaughter anyone who tries to stop me from getting to her. Happy?"

"Deliriously so." Beaux smiled.

***

Chained. Tossed into a stinking prison cell and chained like a common criminal. Oh, how the mighty had fallen.

Elise glowered through the prison bars at her twin brother. As usual, Ardon was perfectly styled, with his brown hair slicked back from his head and his body adorned in the finest silk the fey had ever conjured.

He was on the other side of the bars. Just smiling and staring at her.

"If you're going to kill me," she finally snapped at him. "Do it. Come at me. Get those pristine hands of yours dirty and stop just friggin' standing there!"

He...laughed.

His laughter was charming and deep. Warm. Another part of the deceit that cloaked him. Ardon always looked so harmless. Back in the mortal world, people would have thought he was some kind of model. Such handsome features. Such a perfectly toned body.

Such a load of utter bullshit.

"I missed you, sister."

She yanked at the chains around her wrists. She'd been yanking ever since she'd woken in there. Her magic was still gone—weak, trapped, cursed—whatever. It wasn't working, and she didn't know how to turn it back on. Since she didn't have any magic at her disposal, Elise hadn't been able to fight him when he'd blasted her with his magic. He'd knocked her out after he'd hauled her back to the fey realm, and she'd woken up in the cell.

The question, though, was…why had she woken up at all? Why hadn't he killed her already? "What are you waiting for?"

He mock pouted. "Didn't you miss me? We have been together since before birth. We came here together, shared life and power, and —"

"And then you used some dark mojo to strip me of my power and you kicked my ass out of my realm. I don't need the recap, thanks so much. I sort of lived through everything, in case you forgot."

Ardon stepped closer to the bars. "Father always hated you."

"No, no, please!" She gave a dramatic exhale. "Don't try to hurt my feelings! Don't! It's just too much."

His eyes turned to slits.

Now it was her turn to laugh. "Dear old dad was a sadistic prick who should have never ruled. He used our mother. Bonded to her for power, and if you want to know the real truth, I always suspected he killed our mother. I don't think she died in childbirth. I think he offed her."

Her brother shook his head. "No."

"Yes. That's what I suspect. You know I can't lie. I asked father if he killed her. Did he tell you that? On our sixteenth birthday, I asked him…and do you know what he told me?"

Ardon waited.

"He said, 'She was meant to die.'"

Ardon shrugged his wide shoulders. "So the fates willed it, so —"

"He played with words, just like you and I have done all of our lives. If he hadn't killed her, he could have just said no. *No!*" Elise yelled. "See? Not hard. Not hard at all. But he didn't say no, and in that moment, I knew the truth. I knew it. He knew it. But...you...did *you* ever know it?"

His eyelids flickered. Was that a yes? Or a no?

"Take this damn curse off me," she snarled at him. "Prove that you're not the biggest asshole in the realm. We don't have to be like him. We can be better."

"That's the problem." His lips twisted. "I'm not so sure I am better."

She wasn't certain either. Oh, yeah, Elise would have loved to throw out some BS about how, as his twin, she knew his heart was pure. That he had a core of good inside of him. Blah, blah, blah. But the truth was, most days, she didn't even know if she had any good in her. Maybe she was too much like her father.

Maybe they both were.

Not like she'd spent much of her life doing anything good.

Now she was chained in a cell, powerless, and just waiting for death. It was enough to make anyone gloomy. "Take the curse off."

"It's not my curse to remove."

Her back teeth clenched. "Call your flunky, call whatever witch of the hour you were screwing when you magically hit me, and get this curse gone."

He laughed. "I can't."

"This is not funny!"

Ardon sobered. "No, I don't suppose it is." His gaze sharpened on her. "He told me that loving you would be a mistake."

Her throat dried. "Who told you that?"

His lips pressed together.

She nodded. "Oh, got it. Dear old dad."

A fat spider raced through the bars. She didn't look directly at him. Just saw the spider from the corner of her eye. Elise cleared her throat, wanting to make sure that Ardon's attention stayed on her and not on that cute—no, gorgeous, amazingly precious—spider. "How old were you when he told you that warm and fuzzy sentiment?"

"Five."

Damn.

Ardon rocked forward a bit. "Did he tell you the same thing? Did he tell you not to love me?"

"No. He barely wasted any time with me. I wasn't important to him."

"Maybe you were lucky."

She jangled her chains. "This isn't what lucky looks like." Dumbass. "I'm losing my patience, Ardon. *Remove the curse.*"

He laughed again. That jerk needed to stop that crap. "I *can't.*" He pointed at her. "You were the firstborn." His voice was all hushed and silent. Probably because he didn't want everyone else figuring out that he was a giant fraud. The dark fey king. Or, would-be king, anyway. "The curse falls on our family. It isn't our doing." Again, his words were so low. "I just knew when it would occur, so I used that to my advantage. You thought I'd done the wicked deed to you, but, sister dear, it wasn't me."

She found herself inching toward him. "What are you talking about? You took my power and then you kicked me out."

"I kicked you out, yes, but I had nothing to do with your power vanishing. I waited until the power was gone, and *then* I banished you. Don't you see? You losing your power—it's a test."

"Trust me, I feel tested." Understatement of the century.

"A would-be ruler's powers are stripped right before ascension because you have to prove you are worthy. Prove that you can triumph, that you have good in you, before you touch the crown. Because if you don't..." A roll of one shoulder. "When you touch the crown, it sees your truth. If you're dark, the whole kingdom goes dark. If you're light..."

Her breath caught. She remembered stories. Stories of a beautiful, glittering fey kingdom. It had been a long time since the kingdom had been truly breath-taking.

"The right ruler brings back the light. So the stupid legend goes."

She was struggling to follow along with everything. "You didn't curse me. That's what you're saying? Our bloodline did? Or…the crown did?"

"It's testing you."

She lunged forward, only to be yanked back as the chains bit into her wrists. *Ow!* That would leave a mark. Or two. "You waited until I was helpless and then you cast me out. You thought without my magic, I'd die."

Another roll of his shoulder. As if he didn't care whether she lived or died.

"With me out of the way, you'd be next in line. As soon as I'm dead, you get to touch that precious crown." So why was she still breathing?

"It's harder to kill you than I thought." A furrow deepened between his dark eyes. "You thrived in the mortal realm." He glanced around. "And the kingdom withered all the more. People were starting to think that *I* was to blame."

"Spoiler, you are."

"I brought you back here so I could finish the job myself."

"Oh, really? You expect me to believe you're going to get your hands dirty?"

"You survived vampires."

"Their bite isn't so bad."

"Werewolves…"

"I gave them something to howl about." With some help.

"And even my wraiths." Anger shook his words.

She blinked innocently. "Oh, no! Did someone lose his favorite toys?"

"*Someone* is about to lose a favorite toy. Only that someone isn't me."

Her heart thundered in her chest.

"You had no power, sister. You didn't defeat your enemies on your own. I have spies in that realm. Spies who were closer than you realized. They told me all about your relationship with a certain hunter."

The situation had just gone from bad to horribly, terribly screwed. "A hunter?" Her chained hand lifted as she tapped her chin. "Can you refresh my memory a bit?"

"The hunter you fucked...Harrison Key. You used him to stay alive."

"*Used* is a strong word. I don't like it. Enjoyed is better. I enjoyed him." Another tap on her chin. The chain made a grinding sound as it dragged across the stone floor. She felt a tickle on her foot. She didn't glance down, but she knew the spider was beside her. "What does the hunter have to do with any of this? I left him behind when you so forcefully pulled me home."

"He's not just a hunter, is he?"

"No. He's *the* best hunter. The most amazing one out there. I don't sleep with losers."

Her brother's eyes gleamed. "I know."

"You know…what? That you're annoying? A dick? Delusional? That you were brainwashed by our father and the little bit of *real* you is buried under a shitload of his deceit? How about try digging deep, finding that real part, and *letting me out of this cell?*"

"You don't let bait out. You use bait. After she brings in the prey you want, then you eliminate her."

Elise shook her head. "What?"

"I told you, I had spies close. A spy —"

"In the group of hunters," she realized. Dammit. *Who?*

He gave a knowing smile. "You were trying to wake the beast, weren't you?"

"What beast? You'll need to be way more specific. There are lots of sleeping beasts out there, and, according to a friendly child I met, even some woman named Snow White who enjoys being kissed while she sleeps —"

"You thought you'd use him against me."

"To be honest, I plan to use everyone and everything against you. I'm not just going to sit back and die."

"No, you'll sit back and burn. The beast you were planning to use against me…he'll destroy you. He'll come for you." More of the laughter that she hated with her soul. "I've heard that he's already crossed into this realm."

Hope flared. A quick spurt of joy. Did she mask it? Did Ardon see it?

"Poor Elise. You don't know what will happen to a being like him in our realm, do you? Think about it."

"Um, he'll kick your ass?" Excellent plan. Brilliant. "He'll—"

"Be overwhelmed by the magic here. It will stir his beast into a frenzy. Oh, sure, if he'd been shifting his whole life, if he had control of the beast, there would be no problem. But he doesn't have control, does he?"

She didn't speak.

He winked. "My spy told me he doesn't. Don't feel bad. You're not betraying any confidences."

"Um...could you do me a huge favor?"

His eyebrows lifted expectantly.

"Go screw yourself," she snapped.

He wagged his finger at her. Wagged that shit. "His beast will take over. He'll be consumed. He will attack anyone and everyone near him. Guess who will be the closest when that momentous event occurs?"

She did not like where this was going. Elise turned away from him. She didn't want to give him the satisfaction of seeing any pain on her face. When she whirled away, the spider rushed up her body. His feet flew over her arm, then her shoulder, and he stopped for shelter in the crook of her neck. If spiders could hug, she thought he might be hugging her.

When Ardon had spoken, of her impending, fiery death, he'd sounded so satisfied and smug.

She needed to shake that certainty. "How can you be sure of what will happen?"

"Because I know more about dragons than you do. You had some two-bit priestess feeding you information. I had the power of ancient fey. Want to know what they told me?"

"Not particularly."

"They said that a dragon's fire wouldn't hurt a blood-born fey with power. Did you hear that last part? The key part? *With power.* Your power is gone until the next full moon, so that means if your lover breathes his flames on you, you will die."

"I don't believe that."

"Why not? It's true. A dragon's flames will kill you unless your power is back." His voice dropped, as if he wanted to share a secret. "I have all my power right now. I have *more* than my normal amount. When you were cursed, it's like your magic jumped to me. If your dragon breathes his fire on me, it won't even mar my skin."

"Oh, please." She spun toward him. "You're basing this whole evil plan of yours on something one of your crappy advisors told you? One of dad's old flunkies? Those guys should have been executed long ago. They are as corrupt as they come, and if I were you, I wouldn't buy their stories."

A muscle twitched in his jaw.

"Maybe they are carefully deceiving you with their words. Or maybe they just have wrong information. You won't know for sure. You won't know anything for certain. Not until my beast opens his mouth and pours fire all over you."

Her brother backed up a step. "You don't have your power. The only other way you can possibly survive a dragon's fire...well, that would be if you're his mate. The dragon's true mate. He would have to give you his very heart, and only then would you be safe." A mocking smile. "We both know he doesn't love you. He might want to fuck you, but he doesn't love you. Love isn't in the cards for you."

"You don't know him, and you don't know me. You sure as hell have no idea what I feel for him." *Or what he feels for me.* She had to think this through. Had to figure out a way through the darkness. "There is still time to change things." Didn't he see that? "Just let me go. Try being my brother and not my enemy."

"If you take the kingdom, I have nothing."

"That's just what father wanted you to believe."

"You're going to let me rule at your side?"

Um, no. You're crazy. You're trying to kill me.

"Didn't think so." He turned on his heel. "We'll test out the burn theory. We'll let those flames rage on you first. Then maybe...you know what? Maybe I'll just slay your dragon. I'll find a way to pierce his heart, and it won't even matter what he can or cannot do to me."

"*Don't!*" The cry tore from her, and, yes, she'd lunged for the bars again. Apparently, she was a slow learner. The spider went flying and the chains bit deeply into her wrists. She could smell her own blood.

Her brother stopped. "That was a mistake."

Her breath heaved in and out.

"I may not know how to pierce his heart, not yet…" Now Ardon was the one to glance back. Torch light flickered over his face and made him appear extra sinister. As if he needed that additional touch. "But I know how to pierce yours, don't I?"

She had to deny his words. "He's a hunter. Hunters don't fall for monsters."

"But monsters fall for hunters. You did. Poor Elise. You went out into the mortal realm, and you fell for a man who will always hate you. Even if he does have a beast on the inside, he was raised as a hunter. Why do you think he even came to this realm? Not to save you. To destroy you. My spy said that was all Harrison wanted. He was enraged by what you'd done."

"No." They'd talked at the hotel. Things had been getting back on track before Ardon grabbed her. Hadn't they?

"Yes. He left the house in that silly suburban neighborhood—"

"There is nothing silly about that house or the people who live in it!" Holly and Cassie were quite wonderful.

"Your Harrison left that house with one goal. To find you. To end you."

He had been incredibly angry when he found her at the hotel suite. But...he hadn't been planning to kill her. He'd said that he wouldn't kill her.

"Oh, Elise. You were always too trusting. I mean, you believed I was the ruler for most of your life even though you had to see the signs of your own power. Until the curse kicked in, you were always stronger than me. You should have fought me long ago. *Before* it became too late. Instead, you believed the careful deceits father and I gave you..."

"You are my brother!"

"And you are in my way."

"Technically, I'm in a cell."

"You can't count on your lover to save you. He's coming to kill you. I'm just making it easy for him. When he arrives, he'll join you in that cell. His beast will take over, and then everything will burn."

"Well, that explains why you didn't put me in a cell inside *your* castle. You just shoved me in the pit on the side of a mountain because you didn't want people questioning a giant blaze."

"They'll still question it. I'll say your lover killed you in a furious rage. Truth. Because you know, fey must always tell the truth." With that, he left her. His steps echoed over the stones.

"We don't have to tell the truth," she whispered. "Not when we can just twist our lies."

The spider rushed toward her. She knelt. "Beaux, what in the hell are you doing here?" She carefully stroked the top of his head with her pinky as she whispered to him, "It's time to cut your losses, buddy. You're not on the winning side. Maybe you should consider going to the mortal realm. Find some sexy guys over there that tickle your fancy and party like there's no tomorrow." She had to gulp down the thick lump in her throat. "Because for me, there isn't gonna be a tomorrow. There isn't going to be anything else."

A circle of blue light surrounded the spider. She sat back, slumping on the dirty floor as more effervescent blue swirled around the spider. Beaux grew and, in a burst of brilliant light, he stood as a man.

She stared at his face. His gorgeous face. Beaux never worked his concealment magic on her. She always saw him exactly as he was.

"You're a sorry sight," Beaux told her as he raked her with his stare. His hand motioned toward her. "What is that precious fragrance you're wearing? The scent of defeat? And maybe a little urine?"

"Get out of here," she told him as she refused to let her nostrils inhale that stench. "My brother will be back or he'll send in some of his lackeys, and if they find you with me, you'll die, too."

He drew himself up. "I'd rather die at my queen's side than run away like a coward."

"I'm not a queen. I'm not even a princess right now. I'm a prisoner. Besides, did you hear what Ardon said? Harrison is going to kill me. I thought he'd be my big gun in this battle, but he's just—"

"I'm right here."

And...he was. He stood on the other side of the cell, just beyond the bars. She wanted to run to him, but Elise wasn't in the mood to be wrenched back by the chains again. Also, the fact that Harrison's eyes were swirling with flames? That would be reason number two why she stayed rooted to the spot.

"What have you done?" Elise asked Beaux.

"Oh, you know, the usual. Avoided detection by all the bad guys, snuck in a hunter, and arrived to save *your* ass." He gave a perfect bow. "Always happy to save that, my royal prince-ass."

CHAPTER FIFTEEN

It wasn't true.

He wasn't a beast. Sure as hell not some dragon. Dragons weren't even real. All hunters knew the last of the dragon shifters—a savage, brutal group—had died out long ago.

"He looks like he wants to eat you," Beaux loudly whispered as he eyed Harrison.

But she shook her head. "No, it looks like he wants to burn me alive." She hunched her shoulders as she sat on the dirty, stone floor. "You walked into a trap, you know. My brother is going to jump out of the shadows at any moment and watch you roast me. This whole sorry deal will end poorly for everyone involved."

She couldn't lie. She really thought that was the end?

He eased out a low breath. Surely smoke had not just blown from his mouth? Harrison shook his head. "I'm a hunter."

Her head turned toward Beaux. "Did you tell him?"

"Gave the guy his entire tragic back story. Don't think he believed me. I mean, sure I get it.

We're strangers. I could be some crazy psychopath who makes up dramatic back stories for kicks. I'm not, of course, but he doesn't know that. Why should he believe me? Why should he —"

"Does he always talk that much?" Harrison interrupted curtly. "I noticed when he starts, he doesn't stop."

Slowly, her gaze tracked back to Harrison. "Beaux grew up alone until I found him. The other fey children shunned him because he was different. Sometimes, children can be very cruel."

Harrison nodded. "So can adults."

"Beaux decided he didn't need those others, so he just talked to himself."

Beaux cleared his throat. "I like to hear my own voice. I find it quite beautiful and melodic. I don't see where the problem —"

"Your voice *is* beautiful and melodic," Elise agreed immediately. "But if we're going to live, we need to get out of here and save some of that beauty for later."

An excellent plan. Except for the fact that Elise was still staring at Harrison as if she expected him to attack her.

"I'm *not,*" he gritted.

Beaux moved in front of her. A protective stance.

"I'm not going to let either of you die," Harrison clarified. "We're all getting out."

"Good luck." Elise waved toward the bars. "Do you have any idea how heavy those—"

He yanked the cell door right off the thick hinges.

"Oh." She blinked. "That was sexy, and I'm working hard not to find anything about you sexy because I'm afraid you're going to burn me."

He stalked toward her. Distantly, he heard an echoing bell.

"Alarm," Beaux snapped. "Shit, probably tied to the cell. If her door opened—"

"Or got torn off by a powerful dragon," Elise added smoothly.

"It must have been set to blast an alert." Beaux winced. "That means Ardon will be rushing here any moment."

She curled her hand around Beaux's wrist. "Get out of here, *now.*"

"No, no, I will not leave—"

"You have to stay free in case something goes wrong. *Get out of here.*"

Blue light flared. As Harrison watched, Beaux shrank down to become a spider again. The spider rushed toward the shadows.

Harrison had to admit, "That shit freaks me out. Seeing a man turn into a spider takes some getting used to."

"If you think that's bad, wait until you see a guy turn into a dragon." She stared pointedly at him.

"I'm confused as hell."

"Yes, and I'll help out with that, but for now, I could use some help."

His focus sharpened on her.

Elise licked her lower lip. "Help if…you're not planning to torch me."

Rage burned through him. He stalked across the cell. He expected her to cower more and the idea of her cowering before him—*no, I don't want her fear.*

But she didn't cower. Elise shot to her feet. She tipped back her head, sending her hair sliding over her shoulders. She was dressed in some fancy, fantasy-like gossamer dress and if they weren't in the pits of hell, he would have appreciated her outfit a whole lot more. As it was…he saw, he appreciated, and he planned to revisit later. *After* they were out of the cell.

He closed his hand around one of the chains that circled her wrists. "Been over this before." He yanked the chain and it broke, freeing her wrist. "I'm not planning to hurt you. I would never hurt you."

She sucked in a breath and held out her other wrist. "That's what the man says. But that beast inside that you want to pretend you don't carry? What does he say?"

Mine. The dark, possessive cry slid through his mind. He wanted to deny there was a beast. Wanted to say everything was a lie. A terrible, crazy lie.

But…

He'd been hearing that dark whisper all his life. Trying to ignore it. His father had told him that it was nothing. He'd even given Harrison drugs to shut up the voice. He'd made Harrison think he was insane.

The drugs hadn't stopped the voice.

Nothing had stopped it.

He broke the second chain. "The beast says he's keeping you."

Her lips parted. "What? You—you believe me?"

He held up his hand to her. His fingertips were burning. "This shit started when Beaux and I were running across the fey land coming to save you."

She swallowed.

He fisted his hand. The flames died. "I don't know what I believe right now. Could be some fey trick. Could be..." *A beast inside. Something that wants you, Elise, just as much as I do...*

"It could be truth," she told him. Her fingers lifted and hesitantly curled around his fist. "It could be the first time you've heard truth in a very long while."

"Knew you'd come for her!" A mocking voice called out. "Just couldn't stay away, could you? Don't feel bad. My sister has always been irresistible to her lovers."

Harrison stared straight at Elise.

"That's Ardon, my brother," she told him. "He's a dick."

Her hand was still on top of his, and her touch seemed to be soothing Harrison. He wanted to spin around and rip off her brother's head. He wanted to destroy and savage but...

Her fingers stroked over his.

"I think we need to get out of here," Elise added. "He's got magic, and I don't, and I don't know what he's going to do with his magic, but I know it won't be anything good."

Fair enough.

Harrison scooped her into his arms. He turned toward the door. Or what had been the door, before he'd ripped it from the hinges.

Her brother stood there with his arms folded over his chest and with four of those wraith guys behind him. Did they always come in groups of four? Was that a wraith thing?

Harrison frowned. "Seriously, more of you assholes?"

"Dark magic controls them," Elise explained quickly. "Until Ardon is taken down—"

"I will have a pretty much unlimited supply of wraiths," Ardon concluded with a little shrug. "Eager soldiers ready to follow my every command."

Well, shit. No wonder Elise wanted out of the cell.

"You're not leaving this place." Ardon pointed at him. The guy was all pompous and smug with his creepy smile. "My wraiths will keep you here. The longer you are here, the more magic will seep beneath your skin and unlock your beast, and when he finally emerges…" The creepy smile stretched. "You'd better pray you aren't touching my sister. You'll burn her flesh away and all you'll know will be her screams."

Harrison's chest squeezed. "I can see it now. You're right, Elise. He's a total dick."

Ardon's face tightened with fury. "While you're a monster hunter *with a beast inside*. That beast will rip you apart when it breaks free, and then you'll kill her. The man won't be able to live with what the beast has done because, obviously, you have a soft spot for Elise. Not surprising, considering the way she's manipulated you. She had you addicted to her before you even knew what was happening."

"Uh…you know…" Elise coughed. "I do need to explain a few things to you, Harrison."

Harrison's head turned. He stared into her eyes. Her gorgeous eyes. Her ever-widening eyes.

"Have I told you…" Elise's voice grew huskier. "When you get mad, your eyes turn to flames?"

His back began to…ache. To itch. He rolled his shoulders. "Hold on to me."

Get our mate out. Take our mate.

The dark whisper needed to shut the hell up. He was trying to figure things out and—

Pain tore through him. Absolutely flayed him. Harrison dropped to his knees as the agony pierced him. It felt as if someone had taken a whip to his back and—

The memory was there. It broke through and exploded in his mind. A time long ago. A time he'd fought to banish.

His father...slamming first his belt and then a whip into Harrison's back. They were in a barn. Everything was quiet...except for the slapping of the belt—then the whip—against his flesh. He could smell the hay. Could smell his blood. Could smell...ash?

"If I beat them hard enough, maybe they won't ever grow. Maybe they'll never come out...maybe I can break them. Maybe I can break him." His father's voice. A memory, unlocking?

Then...darkness. The pain had overwhelmed him. He'd passed out and...

Woken up with no memory. Woken up with wisps of a nightmare. When he'd looked in the mirror, his back had been unmarred. He'd stared at his father, shocked and scared to death, until his dad had whispered...

"Ah, son, did you have a bad dream?"

"This is so not the time to zone out on me." Elise tapped his cheek.

His gaze sharpened on her beautiful face.

She smiled at him. "Hey, there. You went away, and I'm glad you're back."

He was back, with her, and his shoulders were still splitting open. He could feel a phantom whip slamming into the skin over and over, ripping him open.

"I'm really sorry you're trapped here with me. If you will just put me down, I'll try to kick some wraith ass and while I do that, you can run."

She thought he was going to run and leave her? That was just fucking wrong. Harrison growled.

"No one leaves!" Her brother bellowed, "You won't make it out of here, Elise. I can't risk other fey finding out—"

"That you're a giant liar with a soul black as night? Huh. I think some of them are going to wise up to that sooner or later."

Her brother glared at Harrison. "Why aren't you killing her? Burn the bitch."

Something snapped inside of Harrison. "Don't call her that."

"She lied to you—"

"She doesn't lie. She just gets creative with the truth."

"She used you—"

"She saved my ass. And the life of a kid."

Ardon opened his mouth. Closed it. Opened— "*She tricked you and used you!*"

Harrison laughed. "There was no trick. I wanted her. I willingly joined with her, and from here on out, it's gonna be us against the world. You stand with us..." His gaze flickered to the unmoving wraiths with their blank expressions and black eyes. "You get to live." His stare returned to Ardon. "You stand against us, and you die."

Ardon's lips twisted as fury sharpened his face. "Let's get this party moving, shall we?" He lifted his hands and blue light shot from his fingertips. The blue light leapt straight at Harrison. It looked like the same light that had surrounded Beaux when he'd transformed into a spider.

Was the blue light fey magic? Had to be. And it was launching straight at Harrison.

"*No!*" Elise hurtled out of his arms. She planted her body in front of Harrison. She took the hit from the blue light. A blast that had been aimed right at Harrison.

Her whole body jolted, as if she'd just been struck by lightning.

Her brother's face went slack with shock. The blue streaks of light vanished. "*Elise?*"

She staggered to her knees.

A savage, unearthly roar shook the cell.

Her brother froze. His wraiths stared in dawning horror. Elise fell forward, but Harrison grabbed her. He snatched her up into his arms.

"*Stop it! Put her down!*" Her brother sent more blue light at Harrison. Harrison turned his body, shielding Elise from the blast, and that blue magic pierced his shoulders.

He expected pain. Instead, there was just pressure and then...

He felt his skin split open as if he'd been cut with a razor-sharp scalpel. The skin parted, and there were screams and he didn't understand why the wraiths were screaming because he was looking down at Elise and he couldn't be bothered with seeing anything else.

"Oh..." Her lips tried to curl. The normal red color of her lips had bled away to the palest of pinks. All of the color had faded from her skin. *Too pale. Far too pale.* Her eyes even seemed weaker. "They are...beautiful."

"Elise..."

"How about..." Such a weak whisper. "Use them...fly us out of...h-here..." Her eyelids sagged closed.

The screams had stopped.

Harrison became aware that he wasn't standing on the floor. He was floating —*flying*— near the top of the cell. His head turned and he could see giant, scaled, black wings batting at the air. Wings that came out of his back.

He dipped and almost crashed into the floor.

"Why aren't you killing her?" That was her brother again. Pissing off Harrison.

He glared at her brother. "Because I'm going to kill *you.*"

Fear burst across the dark fey's face. "Kill him!" he shouted.

The wraiths surged forward. They gripped silver knives in their hands.

"Silver worked on your father. It will work on you!"

Shit.

More wraiths were rushing in behind Ardon. A whole army of silver-armed wraiths. Harrison was way, way outnumbered.

"F-fly..." Elise whispered.

He couldn't fly toward the wraiths, but there wasn't another way out. There were only the stone walls.

So...

Screw it.

He flew right at one wall. He turned his body and let one powerful wing crash into it first. The stones exploded outward as if they'd been hit by dynamite.

"No! Stop! Come back!"

He didn't stop. Getting Elise to safety was his number one priority. He found that if he flexed his back, the wings moved on command. It took some effort, he could feel one big-ass strain, but he could also soar high into the sky. So he flexed, he flew, and he held tightly to his fey mate. His black wings beat against the air. Wings...wings of a dragon.

Because that was what Harrison truly was.

Not a hunter.

Not a man.

He was a beast.

***

He had to send them back.

Ardon raced toward the giant hole in the wall of his thickest prison cell. The dragon was flying away. Well, it wasn't a full dragon. It was a man with dragon wings. Maybe the bastard couldn't change all the way. After all, his mother had been human. Ardon hadn't factored that into the equation. Maybe the reason the dragon hadn't taken over was because Harrison Key was incomplete. Otherwise, surely the beast would have killed Elise.

It had to kill her. She'd betrayed it. She'd tricked it. She'd...

Mated a dragon?

The suspicion slid through him. If they were well and truly mated, a dragon would never attack his mate, no matter what. According to legend, a dragon's mate was the only one safe from his rage and his savage nature. But...

But a true mating required love. On *both* sides.

Elise couldn't love. His father had always told him that Elise had an ice-cold heart. That she would never love anyone. That she could never be trusted. But...

She put her body in front of Harrison. She protected him from my magic.

Ardon's breath came faster and faster. Elise might love the dragon. But how did the beast feel about her?

There was only one way to find out.

"If she gets to the other fey, she'll tell them what you did," one of the wraiths warned.

"She won't get to the others."

"What about the spider? He knows, he—"

"I'll take care of him. He's nothing. Forget him." Ardon lifted his hands, calling up his power. His gaze remained on the dragon and on the woman clutched in the dragon's hands. Elise was limp. Unconscious. She'd taken a powerful hit of magic. A deadly hit.

Elise. For a moment, he remembered her as she'd been. The girl with the long blonde hair who'd trailed behind him, asking to play. Asking if he wanted to work magic with her.

She'd never seemed like a threat.

But his father had told him otherwise. His father had said Elise hid her darkness deep inside. She was the threat. If Ardon didn't eliminate her, then Elise would one day destroy him.

His magic had hit her in that cell. Now, he lifted his hands again, and he sent the blue streams jerking from his fingers and into the air. The dragon dodged, as if he thought the streaks were intended to knock him out of the sky.

Silly shifter. That wasn't the intent at all.

The magic was designed to rip a hole in the sky. Thunder rumbled.

The sky tore open. Wind whipped right before the dragon and Elise were sucked out of the fey land. Boom. No mirror needed, not when he was riding high on a combination of his power *and* his dear sister's.

"Thanks for visiting, sis," Ardon murmured. "Hope you enjoyed your last view of home."

He turned away.

The wraiths waited with their expressionless faces. He controlled them because of the dark magic his father had gifted to him long ago. The wraiths were dangerous, deadly predators. They also enjoyed giving pain far too much.

One wraith cleared his throat. "Why did you let her go? You brought Elise back to stop the decay in the land..."

"No, I brought her here because I thought killing her would be a breeze. The dragon was supposed to burn her alive." Why did he have to explain himself? "But the idiot just wants to fuck her. I couldn't let her stay here. She'd stir up opposition to me. So I had to send her back to the mortal realm where I had spies waiting who could get the job done."

Spies...Harrison's friends. This would be Harrison's test. Would Harrison choose Elise over the people closest to him? Only if he really loved her.

And I say he doesn't.

"But if they don't kill her..." The wraith smiled, flashing teeth that were far too sharp. "Then it will be our pleasure to take the skin from her body."

"You're just pissed because she ended Soloman. That was his fault. He was always a cocky bastard." Ardon straightened his shoulders. "You're not touching my sister. If my spies don't kill her, then I'll do the job." He nodded. "I'm going to the mortal realm. I'll make sure only one twin returns. *Count on it.*"

He opened up a gateway and marched inside…

And he didn't notice the spider that was sitting on the back of his shoulder.

CHAPTER SIXTEEN

"Elise, baby, open your eyes."

She didn't. She groaned. It felt as if she'd been hit hard by a bus or a semi or…something really, really big. After she'd first come to the mortal realm, she actually *had* been hit by a bus. So she had a pretty good point of comparison. She'd jumped out of the garbage bin and — wham. That was the moment she'd discovered that while most of her magic had been gone, she'd — luckily — maintained her healing powers.

"Okay, you're groaning. That's good."

It was?

Callused fingertips stroked her cheek. "I don't know how it happened, but we're back in the honeymoon suite."

Uh, oh, that wasn't good. And if she wasn't aching, she'd be more worried.

"You're scaring the hell out of me. *Please,* look at me."

It was his voice that got to her. The fear. The pain. Especially the ragged "please" from him. She forced her heavy eyelids to lift. "Don't…be scared."

His expression was so tense and worried.

Elise tried to smile. "I'm here...I'll...keep you s-safe."

A relieved laugh broke from him. "You're talking. You're staring at me. *You're going to be okay.*"

Well, she couldn't promise that part. "I...n-need..."

"What? Tell me. Because, baby, I'm freaking out. You took one massive hit from the blue light crap that shot out of your brother's fingers."

"I...remember." She also remembered wings. His, not hers.

"What can I do?"

She tried to peer over his shoulders. "Did you have wings?" She was feeling stronger. The pain fading. Her brother might not have realized it, but he'd saved her life by sending her to the mortal realm. If she'd stayed in the fey land after taking such a powerful hit, his magic would have spread through her body like poison.

But in the mortal realm, it slid from her with every breath she took.

Or...had Ardon realized it?

"I had wings, but they're gone now."

"Join the club."

His fingers brushed back her hair. "Why did you take that hit for me?"

"Because I'm helplessly in love with you." After the confession popped out, Elise slapped a hand over her mouth.

Oh, no. No, no, no.

His eyes widened. "Say that again."

She kept her hand in place. An unfortunate side effect of waking up after taking one uber powerful hit of fairy fire? She didn't have the mental strength to think of careful deceits. She was spitting out truths.

Harrison seemed to realize what was happening. "You can't twist your truth, can you?"

She could...in about five more minutes. Maybe ten.

"Did you say you loved me?"

She shook her head no. She'd actually said that she was *helplessly* in love with him.

He leaned forward and lightly pressed his lips to hers. "Now who is afraid?"

She was. Utterly terrified, in fact.

He started to pull back.

Her hands flew out and locked around his shoulders. "If you want to help me, kiss me again."

"Elise..."

"Fey are very sensual creatures. Sex makes us stronger." Especially if the sex was twined with love, the way hers was with him. She'd tried to tell him before that they wouldn't be fucking. They'd be making love.

A half-smile curved his lips. "Sex makes you stronger, huh? That sounds like a very good deal."

"It is, provided you have the right partner." With the right person, everything was better, and she could see that now. She could see so much. Fey weren't supposed to have mates — that was a shifter thing. There was no belief in one, true soulmate in the fey realm. But feys did believe in love. Oh, yes, they believed in it. If you were lucky enough to fall in love, to feel the true magic that could come from giving your heart completely to another, then you did anything necessary to protect that love.

Love was deeper than mating. Mating — to the fey — was all physical.

Love was so much more.

I love him. I fell for him hard and fast. Using Harrison wasn't part of her equation any longer.

"You think I'm the right one?"

"I think you are my only one." Her fingers toyed with his hair. Such thick, soft hair. "I planned to use you."

"Uh, baby, if this is your attempt at sexy talk…"

"As if." A fast smile came and went on her face. "When I talk sexy, you'll know it." She swallowed. "This is my attempt to be completely honest with you because I think you deserve that from me."

He waited. She could feel the tension coursing through his body. The waves of heat and power.

"I intended to use you. Because what beast could be stronger than a dragon?"

"I'm not—"

"I think we're past the denial point, don't you? I'm pretty sure I remember wings and they weren't mine."

His nostrils flared. She could see the sputter of flames in his gaze. "I was going to say I'm not really sure what the hell is happening with me. I thought I was a hunter."

"You're so much more." *You're everything.* She almost said those words. Her lips pressed together.

His gaze dropped to her mouth. "Everything is screwed up right now."

Absolutely. One hundred percent. "My brother will send people to kill me."

"They won't touch you." His gaze rose back to hers. "I swear it, and I don't give a shit if you are just using me for protection."

She shook her head, sending her hair sliding over the pillow. "I'm using you for incredible, mind-blowing sex. The kind of sex that comes from loving someone."

"No, you don't have to say that, you don't have to—"

"I love you." She waited a beat. "No way for me to twist the truth when the statement is so simple. I'm not using you for protection. In fact, after we have our mind-blowing sex, I'd like for you to get as far away from me as you can."

"What?" One eyebrow notched up.

"Far, far away. Until this mess is over. Until the whole deal is settled with Ardon." *Until the battle is over so I don't have to worry about you dying.*

"Fuck that." His lips crashed down onto hers.

Fuck me. No, love me.

The kiss was hot. Hard for it not to be since Harrison was a dragon. He kissed her with a voracious hunger and a desperation that said he was starving for her. Oh, she liked that. What woman wouldn't like for a man to kiss her as if she was the most important thing in his world? To kiss her with a consuming lust? With demanding need?

With sweet, sweet possession?

He wasn't wearing a shirt. She had no idea what had happened to it. Maybe his wings had shredded it? The wings were gone, the shirt was gone, and her greedy hands stroked over his skin. All of that muscle. All of that sexiness. All of that delicious heat.

She wanted to touch and taste all of him. Every single inch.

But he'd just torn his mouth from hers, and he was kissing his way down her neck.

"What the hell is this outfit?" Harrison rumbled. "It's sexy as fuck."

She tipped back her head and moaned. She loved it when he gave her those quick, teasing little licks along her skin. "It's…ah…traditional garb for fey. We like…yes, yes, do that *again*. We like light-weight clothing. And in the back, there's a place for our wings to—slip—ah, to slip—*Harrison!*"

His hand had *slipped* between her thighs. "The material is so thin and soft."

Gossamer…that was kind of a fey thing.

"It feels like my fingers are touching your clit right now, doesn't it? The fabric is still between us, but it feels—"

It felt like he was strumming her clit over and over, and her orgasm was building fast. Elise didn't bother with words. Mostly because she didn't have any. She was too busy gasping and lifting her hips and feeling her muscles tighten in preparation for what she knew would be a mind-melting orgasm.

"Let's try this." He yanked his hand away.
Dammit!

But he just spread her legs and put his mouth on her. Blew through the fairy garb and licked her clit. Kissed her. Sucked. Blew again…*Lick, kiss, suck, blow—*

She screamed his name.

The orgasm whipped through her, and it brought a surge of strength. Of power. For a moment, she could have sworn she even saw a glow light her skin.

"Beautiful," Harrison told her.

Her breath kept coming in wild pants as she stared at him. At the gorgeous eyes that danced with flames. "Yes," she said, voice husky. "You are."

His brow furrowed.

She launched at him. Tumbled Harrison back on the bed.

"Someone is feeling better..." he murmured. His teeth flashed as he shot her a wide grin that made him look younger. Boyish. *Happy.*

I want him to always be happy.

Only life with her didn't promise happiness.

"You make me better, Harrison." That was perhaps far truer than he realized. Her fingers grabbed for the snap of his jeans, and she yanked the snap open. She pulled down his zipper and the thick, wide length of his cock shoved out at her.

"Let's see if I have your order right..." Elise lowered her head. "I think you started with a little blow..." Her breath blew lightly over the tip of his cock. "Then a lick." She licked him.

"Fucking hell." He grabbed for the covers.

"I think a kiss came next." She kissed the head of his cock. A slow, savoring kiss. "Then a suck?" She took him inside. Sucked and licked at the same time, and damn but he tasted *good.* She took him in deeper. Savored him and then —

Let go.

Elise licked her lips and looked up at him. "Did I have the pattern right? That's what you did for me, so I just wanted to make sure I did the same for you."

His eyes were blazing. Such gorgeous flames.

"Let's try that again," she murmured. "Just to make sure." She blew over his cock. She licked. A long, savoring lick. She kissed. Open-mouthed again. Then she took that wide head into her mouth. Her cheeks hollowed as she tried to savor every single—

She was on her back. He'd flipped her back and lodged his cock at the entrance to her body. He'd snatched her clothing off in lightning-fast movements. Behind him, she could see his wings. Those amazing wings had shoved through his skin and were stretching wide. Ah...no wonder he'd moved so fast. Her hand lifted so that she could stroke one of his wings. It was rough, scaled, and warm.

"Amazing," Elise breathed.

He drove into her. Her legs wrapped around him. Held onto him as tightly as she could as he pounded into her and as she pounded right back up against him. She clawed at his arms. He kissed her neck. Bit her lightly on her shoulder. Every move of his dick inside her body was just making her wilder, just making her need him all the more.

He was everything she'd ever wanted. Everything she'd never thought she would have.

The climax hit her, and the whole room went dark. For a moment, she lost herself. The pleasure was so intense Elise couldn't breathe or see—she could only feel. Waves and waves of bliss hit her.

Then he erupted inside of her. She felt the warm, wet release, and her sex greedily clamped around him. His orgasm seemed to double her pleasure. He was snarling her name. She was moaning his, and it was the best sex of her life.

He was the best sex of her life.

Gradually, sanity returned. Not that she wanted it to return, but it still came back, anyway. Her heartbeat slowed down. Her vision went back to normal. He was on top of her, and his wings were still spread wide.

Her hand reached for a wing once more. Her fingers trailed lightly over the scales. Oh, how interesting. It looked like his wings were tipped with talons. That was extra fierce.

"I'm sorry." His voice. All wooden and halting.

He lifted up. Pulled out of her. Even left the bed.

Well, that had been unnecessary. She sat up but didn't bother covering herself. "You're sorry. Why? What have you done?"

His back was to her. Those glorious wings…

"They just…came out. I didn't mean to turn into a freak while we were fucking."

"*Stop.*" Fury blasted in that one word.

Harrison whirled toward her.

She climbed from the bed. Naked, she marched toward him. Elise jabbed her index finger into his chest. "Don't you ever do that again."

"I didn't mean to do it. I could feel them trying to come out. The more I wanted you, the stronger they became. I wanted to stay a man, I wanted —"

"You are a man. You're just a man with some extras. So what if your wings come out during sex? That happens to paranormals. We get turned on and our primitive sides take over. It's a compliment, all right? It means you're not in total control with me. That you *forget* control."

His jaw was tight. "It didn't happen before…"

"Yes, well, that was before you went to the fey realm and got all hopped up on magic. I suspect your, um, hunter father put some safeguards in place to stop the change from happening. The whole time, I've suspected that perhaps he made a deal with a witch to chain up your beast."

His lips parted. "That was what you meant, back at Cassie's place, when you said I was under a spell."

She nodded. "It must have been a spell. Otherwise, you would have known he was lying. He blocked you from scenting his lies." His…and probably the lies of others who had known the truth. "But once you crossed over into my realm, the power there knocked through any spell holding you back." Her hand fell. He should know… "It's not going to get easier. I think you have a full dragon inside of you, and one day, he will come out completely."

Harrison shook his head. "I'm a —"

"Do *not* say freak, got me? Because no one talks about my man that way. No one." She put her hands on her hips. "I have wings, too." She spun, presenting her back to him. "One day, they'll be back, and when we have sex, they'll come out. That is normal for fairies. Hell, we even fly during sex. It will be freaking fantastic, and you'll love it, and you'll start to see what a blessing it is that we both have wings."

His fingers slid lightly over her shoulder blades.

Elise shivered. "They're, um, super sensitive. Fey wings. When you touch them, it's like you're stroking my sex."

His fingers stilled. Then he caressed her again. She leaned back against him and gave a little moan.

That was when everything went to hell.

There was a loud bang from the outer room...as if someone had just kicked in the door to their suite. Footsteps rushed toward them. *Thundered* toward them. Wild and frantic footsteps.

Harrison locked his arms around her and yanked her back against him. One arm over her breasts, one over her sex, shielding her, and his wings swept down to cover her from neck to calf.

The bedroom door flew open and rammed into the wall. Considering the amount of damage that poor suite had suffered since their check-in, Elise had the distant thought that the hotel staff would freak when they eventually came to clean the room.

Three armed men and one very armed woman rushed into the bedroom. The hunters were loaded to attack and, at first, they just look determined.

Then the determination on their faces changed to horror.

Krista's eyes were as wide as saucers as she gaped at Harrison. "OhmyGod." Her shocked gaze flew to Elise. "What did you do to him?"

CHAPTER SEVENTEEN

"Typical," Elise snapped. "You blame me. Had to be something I did, right?"

Harrison saw the hunters exchange a quick, confused glance. But no one lowered a weapon. All were armed with guns, and he was betting silver was the bullet of choice. Silencers were on the guns because, of course, hunters came prepared.

What would silver do to Elise? He wasn't sure, and he didn't want to find out. When he'd tested her—God, that seemed like a lifetime ago—he hadn't used silver against her because he hadn't smelled a beast on her.

"You put a spell on him," Razor accused. "You got him obsessed with you. The room reeks of sex. You put some sex spell on—"

"Oh, please," Elise sighed. "Sex with me is just that good. Yes, I said it. Good enough to obsess a man. No spell required."

Krista kept glaring.

Ward just shook his head in shock.

Razor raised his gun. Harrison knew in that split second that the man who'd been a mentor to

him for most of his life was going to fire and hit
Elise in the head.

Gray seemed to realize it, too. Gray dropped
his own weapon and grabbed for Razor.

And Harrison whipped up his wings,
shielding her head even as he whirled away with
her.

There was a loud clatter. A scream.

Elise shuddered in his arms. "I don't think
your friends like me anymore."

He didn't *feel* a bullet wound. "Sweetheart, I
don't think they ever did." He brushed a kiss over
her temple. "Stay behind me." He faced his *ex*-
friends and kept his wings extended to block her
body.

Razor was on the floor, holding his bleeding
shoulder.

Ward was still gaping. "You're bulletproof."

Krista was to the right of Razor. Gray to his
left. Gray didn't have a weapon. Krista did.

"The bullet bounced off your...shit, your
wing. Man, it bounced off your freaking wing! It
flew back and hit Razor." Ward's eyes were wide
with shock. "You're bulletproof!" he said again.

He was? Good to know.

Krista's face twisted with rage. "Silver bullets
don't hurt him, but I'm sure something does."

Gray looked over at Harrison. Winced.
"Jesus, man, can you put on some jeans? Your
dick is waving in my face!"

"Sorry," Harrison bit out. "Was a little busy trying not to die at the hands of hunters who I'd *thought* were on my side. Didn't realize I needed to stop and dress."

Gray kicked away Razor's gun. "Everyone, stand the hell down." Command echoed in his voice. Gray grabbed Harrison's jeans and tossed them at him. His gaze strayed to the wings — wings that still hid Elise. "Does she need clothes, too?"

Krista had already grabbed them. A t-shirt and jeans that she found in a drawer. She threw them forward.

Elise reached out a hand and caught them. "Nothing is wrong with nudity, you know. It's natural where I'm from."

Harrison yanked on his jeans.

"Where is she from?" Gray asked quietly.

"I'm fucking bleeding to death here!" Razor yelled.

"That's your own fault." Harrison had no sympathy. "You shot at me."

"I shot at *her!* At *her!* She's the one who is screwing you up! She's the one turning you into a monster!

Elise — who'd dressed super fast — tried to charge past Harrison. "I *will* kick your ass — "

Krista pointed her gun at Elise.

But she didn't fire. She bit her lip. Her hand trembled.

"Oh, yes, that's right," Elise practically purred. "Let's just take a minute and remember that I saved you." She nodded toward Krista. Then pointed at Ward. "And you. Is this how you thank people who save you? You interrupt their sexy times and wave around weapons?"

"He has fucking wings!" Razor screamed. Spittle flew from his mouth. "She *took* him somewhere. Probably back to the fey realm. We know it. This suite was empty a few hours ago. We were watching the room the whole time. They just—just magically transported back inside. She's working spells and witchcraft or she's communing with a demon to give her extra power and she's—"

"Slow your roll," Elise huffed at him. "You need to speak to me with a whole lot more respect in your voice. Because you are staring at a real-life fairy tale princess right here."

"Elise…" Harrison sighed out her name. "Get behind me so that you'll be safe."

"No. I told you already, I'm not using you for protection. I stand *with* you. Just as you stand with me. If anyone doesn't like it, they can screw off." Her hand caught his and their fingers threaded together.

Harrison sucked in a deep breath. He rolled back his shoulders and his wings…he felt them pull inward. It was a slight tug, and he realized *he* was pulling them inward. Elise's touch had given him control.

He turned his head to stare down at her.

She wasn't looking at him. Her gaze was on the hunters.

"We came to save you," Gray mumbled.

Harrison slowly swiveled his head until he was focusing on Gray. Gray stood near Razor and Razor — he still had one hand clamped over his bleeding shoulder.

"Razor says she's going to be the death of you," Gray added grimly. His head tilted as he looked up at Harrison. "Got to say, man, I did not expect to see the wings."

His shock seemed genuine. "Can't say I expected them, either."

"What are you?" Ward asked.

Harrison's shoulders stiffened.

"He's the same guy he's always been," Elise immediately threw back. "He's the guy who has had your back for years. I'm betting he's saved you over and over again, hasn't he?"

"How do you know that?" Krista demanded. "Did he tell you —"

"It's who he is," Elise fired. "Harrison saves people. Even when those people don't always deserve it." She tugged her hand from his.

He grabbed her hand and twined their fingers right back together. When he felt her start of surprise, Harrison merely tightened his hold on her.

"He has freaking *wings!*" Ward seemed to still be processing that fact. "She had wings at the speakeasy. Now he has wings." He glanced over his left shoulder. "Is everyone getting wings?"

"I don't have wings." Elise hesitated, then clarified, "Not at the moment. If I did, I'd be flying out of this place and away from you people. Because, obviously, one of you is a spy."

"What the hell?" Krista marched toward her. "A spy for what?"

"For my brother. For the dark fey. You're working on the side of the supernaturals while pretending you hate us. Pretending you're a good hunter, while really you're just a sell-out." Her gaze swept over them. "One of you is trying to kill me."

"Trust me," Razor muttered as the blood seeped through his fingers. "We all want to kill you."

Gray cast him a quick, hard glance. "Speak for yourself. She saved my daughter. The last thing I want is for Elise to die." He bit his lip. Straightened his shoulders. "I don't care if she is a fairy or the devil himself, Elise saved my girl. I won't forget that." He released a breath and focused on Harrison. "I came here to make sure no one hurts you. Or your lady. I'm no spy. I'm your friend."

"One of you is a spy." Elise was definite. "My brother told me that the spy had been close to Harrison all along. You hunters...apparently lies are easy for you. I'm sure a spell was used so you could tell lies without the scent of betrayal giving you away." She sounded furious. "Harrison's true nature was hidden from him. And one of you has been selling secrets to the paranormals."

Ward raised his left hand. "I'm sorry. Um, could you tell me exactly what Harrison's true nature is?"

"After you all put your guns and any hidden weapons on the floor," Elise snapped. "I'll be happy to. But I'm getting tired of having weapons pointed at us."

"So the hell am I," Harrison added. His stomach felt hollow, while his heart felt *hot*. One of these people — one of them had been working with Elise's brother. One had been setting her up to die, and one had been helping Harrison's *so-called* father hide the truth of his birth for years. Harrison swallowed and ignored the taste of ash on his tongue. He was learning more about his beast. He knew what that ash-taste meant.

The dragon was close.

Ward put down his gun. The gun he'd been holding. And the gun he'd had hidden in his ankle holster. He placed two knives on the floor. One set of brass knuckles. A tube of holy water. "That's all I had on me." He held up his hands. "Tell me what you are, Harrison."

Harrison's lips parted, but he couldn't respond. Couldn't actually say the words. His whole life, he'd believed he was one thing...

Hunter.

He hunted the monsters. He stopped them.

But now…now…he *was* a monster? No, he hadn't just become a monster. He'd been one all long.

"I still see too many weapons pointed at us," Elise called out. "Hey, bleeding shoulder."

Razor's head jerked toward her.

"You're the one who came in shooting first and not asking questions. So when I hunt for a spy, my money is on you."

Razor staggered to his feet. His face twisted in disgust and rage. "I know the fey. I told you that before. I know you trick and deceive, and that's what you're trying to do right now. You're trying to trick and deceive Harrison. You're trying to get him to turn on the only family he's ever known. It's not going to work. You aren't going to use him. You aren't going to draw him into your war. I won't let it happen."

Her gaze cut to Harrison. "That's a confession. On that awesome show, *Law and Order,* that I caught right after I dragged myself out of the dumpster—"

He growled. The *what?*

"On that show, the perps—they called them perps, you know—anyway, they tripped themselves up like old Razor just did." A pause. She wiggled her eyebrows. "How did he know I was in any war?"

Harrison had already put those pieces together. He brought their joined hands to his lips and pressed a kiss to her knuckles.

The fury on Razor's face deepened. His skin flashed and mottled purple.

"He knew," Harrison said quietly, "because he knows your brother. Because he's been feeding your brother information on me. On all the hunters."

"You can't trust the fey!" Razor shouted.

The other hunters all stared at him in shock.

"Razor?" Krista's voice. Shaking. "You...you're not working with the fey. Tell me you're not."

"Oh, sister," Elise cut in. "He's not working with just *any* fey. He's working with the darkest fey out there. My brother."

"Fey deceive!" Razor roared. He leapt forward and swung a knife right toward Elise.

Gray tried to knock the weapon aside, but Razor heaved him away. When Krista and Ward grabbed at him, he swatted them aside as if they were flies.

"Someone has a supernatural boost," Elise exclaimed right before Razor swung his knife—

And Harrison kicked it out of his hand. "Yeah, someone does." Harrison grabbed Razor around the neck and lifted him high into the air. Razor clawed at Harrison's fingers, but Harrison didn't let him go.

"I was always stronger than the other hunters, but my father said I was just lucky." Harrison had to force each word past gritted teeth. "He told me to hold back my true self, only to use it in combat. *You* told me the same damn thing." Harrison had to choke back his rage. "You knew what I was all along, didn't you?"

Razor scraped his nails over Harrison's wrist.

Elise tapped Harrison's shoulder. "He can't talk. I think you're holding him too tightly."

Harrison let go. Razor fell to the floor. Gulped in desperate breaths.

"He was using some supernatural strength of his own," Elise noted as she circled Razor. The other hunters eased forward, all hesitant and suspicious. "I'm betting my brother was paying him with magic. The more secrets he shared, the stronger Razor became."

"Your brother can bite me!" Razor gasped.

"Uh, he's not a vampire. He wouldn't be interested in doing that. He'd just want secrets. You gave them to him but..." Elise glanced over at Harrison. "It was awfully fast for Ardon to get a spy in place. I've only been in the mortal realm since the last full moon. I...I wonder..." Her gaze flickered back to Razor. "How long had he been using you?"

Razor grabbed for the tube of holy water that Ward had put on the floor. He ripped the top off and hurled it at Elise. "The fey *burn!*"

The droplets poured over her. She didn't burn. "I'm not a demon."

Razor gaped. "But...but your brother...I-I saw..."

Elise frowned at him. "What did you see?"

"I saw your brother burn when holy water touched him."

She took a step back. Was silent a moment. Seemed to go pale. "I am not my brother." Her shoulders slumped.

Harrison stalked to her. He lifted his hand and carefully wiped the water from her cheeks.

Her fingers curled around his wrist. Sadness slid over her delicate features before she told him, "Our families are pretty screwed up."

He didn't have a family. He had a lying SOB who had deceived him.

And I grew up with him. He raised me. I wanted to be like him. I wanted to make him proud of me.

I wanted him to love me.

The bastard who'd killed Harrison's real family.

He backed away from Elise and smoke drifted from his mouth.

"I'm…thinking that's not a good sign," Gray mumbled.

Harrison tried to pull in a breath. Instead, in a blink, he found himself towering over Razor. "How long have you worked for the fey?"

Razor tipped back his head. "Only…did it…to help you."

He didn't want to believe it. But everything was falling into place. "You went to the fey, and you got them to bind my beast."

Razor nodded. "They…there was a witch they used to help us. Your father and I — we — "

"He is not my father!" The words tore out as a roar. *"My father…my father —* " He just had to say it. "My father was a dragon. My real father…" His wings broke through his skin. "My father was a dragon."

Fire seemed to race along his skin.

"Oh, dear," Elise breathed. "I think…yes…we all need to get out of here. *Right now.* And we need to pull the fire alarms while we flee."

No one moved.

"*Flee,* people!" Elise screamed. "You've never seen a dragon shift, and I haven't either, but if he shifts and has no control — I'm thinking fire will go everywhere. Humans don't do so well with fire. Get the hell out!"

Harrison couldn't look away from Razor. "You were my friend."

"I *am* your friend."

Harrison's skin felt funny. Itchy.

Razor was at least twenty years older than Harrison, and he couldn't help but wonder… "Were you there…when they died?"

Razor blanched. That was Harrison's answer.

Fire shot down his arms as he reached for Razor —

"We need answers!" Elise jumped in front of him. "You kill him now, and you don't get answers."

He saw her…through fire. Through rage.

"Last chance!" Elise yelled. "You hunters either run or you burn!"

He heard the distant thud of footsteps. Someone was running away. Two people from the sound of things. And one person—

Gray appeared beside Razor. "Let me get him out of here."

Razor...

Friend.

Traitor.

Killer?

Razor had tried to kill Elise over and over again. As he stared at Razor, Harrison remembered the attack on the speakeasy. He'd thought only the werewolves were responsible for that attack. Gustave's crew. But... "You weren't at the speakeasy when it was under attack. You weren't there..."

Razor lowered his head.

"*You sonofabitch!*" Gray's roaring voice said he understood. "You sent those people in to attack Elise? To hurt Ward and Krista? You sent them after your own?"

"I...worked with Gustave."

Fucking hell.

"The Fey deceive." Razor clenched his left hand into a fist. "First her father...then her brother...they promised me so much, but only gave me tastes of power. Said that I'd have everything. That I'd even be able to bring *her* back." His head lifted. Tears gleamed in his eyes. "I loved her."

Harrison breathed in and out, in and out. *I only taste ash.*

"I loved her, but she fucked a dragon shifter. Got pregnant with you. I told Jason about the dragon...I thought he'd help me kill the bastard. How was I supposed to know Jason would kill Michaela, too? How could I know?" Pain choked his voice. "But she died and the dragon went crazy, and the next thing I knew, you were all alone."

No, no, no, no, no.

Elise reached for his hand, and Harrison realized his nails had turned into black, razor-sharp claws.

"I couldn't kill you." Razor's voice shook. "That was what Jason wanted..."

Jason...the hunter who'd claimed to be my father.

"I begged Jason to let you live. I told him we could find a way to keep you in line." Razor nodded. "You...you had Michaela's eyes." Razor's breath heaved. Blood poured from his shoulder. "The fey ruler used a witch to bind your beast and, as payment, he said we had to work for him. Had to take out his enemies. We...we did what he wanted. He gave us power." His words seemed to come faster and faster. "We got stronger. We got stronger because we *had* to be stronger in order to take out the monsters. You grew up. You didn't know. You weren't a beast.

You were a man. But that bitch you're screwing was going to change everything. You —"

Harrison loomed over him, nose to nose. "Do I have my mother's eyes *now?*"

Razor gave a trembling shake of his head. "Y-your...f-father's..."

"My real *fucking father!*" A roar. The whole suite seemed to shake.

Somewhere, a fire alarm was sounding. The fleeing hunters must have set it. Or maybe...

Was there fire racing across the floor? Yes, yes, it was...fire that came from...

Me.

Sprinklers burst on from overhead and dowsed Harrison in water. The pouring water didn't calm him. The burning was coming from inside. Surging up. Spreading through him.

"I won't let you be like him!" Razor jutted up his chin. "I *won't!* The bitch did this. She *did it.*"

Razor leapt up. A hunter always had plenty of weapons hidden on him. Harrison knew that. Hunting 101. Always have backups. So he wasn't particularly surprised to see Razor snatch up a knife from this ankle sheath. The bastard tried to go for Elise, though.

So he became a dead man.

No more chances. You're done.

Harrison slapped his hand on Razor's chest. Fire ripped from Harrison and surrounded Razor. Razor opened his mouth to scream but —

But it was over too fast. The fire ignited and burned through Razor. Burned so fast that he didn't even get the chance to scream. He was there one moment. Turned to ash the next.

Power surged through Harrison. Dark and malevolent. Red-hot and consuming. The beast was free. Finally free. And he wanted vengeance.

"Elise, *come on.*"

Harrison whipped around at that voice. Gray stood in the doorway, with his arms wrapped around Elise's stomach. He was trying to haul her away as the fire spread all over the bedroom. Gray was coughing. Elise was coughing. And...

They will burn.

"I'm not leaving him!" Elise yelled. "Harrison, Harrison, it's okay! You just have to calm down!"

There was no calming down.

He took a step toward her, and fire seemed to burst all along his body. Harrison lifted his hand. Scales. Scales and claws. And fire. Pain tore through him and he slammed down, falling to his hands and knees as he burned, but...

He was changing.

His bones were breaking. Reshaping. The scales were everywhere, and he could feel razor-sharp teeth exploding in his mouth.

Dragon. The beast...he was the beast.

And Elise was still trying to get to him. If she touched him, if she got too close to the fire...*she's dead.*

"Get…her…out…" Deep and booming. More like the voice the devil would possess. Not the voice of a man.

Elise stopped fighting Gray. "Harrison?"

He couldn't speak. He wasn't sure he was Harrison any longer.

He was something else.

"Harrison, you have to pull back." Tears streamed down her cheeks. "This hotel is filled with humans. Your fire — it will kill anyone who doesn't get out!"

That was why she had to go. Why she had to get far, far away from —

He roared. There was no more voice for him. There were only roars and growls as his body grew bigger and bigger and he was too strong and the night called him and the bloodlust consumed him. Fire. So much fire.

Fire.

Rage.

Vengeance.

His wings stretched. So big and powerful now. They scraped the walls and the ceiling.

"Holy shit," Gray whispered.

We kill. We destroy. Was that the dragon? No, no, *I am the dragon.* He was the dark voice he'd heard so long in the depths of his mind.

And the dragon — it was finally free.

He looked back at Elise, one final time.

She stared straight at him. "It's still you," she told him. "It's still you in there. I can see you. I love you!"

No, no, she didn't love fire and fury. She didn't love razor-sharp teeth and death. It was a lie. A trick.

He roared again and then he took flight, crashing through the balcony doors and soaring into the night. Soaring after his prey.

We kill. We destroy.

***

The sprinklers kept pouring down water. Elise swiped at her eyes. Her hair was soaking wet and her t-shirt clung to her like a second skin. Gray finally eased his death grip on her as the flames sputtered away.

"You saw that shit, too, didn't you? I'm not having a breakdown?" His voice shook. "Harrison turned into a giant dragon and flew away. *After* he turned Razor to ash."

She swallowed and crept toward the balcony doors. Glass and broken wood littered the floor. The glass crunched beneath her bare feet. She'd put on jeans and the shirt, but no shoes. She felt the glass cut her, but she ignored the sting. Her eyes were on the view outside. On the night sky and the dragon that she could see flying beneath the starlight. "I saw it, too."

"He was a dragon, all along?"

"Yes." He'd flown away from her, and Elise had a sinking suspicion about where he was going. "I need your help."

"Lady, you saved my daughter. Haven't you realized it yet? I'd pretty much put down my life for you."

She glanced back at him. "You don't care about what I am?"

"My daughter says you're a fairy princess."

Her lips twisted.

"You're her hero. That's good enough for me." He nodded and shoved back his wet hair. "What can I do?"

"I need you to take me to the man who raised Harrison. The man who claimed to be his father."

Gray winced. "Why would you want to see him?"

"Because I think that's where Harrison is going. Harrison is off to hunt him." Hadn't Harrison told her that Jason Key was supposed to be returning to Savannah? Was Jason already there?

"Oh, hell." Understanding flashed on Gray's face.

"Hunt him...and kill him."

Gray came closer, crushing glass and peering into the night. "Think anyone is going to report seeing a flying dragon to the cops?"

"If they do, the cops won't believe them. They'll just think the callers are drunk or high. Any video footage will be assumed to be edited."

Humans were so good at hiding the truth, especially from themselves.

Sirens screamed in the distance.

"They're coming to the hotel," Gray muttered.

"Then we need to be gone." She turned toward him. "You'll take me to the hunter I seek?"

He hesitated. "Look, I'm confused as hell, but is it such a bad thing if Harrison has a go at the guy? I mean, if I'm following along right, Jason Key killed Harrison's real father. Harrison deserves some payback."

"Yes, the hunter killed Harrison's real father. That means the bastard knows how to kill a dragon." She let that super bad part sink in. "Harrison has just shifted for the first time in his life. He may seem all powerful, but he's not. No one is. This Jason Key? He killed a dragon before, and I have to make sure he doesn't do it again."

A low whistle. "Damn."

"We need to go. Take me to Jason Key, *now*."

Before it was too late.

Everything else — her brother, the loss of her magic, the war for the fey crown — all of that would have to wait. Harrison mattered. He had to be protected.

She was just the fey princess for the job.

They hurried out of the suite, and she barely paused as she swiped up the knife near the pile of ashes. The knife Razor had intended to use on her. She knew it would come in handy later.

CHAPTER EIGHTEEN

"We beat him." Gray slammed the door of his truck as he stared at the old cabin that waited beyond the sagging, wooden gate. "If a giant, fire breathing dragon were here, I think we'd see him."

Elise climbed out of the passenger side. When they'd raced out of the hotel, they'd blended in with all of the other fleeing guests. They hadn't seen Krista or Ward, and she wondered where they'd gone.

She also wondered where Harrison was because no way should they have beat him. A dragon could fly one heck of a lot faster than a truck could drive. "You're sure Jason Key is here? Harrison could be tracking him by scent." She wasn't sure how the whole dragon thing worked. "Maybe they're a hundred miles away and we're about to be screwed—"

Gray headed for the gate. "I can see Jason's car. And Ward's."

Chills skated down her spine. "Ward?"

"Yeah, they're all here." He looked back at her. "Makes sense. When you're under attack, you regroup." A sigh. "And when you've been betrayed, you go and confront the asshole who's lied to you."

"So he was on the outskirts of town? When did he come back to Savannah?"

"When you and Harrison were taking that trip to wherever the hell you're from, that's when I got word that Jason Key was back in Savannah." His lips twisted. "Though now that I think about it, the timing seems suspicious as hell." He studied the cabin. "Starting to wonder if maybe he's been here a whole lot longer. Not so sure that I can exactly trust what I'm being told these days."

She glanced around, not liking this setup at all. It was so dark and the shadows stretched and danced everywhere. Walking into a cabin full of who knew how many hunters? Um, hard no.

A spider skittered across her tennis shoe, one she'd stolen on her way out of the hotel. It had been easy enough to do a little snatch and grab action at the hotel's boutique before her mad dash of an exit.

The spider rushed across her shoe once more. Elise spared the spider a glance as her breath eased out. Such a big, fat, gorgeous spider.

Okay, so I have backup. Relief flooded through her.

But...

A scream cut through the night. A scream that had come from inside the cabin. She and

Gray both took off running. She leapt over the fence faster than he did. Elise reached the cabin first. She wrenched open the old door —

Ward was on the floor, blood pooling from his body as he sprawled face down. His eyes were closed. His form far too still.

And the scream? It had come from Krista. Blood dripped down her neck. A man stood behind her. His left arm circled her waist while his right hand held a knife to her throat. The knife had already cut her once, obviously. The slice hadn't been deep enough to kill, not far enough to stop her cries, but just enough...

To bring us running.

Krista's eyes were wide and terrified and as for the man...

"I'm guessing you're Jason Key." Elise ran her gaze over him. "I thought you'd be bigger."

He was a muscular, stocky man, not too tall, though. His black hair was sprinkled with gray, and his brown eyes blazed with fury. He had a rough, dangerous face, and some might have even termed him handsome.

Elise didn't. He was soul ugly to her.

"I'm Key." His lips twisted in a sneer. "And you're the fey bitch who ruined Harrison's life."

She made a tut-tut sound. "You're going to regret calling me that."

"You're about to die. I won't regret shit."

Elise shrugged. "We'll see." Her gaze darted to Ward. Gray crouched at his side and his fingers pressed against Ward's throat. "Is he alive?"

Gray's head whipped up. Fury hardened every inch of his expression. "Barely." His gaze locked on Jason. "Why the hell would you attack him? He's *human.*"

Elise laughed. "I don't think he cares about whether his foes are human or supernatural. I'm suspecting that is way low on his priority list."

"You know nothing about me," Jason thundered. The knife was still at Krista's throat. She stood statue-still.

"I know plenty. Like the fact that you used spells to hide your lies and deceit for years." After a hard glare, Elise let her gaze dart to Gray once more.

Grimly, Gray told her, "If Ward doesn't get help soon, he's dead."

Based on all the blood around him, Elise was surprised Ward hadn't already died. "Get him out of here."

Gray looped one of Ward's arms around his neck—

"No!" Jason bellowed. The knife nicked Krista. She sucked in a quick breath. "No one leaves or I will slit her throat from ear to ear!"

"Will you now?" Elise smiled at him. She didn't take her gaze off him, she wouldn't risk that again, but she asked, "Gray, do you trust me?"

"Yes."

Wow. That answer had been fast. How lovely. "Good. Then take Ward and leave. He won't slit Krista's throat."

"I attacked Ward!" Spittle flew from Jason's mouth. "I'll kill anyone in my way!"

"Take Ward," Elise ordered flatly. "Get him help. He doesn't need to die here."

"*I don't want to leave you alone.*"

She felt a spider race up her arm. "I'm not alone. *Go.*"

Gray rushed out, hauling Ward with him. A moment later, she heard the sound of an engine and then the screech of tires.

"Funny." Her head tilted as she kept her attention on Jason. "Krista's neck hasn't been sliced from ear to ear yet."

He lowered the knife. Smirked at her. "Funny...you just let the only two men who might save your ass drive away."

Krista laughed.

Laughed.

Elise rolled her eyes. "Did you really think I didn't know Krista was on your side?"

That stopped the laughter.

"FYI, sunshine," Elise said to Krista, "I so regret saving your life at the speakeasy. I won't be making the same mistake again."

"How did you know?" Jason demanded.

What? Was this freaking show and tell? Was she supposed to reveal all her secrets? But her dragon hadn't appeared yet, and Elise was still thinking out her plan of attack so she decided to be a wee bit chatty. "Krista is kick ass. She's been trained her whole life to be a hunter, and when her good buddy Ward is bleeding out on the floor, you expect me to believe that she's just going to stand there and not try to get away from you? I mean, really, one hard elbow back and you would've dropped your hold on her. And, obviously, you wanted her to scream. Timed that a little too perfectly, didn't you?" Elise shook her head. "If you wanted her silent, you would have sliced way deeper into her throat. The setup was obvious from the word go."

His face darkened. "Then why did you let the two others leave?"

"Because I have no desire to kill them." She lifted her knife. "But you two? Oh, you assholes are going down."

Now Jason laughed. So insulting. Did he not get that she was dead serious?

Obviously, he didn't. Jason mocked, "You're a fey princess. A princess with no power. Yes, I know all about you. In fact, I suspect that once I carve out your heart, your brother will be incredibly grateful to me."

"Don't be so sure about that."

"I bet he'll give me even more magic than I already possess."

"Oh, wow." She widened her eyes. "You're hyped up supernaturally. Got it. Am I supposed to be impressed?"

His lips thinned.

"Scared? Am I supposed to be scared?"

Krista had snatched out her own knife.

Elise winced. "Sorry. Can't say I feel impressed or scared. But you know what I do feel?"

They waited.

She smiled. "Bored."

"Kill her!" Jason shouted. "Kill her because when Harrison comes and he finds his dead mate, it will wreck him, the same way it wrecked his father! Then we can kill him! We can kill —"

"Not happening," Elise snarled. "Beaux, get your little spider buddies and take out Krista. I'll end Jason."

Spiders swarmed from the darkness and rushed right for Krista. She screamed as they swarmed her. They flew over her body, and she *flipped the fuck out.*

"I hate spiders! No, no, no!" Krista screamed.

Seriously?

Krista swiped with her knife, and the crazy hunter stabbed herself. Not once, but twice, three times and —

"*Krista!*" A wild, pained bellow from Jason. He seemed to lose his shit, too, as he ran for Krista, and he shoved the spiders off her. They were everywhere — on her body, in her hair, in her mouth.

The mouth part was just gross. Beaux and his spiders. He'd always had an affinity for them. Not only could he transform into one, but he could command any spiders who happened to be in his vicinity. She suspected he had a long-ago descendant who'd been a shifter. A spider shifter. She'd always told the guy he was special. It was wonderful to see how much stronger he was becoming.

Hopefully, he'd start believing that truth for himself.

"Baby, baby, look at me..." Jason crouched over Krista. His voice had gone tender. Worried...

Elise's jaw dropped. "She's your daughter. Like, you didn't steal her from someone, the way you stole Harrison. She's really yours."

"*She's mine.*" His head whipped toward Elise. "And they'll stop attacking...*when you're dead!*"

He lunged at her. She lunged right back at him. She brought up her knife, ready to carve out his black heart, but he — he swiped down with his knife in a lightning-fast move.

A move far too fast for her to see. He moved faster than the most powerful fey, faster than vampires, faster than should have been possible.

The knife cut deeply into her shoulder, sliding straight to bone, and her own weapon fell from her nerveless fingers.

It fell…and she realized…

Jason hadn't been talking to *her* when he said "They'll stop attacking…when you're fucking dead." Because though his knife had cut into her shoulder…he'd been aiming at…

At the big, dark spider that perched on her. At the spider that controlled the others. At her precious Beaux.

"*No!*" Elise screamed as pain ripped through her. Pain that was so strong and consuming because Beaux…Beaux wasn't just some servant. Some guard. He wasn't a follower. He wasn't even simply a friend.

He was family.

Her family.

And no one messed with her family.

"*No!*" Elise tossed back her head as grief and rage ripped past everything and as it did, a bright, blue light shot from her fingertips. Beaux had transformed at her feet, shifting from a savaged spider into the form of a man who was bleeding and broken. The blue light poured from her fingers and surrounded him. Her wings stretched behind her, she felt them grow and quiver as she poured all that she had into Beaux. She wasn't going to let death take him. Not happening. Not—

"That's right. Drain all that magic out of you! Drain it until there's nothing left!"

The blue light died away.

Beaux pulled in a shuddering breath.

Elise collapsed and her fragile wings covered her body.

"Th-the spiders are gone." Krista's voice. Weak. Thready.

A fucking hunter...scared of spiders. If Elise hadn't been hanging on to consciousness by a teeny, tiny little thread, she would've laughed.

"Of course, they're gone. I killed their ring master," Jason boasted.

He was wrong. She'd seen Beaux take a breath. Hadn't she? Elise wanted to look but couldn't lift her head.

"And now she's helpless. Such easy prey. We'll start by slicing off her wings. Those will get us a hell of a lot on the black market. Then we'll cut her open so that Harrison can find her." He grabbed Elise's head and wrenched it back. "Guess you didn't really love Harrison after all, did you? You gave up all your power for another freaking fey instead of saving it for the dragon."

"D-dumbass..." Her breath heaved. "Can l-love...more..." More than just one person. She could love Beaux as family. She could love Harrison as...

Everything.

Jason yanked the blade from her shoulder. She was too weak to even cry out. Honestly, she'd forgotten the blade was still *in* her. He grabbed one of her wings. "Not like you'll need this much longer."

Her wings were back. So the curse was gone? Broken? Did it even matter? He was about to slice her wings away, and she couldn't even fight him. What she *hated*...she hated for Harrison to find her. She wanted him to remember her as she'd been. Not the horror she'd be when Jason was done with her.

"I-I think...I'm cut too deeply..." Krista's choked voice. "Jason...*Dad*...help me."

He didn't let go of Elise's wing. "Yeah, I'll be there in a minute." He smiled at Elise. "This is going to hurt."

She closed her eyes. Not because she was afraid, but because she would be damned if she looked at him while he—

Fire. She could feel the heat coming from above. A hot blast that made her eyes fly open because if there was fire, there was Harrison. She wanted him to be the last thing she saw.

The top of the cabin ripped away and a dragon swept down, fire blowing from his giant, gaping mouth.

CHAPTER NINETEEN

The bastard had his knife against Elise's beautiful wing. A wing of the purest blue and the darkest gold. Silken. Fragile.

Elise sagged in Jason's hold, her skin far too pale and her eyes circled by dark shadows. But she looked up at the dragon, and she smiled.

My mate. Mine.

Fire poured from his mouth. Fury churned from him as his wings flapped. He would rip and tear and—

"If the fire touches me, you will kill her, too."

Harrison sucked in a frantic breath, heaving all of the fire back inside.

Jason smiled at him. Jason...the man who'd raised him. The man who'd trained him. The man who'd lied to him.

"That was a cute trick." Jason kept the blade at her wing. "Now ditch the dragon body. If you're going to fight me, do it as a man."

He didn't know how to change back. Rage was too strong. He touched down, his massive claws cutting into the wooden floor.

The scent of blood filled his nostrils. His gaze cut to the right. Krista sprawled on the floor. Her bloody hands pressed to her stomach.

There was a still body near Krista. A familiar figure. Beaux?

"Shift now, or I will slice her wing right off her body. Do you know how sensitive a fey's wings are? Did your precious mate ever tell you that? Wings are the most sensitive parts of a fey's body. The pain from me taking her wing will be like nothing you can imagine."

He could imagine a fucking lot. Mostly ripping Jason's head clear from his body. But Harrison couldn't speak. Not as a dragon. He couldn't say a damn word. Smoke drifted from his massive nostrils.

"Took you a little while to get here, son. I was starting to think you wouldn't show." The knife nicked her wing.

Elise screamed.

You will die. And I am not your son.

"Did you have trouble finding me? Bet you did." A smug smile. "See…as soon as you crossed over into the fey realm, I knew the dragon would be breaking free. Had to, with all that magic surrounding you over there. So I got Krista and Razor to help me. They spread my scent all over town. That way, you'd be confused. Bet you went to a dozen different places before you found me here."

He had, dammit. He'd lost valuable time.

"You haven't shifted yet. I guess she doesn't matter to you, huh?" Grating laughter. "Not like your father. He was ready to do anything for your mother."

But his father hadn't survived. Neither had his mother.

Jason smirked at Elise. "He doesn't love you. Die knowing that, will you? You thought you'd tamed a dragon, that he'd be there to defend you against any threat, but he never loved you. He fucked you. Nothing more. When the chips were down, he wouldn't even shift to save you." He lifted his hand up high. "This is going to hurt."

Harrison couldn't breathe fire at the bastard. If he did—Elise could burn.

That was what Ardon had wanted. For him to burn Elise.

I won't. Not ever.

Elise stared at Harrison. She smiled. "I...love you."

The dragon's heart iced. *I love you.* He hadn't told her that. And now, he couldn't tell her how he felt. He had no voice.

"B-burn the bastard," Elise urged him. *"Burn him..."*

The knife sliced downward. It moved so fast, and there wasn't time to choose. There was only time to act. There was only time—

Harrison's fingers closed around Jason's wrist.

Jason gaped at him. "You...you shifted...*that fast?*"

Yes, he sure as hell had.

The knife clattered to the floor.

"Krista!" Jason screamed. "Attack him! Stab him!"

"Krista is a little busy right now," Harrison snarled. "She bled out, and she's dead on the floor."

Jason blanched. "No, no, I —" His head whipped toward Krista. "*Krista!*"

"The dead can't move, dumbass."

Jason's breath sawed in and out as he swung his stare back to Harrison. "She...she was always weak. Should've known she'd let me down."

You're the weak one. "You killed my mother."

Jason's eyes darted to the left. To the right. Found no escape.

"You murdered my father!"

"He was a monster!"

"*So am I.*" Harrison wrapped his fingers around Jason's thick neck.

"I...raised you!" Jason gasped out.

"You tortured me. I remember..." Memories that Jason had used magic to block out. "You tried to whip away my wings."

"I-I was making you *human!*"

"But I'm not." Harrison could feel the fire rising within him. "I'm just like my father." He leaned in close. "I. Am. A. Monster."

"*Don't! Don't kill —*"

"You were going to cut off Elise's wings." Her beautiful wings. "You were dead when you touched her."

"No, no—"

Ash. That was all that remained. In a blink, Jason was gone. Ash drifted in the air as Harrison spun away from him. He lunged for Elise. She'd slumped to the floor and wasn't moving. He reached for her—

"Don't touch her!"

Ardon appeared beside Elise, as if he'd just materialized from the shadows. He probably had.

Harrison's lips pulled back in fury. "I will *end* you—"

"You will end my sister if you touch her! Look at your hands. *Look!*"

Harrison looked at them. Just beneath the skin, he could see fire. His hands fisted. "She's hurt."

"She's a lot more than hurt. She's dying." Ardon crouched beside her. Spared a glare for the figure near Krista's dead body. "Elise gave the only magic she had to Beaux. She was willing to die for him, and he's not even her blood! He was nothing, but she gave her essence to bring him back!"

To bring him back?

Ardon's hands fisted at his sides. "If she's so evil, if she's nothing but darkness inside, why did she do that?"

Harrison couldn't make the fire banish from beneath his skin. All Harrison wanted was to scoop Elise into his arms, but what if he killed her with his touch? What if Ardon was right?

Fairies can't lie.

But they could twist the truth so easily.

"Why did she do that?" Ardon yelled.

"Because she's not fucking evil! You are!"

Ardon blinked. "No. No, I am meant to rule." His hand reached out and stroked back Elise's hair. An oddly tender touch that made no sense given what Harrison knew about the guy.

Wait a minute. He's playing me. Harrison tried to push past his fear and think. *He rules only if Elise dies.* A cold laugh erupted from Harrison. "That's why you don't want me to touch her. You want her to lay there and die."

Ardon shook his head. "You will burn her to ash. You have no control!"

"I had control when I shifted. I turned back into a man."

"You *aren't* a man. You have fire breathing beneath your skin."

Well, maybe.

"I will take Elise back with me. In the fey realm, she may get stronger."

You aren't taking her anywhere. "May being the key word, huh? Or she *may* die when you drive a knife into her heart. Or maybe it won't be a knife. Maybe you'll blast more of your blue light at her.

You nearly killed her the last time she was in the fey kingdom. Going for the win now?"

Ardon's face tightened as rage darkened his eyes. "I was aiming for you! She got in the way." He frowned. Looked down at Elise. Brushed back her hair again. "Why did she get in the way?"

"Because she loves me." Harrison believed it with every fiber of his being. "And I love her."

He heard the rustle of her wings. They were trying to lift, but she didn't have the strength. She was dying, and he was standing there bitching with her brother. *No!*

Harrison fell to his knees beside her. His hands reached out, but he stopped. He wanted to touch her so badly. She'd said…said that love made feys stronger. When they'd kissed in bed, she'd said that she was stronger with him. He just wanted to make her stronger. He *had* to make her stronger.

"You touch her with your fire, and she will die if she isn't your true mate. If your dragon hasn't chosen her, if you don't love her with every bit of your being, then she *will* die. I am not deceiving you. I'm trying to save her."

Now Harrison actually felt like he was hearing truth. There was real emotion in Ardon's voice. Terror.

"Do you love her?" Ardon demanded. His voice had gone low and deep. "Did a hunter really give his heart to a monster?"

"I'm not a fucking hunter." Elise was too pale. "And she's not a monster."

"Do you love her?"

Harrison's gaze stroked over Elise. "I do. I always will." But he still hesitated because this was *Elise*. Elise with her beauty and her grace and her crazy schemes and her fey charm. This was Elise, and if he did anything to hurt her, if she got so much as a bruise, he would never be able to forgive himself.

And I can't live if she dies.

He—

Elise's wing brushed against him. A soft, gentle touch on his shoulder. It was like a cool breeze blew through his whole body. He sucked in a breath, and her fingers touched his outstretched hand. *She* touched him, and his Elise didn't burn.

"I know…" she whispered. "You…love me…"

She wasn't burning. He wasn't burning. Her touch was cooling him, and his touch seemed to be making her stronger. He could see the faint light returning to her cheeks. A glow from within, and Harrison leaned forward and pressed a desperate kiss to her lips. He scooped her up into his arms, and he held her like the treasure she was as he kissed her and kissed her and wished that—

"Look what you've done!" Ardon shouted.

Harrison's head lifted. Fire surrounded him. A circle of flames that he didn't remember making. The flames were reaching for Elise.

"You've killed her. You've killed my sister!"

Harrison's wings sprang from his back. He held tightly to Elise as he shot them into the air, moving her away from the flames —

"It's not his fire. It's mine." Elise's voice. Not weak any longer. Strong and steady. "What's his is mine. What's mine is his. The way it is for mates. That's the way it is when the love is real."

He had *never* heard of magic being exchanged that way. Was it a fey thing?

"The fire is to protect us from *you*, brother."

Ardon backed up as he retreated from the flames that suddenly heaved toward him. When he scrambled back, he bumped into Beaux. A Beaux who was standing up, looking a bit like warmed death, but standing with his illusion back in place. Beaux clamped a hand over Ardon's shoulder.

Spiders swarmed from the darkness.

"Take the prisoner to his cell," Elise announced. Damn, but she actually sounded all queen-like right then. Not weak, but strong and fierce and sexy.

Mine.

Ardon tried to jerk free of Beaux's hold. "Beaux can't take me anywhere. He doesn't have the power. He doesn't have — "

"He has me." Elise pulled from Harrison's arms. Her wings fluttered as she flew down—and the fire eased for her as she passed. With a soft, delicate movement, she touched down in front of Krista's still body. "Such a waste," she murmured. "Sometimes, our families are truly the death of us." She reached down and her hand seemed to snag something from Krista's jacket. "May you find your peace." She turned her attention to Ardon. "May we all find it."

"I don't want fucking peace!" Ardon yelled as the veins on his neck bulged. "I want a kingdom!" He tried to rush forward, but Beaux just yanked him back. "When the hell did you get so strong?" Ardon demanded. Then he snapped his fingers. "Oh, right, when my sister nearly died trying to save you."

Elise flew toward him. All of the fire had died away. The floor was stained black. Her wings sent a gentle wind blowing before she stopped in front of Ardon. "You would have cared if I died?"

His lips pressed together.

Beaux still had a hand clamped on Ardon's shoulder.

Harrison flew to stand behind Elise. He didn't trust her brother. He'd seen just how much power the guy packed back in the fey realm.

"I have my wings again," she told her brother.

"Yeah, I freaking see them. I'm sure you're thrilled." His gaze drifted to her wings, then over to Harrison. Ardon sneered and said, "And you have your champion. I bet you think your big, bad dragon is going to turn me to ash—"

"He's not my champion. He's my lover. He's my mate." Her hand flashed out, and Harrison realized that she'd taken a tube of holy water from Krista. *That* was what she'd lifted from the hunter's jacket a moment before. Elise threw the holy water at her brother's face.

Ardon screamed as he burned.

"Holy water doesn't hurt fey, but it does hurt demons." She dropped the empty bottle and grabbed Ardon's shoulders as she hauled him against her. "Razor told me that you burned when holy water hit you. That's when I knew what had happened to you. What had happened to you all along."

"You know nothing!"

"I know our father was a demon. For a while, I thought that meant you and I were *both* half demon, but...I'm not. That's one of the reasons father hated me. I wasn't enough like him."

Smoke rose from Ardon's skin. Fury and pain swirled in his eyes.

Voice sad, Elise added, "Just like you hate me because I'm not like you."

He hissed at her.

"I have never seen your wings, Ardon." So soft. "It's because they are demon wings, not fey wings. That's why you wanted the power of the fey crown so much. You thought maybe the magic would give you what fate hadn't."

His lower lip trembled. "Why do you have everything...and I have nothing?"

Harrison wrapped an arm around Elise's stomach and pulled her back against him. He was afraid Ardon would attack her.

And I'll burn him to ash.

"You do have something, Ardon," she assured him. "Deep, deep inside, hidden so well that I almost overlooked it, I think you have a little bit of good."

Ardon laughed. "Bullshit."

The spiders had formed a circle around his feet. They weren't attacking. They just seemed to be waiting.

"When I was in that cell in the fey realm, I heard you scream when you hit me with your magic. You were afraid you'd killed me."

Harrison still owed him for that attack. He'd be getting payback.

"And, a few moments ago, you were afraid that Harrison would kill me with his touch. You tried to stop him because you were truly worried about me."

Ardon's expression didn't change. "I'm bored. I'm leaving—"

"I'm stronger than you. The curse is gone. My wings are back, and I have my dragon's power. You're not going anywhere unless I decree it."

When he didn't try to run away, Harrison realized that her brother was under Elise's control. Harrison still wanted to tear the guy apart, though, so he was waiting and watching for so much as a twitch that looked like a would-be attack.

"You didn't want Harrison to touch me because you were afraid he'd kill me. Harrison wasn't touching me because he was terrified of hurting me." Her lips curled. "So I touched him. I knew he loved me, just as much as I loved him. There was no risk."

"How...did you know?" The halting question came from Harrison. How had she been so certain of him?

Elise spared him a glance and a tender smile. "Because when you found out that I was a supernatural, you didn't come at me with a knife or a gun. You rushed to me so that you could protect me. You loved me even then."

"Hell, sweetheart, if you want the truth," he murmured. "I think I started falling for you when I first saw you in that alley. You stood up to those vamps like they were nothing. No fear." Strong was the sexiest thing he'd ever seen.

She blew him a kiss, and he could have sworn she hummed.

"*Uh, can we stop this shit?*" Ardon groused. "You won. You've got a dragon. Why not just go ahead and kill me?"

"I can kill him for you," Harrison offered. "It would be my pleasure."

Elise shook her head. Her gaze returned to Ardon. "You aren't all dark."

Beaux coughed. "Never thought I'd be defending the dick, but you're right, Elise. I hitched a ride over to this realm on him. He had the chance to kill you. He came over right after you, but...I think he was just here to make sure you were okay. He sent you here, I think, so that you could get stronger."

She nodded. "I know. You were worried your magic would be poison in me, so you sent me to this realm. You wanted me better. You didn't want me dead."

His chin jerked up. "You need to end me. You or your dragon. I warn you now, the world is better without me in it."

Elise shook her head. "And I tell you now that you will not die, not while I still can save you." She glanced around. "There's already been enough death."

And Elise reached for Harrison's hand.

CHAPTER TWENTY

"Do you want to talk about it?" Elise asked softly. She turned her back on the view of her kingdom and focused on her dragon. He'd come with her back to the fey realm. Been silent and strong and been breaking her heart the entire time.

Something had happened during that last fight. When she'd poured her magic at Beaux, something had broken inside of her...only to be welded back together when she'd touched Harrison. She was stronger than she'd ever been in her life. So powerful. She'd been able to bind her brother's magic with a wave of her hand.

She'd transported them all back to the fey realm with a snap of her fingers.

Power pulsed beneath her skin.

So did fire. She could summon it with barely a thought.

She hadn't even touched her crown yet. What would happen when she did?

Harrison didn't answer her question. He just stared out at the kingdom. "It's beautiful here."

It was. As soon as she'd come back — as if the realm had known that her curse was gone and she'd won the battle against her brother — magic had exploded. What had been dead or dying had burst into bloom. The darkness was gone. Glittering, shining homes and castles had returned.

"Beauty is only on the surface. It's what's beneath the surface that matters." Beneath all of the shine and glitter of her world, her people waited. People who were ready for a change. Ready to leave darkness behind and step into the light again.

She reached for Harrison's hand. "I'm sorry you had to kill Jason Key."

His head sagged forward. "I hated him."

Elise waited.

"And when I was a kid…there was no one I loved more."

She slipped closer.

"Jason murdered my real parents. I will never know them. And…God, as I was killing him, part of me was still screaming to stop. Still screaming…" He swallowed. "Screaming like I did when I was a child and he beat me with a whip so that my wings were savaged."

Elise's hand went to his back. She leaned forward and pressed tender kisses to his shoulders.

"He wasn't a good man," Harrison said flatly. "And he raised me to be exactly like him."

"No."

Harrison's head turned at her sharp answer.

"He raised you to be a hunter. You raised yourself to be a man. *You* turned yourself into the man I see before me, and you are not a single bit like him."

His gaze held hers. "How can you love me?"

Elise had to laugh. "Oh, Harrison, wrong question. What you should be asking is...how could I love anyone *but* you?" She leaned onto her toes and pressed a kiss to his lips. "You are the one for me. No other would ever do."

"Because I'm a dragon?"

"That's hot and all." She winked at him. Mostly because she wanted him to smile. His pain was a weight on her heart. "But I love you because you're strong and smart. Because you fight for the people who belong to you. Because you do what's right." She bit her lower lip. "I haven't always done what's right. Not until I met you. You taught me how to do that. You taught me how to be better."

He shook his head.

"You did. You helped me."

"Sweetheart, you're so wrong. You *saved* me."

The princess had saved the dragon? That was fun. She liked that. "Maybe we can just say that we saved each other. Will that work?"

He curled his arms around her and pulled her close. "That will work." He tenderly kissed her. "I love you, Elise."

"I know, but I will never get tired of hearing those magic words."

***

She was so nervous that she thought she might vomit. Elise tried to do some deep breathing, but that shit didn't help her one single bit as she stood at the end of the *seriously* long corridor that led to the throne room. Beaux was at her side, casting her frantic, *calm down* glances. She would've calmed down, except this was such a huge freaking deal.

The crown was going on her head. In the next few minutes, it would be placed *on her head*. The fey knew that she was the firstborn. The truth had been revealed. Her brother had been locked away in a cell, and this was supposed to be her big moment.

Except for one small problem...

"The crown judges you," she whispered to Beaux as he escorted her down the corridor. Everyone curtsied or bowed, and she tried to look regal instead of freaked out. "If it finds me lacking, you know that damn thing might kill me. Or hell, if I'm bad on the inside, maybe the whole kingdom will go dark in a blink."

"You're not lacking." His posture was perfect. His voice stern.

"My father was a demon. I've got fey wings, but who knows—"

"*I* know. And so does he." Beaux motioned toward the tall, handsome figure that waited near the throne.

Harrison.

His dragon wings were out. The fey had made him special clothing—apparently, gossamer wasn't his style, so they'd gone more badass for him. But the tunic still had slits in the back for his wings. What a sight those wings were.

Harrison smiled at her as he waited for her to come to him. He would be the one putting the crown on her head. He was her chosen consort, after all.

She couldn't wait to *consort* with him. After she survived getting the fey crown placed on her head.

As she neared him, Harrison's smile faded. He glared. Uh, oh. Who'd pissed him off? Elise risked a glance over her shoulder, wondering who might be behind her.

No one was there.

When she looked forward again—*Gah!* Harrison had flown toward her in a blink. He stood there, blocking her path and nearly giving her a heart attack.

Everyone froze.

"What's wrong?" Harrison demanded.

Her gaze darted around him and landed on the crown that waited — on its own fancy cushion — to be placed on her head.

"She's scared," Beaux whispered.

"Scared of what?" Harrison immediately took her hand and pulled her away from Beaux as he swept the crowd of nervous onlookers. "Is a threat here?"

"It's the crown." If possible, Beaux's voice was even softer. "She's afraid it will find her lacking. Or afraid that it will show everyone she's dark."

Harrison blinked. "What?"

Elise's stomach knotted even more. "If I'm lacking, something bad might happen."

"You are *not* lacking."

"Jeez, lower your voice!" Elise tossed an everything-is-fine smile at the assembled fey. "Nothing to see here, folks. Just a little pre-crown chit-chat."

There were murmurs. Uneasy ones. *I know the feeling.*

"Bad...like how?" Harrison wasn't keeping his voice quiet.

"I don't know. I supposed a worst-case scenario situation would be the whole kingdom plunged into darkness and my black, black heart explodes?"

He scooped her into his arms. "You are *not* lacking."

Good to know he thought so.

"And fuck the crown. If it kills people, it's not touching you."

There were gasps. Some tears and some folks even dropped to their knees when they heard his words.

"Stop," Elise's voice came out oddly calm.

He stopped his frantic dash to the door.

"If I don't take the crown, it goes to my brother. You know what happens then."

His lips thinned. "I can kill him. Then it won't be an issue."

A woman fainted. A very graceful faint into the arms of the man who stood behind her. Fey had flair, everyone knew that.

Elise shook her head. "I have to do this."

He looked at the crown, then back at her. "No, you don't. I'm here to tell you that you never have to do anything you don't want. You can leave the kingdom right now, and I'll help you. Hell, I'll fly you out. You matter. You come first. I stand with you, always."

That was so sweet. She kissed his stubbly cheek. "Thank you." Another kiss. "But I need you to put me down."

Growling, he did.

Her gaze swept those in the hall. The men. The women. The children. They were all waiting. Depending on her.

"We're going to take care of these people." Elise nodded. Her fingers twined with

Harrison's. "We're going to take care of this kingdom. We are going to—"

Something slipped over her head.

She gasped.

There were murmurs. Some more tears. At least two other fey fainted—a man and a woman.

Elise's left hand lifted. "The...crown?"

Harrison's mouth had dropped open. "Was it supposed to fly to you?"

The crown...had chosen. That was what it did. It chose the next ruler. It judged...

It had found her worthy.

Magic poured through her body. Magic and power and joy. So much joy. Blue and gold light swirled around her as Elise let out a laugh of pure delight.

The crown had chosen *her*.

She looked at her dragon.

And she had chosen him.

She locked both arms around Harrison, hauled him close, and kissed her mate.

***

Harrison waved away the guards. "I need a minute."

They hurried to obey. He'd found that everyone was jumping to obey these days.

Almost everyone.

Ardon glowered at him. The fey was chained in his cell, a beard covered his jaw, and his once pristine appearance looked a bit wilted. "What the hell do you want, dragon?"

"Honestly? For you to be dead and no longer a threat to Elise."

Ardon stiffened. "So you've come to kill me? Now that she's queen, you're going to eliminate the last threat to her. I heard you already took out the wraiths."

"Oh, yes, taking out those bastards was step one after I came back to this realm." He considered that situation. "Your father was responsible for them, huh? Bound you to them when you were a kid? Elise said they were made of darkness. She thinks their darkness seeped into you. Tainted you."

"The fact that I had a demon father *seeped* into me."

Harrison's lips twisted. "Guess we both have daddy issues."

Ardon rose. His chains clinked against the stone. "Are you here to kill me or annoy me?"

"I'm not going to kill you...yet." Though a quick death would certainly make things easier. "Elise thinks you still have good in you. I'll see how that pans out first." He unlocked the cell. Stepped inside.

Ardon's chin notched into the air. "If you're not killing me, then what are you doing?"

"I'm here to beat the shit out of you."

"What?"

"Remember when you fired that blue light and hit Elise? And she was hurt?"

"Uh..."

"Yeah, I remember, too..." Harrison drove his fist into Ardon's face.

***

Elise stood in their tower. They had an honest-to-heaven tower. Harrison still couldn't quite believe that. He'd grown up living in motels, hiding in condemned buildings, hunting and tracking every minute, and now he lived in a glittering, fairy-tale castle.

She was waiting for him, standing at the foot of their massive bed. She was completely naked, and her wings—those gorgeous, delicate wings—stretched behind her back. There was no sign of her crown.

"You disappeared on me." Her lips pulled down. "I was worried about you."

"I had to take care of a little business." He stalked toward her. Stopped when he was less than a foot away. Drank her in. "You are the most gorgeous thing I've ever seen."

Her gaze warmed. "Funny. I was about to tell you the same thing." But a furrow appeared between her eyes. She reached for his hand. "Your knuckles are red. What happened?"

"I tripped, and my fists fell into Ardon's face."

"Harrison—"

He picked her up. Scooped her into his arms and took her mouth. The kiss was long and hot and ravenous. The way he always kissed her. His need for her hadn't dissipated. It grew more and more every day.

"I didn't kill him," he muttered against her mouth. "Let him live. For you."

She kissed him back. A long, savoring kiss. "You're awesome, but you have on way too many clothes."

He felt the charge in the air and when he glanced around, he saw little blue sparks dancing around them. And just like that, his clothes were gone.

Harrison smiled. His wings flapped as he lifted them into the air. Hers moved in gentle time with his. He was about to do his new favorite thing—sex in the air with Elise. Apparently, there were some serious benefits to being a dragon.

He kissed her. Her legs wrapped around his hips. He wanted to thrust deep into her, but he had to make sure she was ready for him. His hand worked between their bodies. Slipped over her clit. Oh, hell, yes, he loved it when she moaned just like that. Loved it when she arched against him. Loved it when she—

"I want you *in* me, Harrison!"

Exactly where he wanted to be. He drove into her. They both gasped. Their wings beat against the air. Their bodies heaved. Faster and harder. Deeper. Rougher. She clawed at his arms.

He yanked her tighter against him.

He kissed a path down her throat. Licking. Biting. Marking her. *Loving* her.

Her sex clamped greedily around him as she came, and she whispered his name.

He exploded right after her, an endless release that left him wrung out as they fell and collapsed on the bed. He sucked in a breath. Then about twelve more as his heart drummed madly in his chest. There was nothing that compared to sex with Elise. Nothing. He caught her fingers in his and brought them to his lips. "Elise?"

She stretched drowsily. Sexily. "Yes?"

"Thank you for being my best friend."

Her head turned. Her eyes met his. Misted a little. He heard her give a quick, sweet hum before she told him, "Thank you for being my happy ending."

He leaned forward and kissed her. "Sweetheart, you're *my* happy ending." She was his everything, and Harrison knew that Elise always would be.

The dragon had finally found his treasure, and it was her. He would protect her and he would love her for the rest of his life.

And if anyone tried to hurt her…

He'd burn those bastards to ash.

No one fucked with the dragon's queen.

The End

A NOTE FROM THE AUTHOR

Thank you for reading SLAY ALL DAY. I was so excited to write another paranormal story and getting to release this tale right before Halloween made me extra happy. Dragons, fairies, and monsters...oh, my. This one was such fun to write! Bring on the paranormals!

If you have time, please consider leaving a review. Reviews help readers to discover new books—and authors certainly appreciate them!

If you'd like to stay updated on my releases and sales, please join my newsletter list.

http://www.cynthiaeden.com/newsletter/

Again, thank you for reading SLAY ALL DAY.

Best,
Cynthia Eden
www.cynthiaeden.com

ABOUT THE AUTHOR

Cynthia Eden is a *New York Times, USA Today, Digital Book World,* and *IndieReader* best-seller. Cynthia writes sexy tales of contemporary romance, romantic suspense, and paranormal romance. Since she began writing full-time in 2005, Cynthia has written over one hundred novels and novellas.

For More Information

- *www.cynthiaeden.com*
- *http://www.facebook.com/cynthiaedenfanpage*
- *http://www.twitter.com/cynthiaeden*

HER OTHER WORKS

Wilde Ways

- Protecting Piper (Wilde Ways, Book 1)
- Guarding Gwen (Wilde Ways, Book 2)
- Before Ben (Wilde Ways, Book 3)
- The Heart You Break (Wilde Ways, Book 4)
- Fighting For Her (Wilde Ways, Book 5)

Dark Sins

- Don't Trust A Killer (Dark Sins, Book 1)
- Don't Love A Liar (Dark Sins, Book 2)

Lazarus Rising

- Never Let Go (Book One, Lazarus Rising)
- Keep Me Close (Book Two, Lazarus Rising)
- Stay With Me (Book Three, Lazarus Rising)
- Run To Me (Book Four, Lazarus Rising)
- Lie Close To Me (Book Five, Lazarus Rising)

- Hold On Tight (Book Six, Lazarus Rising)
- Lazarus Rising Volume One (Books 1 to 3)
- Lazarus Rising Volume Two (Books 4 to 6)

Dark Obsession Series

- Watch Me (Dark Obsession, Book 1)
- Want Me (Dark Obsession, Book 2)
- Need Me (Dark Obsession, Book 3)
- Beware Of Me (Dark Obsession, Book 4)
- Only For Me (Dark Obsession, Books 1 to 4)

Mine Series

- Mine To Take (Mine, Book 1)
- Mine To Keep (Mine, Book 2)
- Mine To Hold (Mine, Book 3)
- Mine To Crave (Mine, Book 4)
- Mine To Have (Mine, Book 5)
- Mine To Protect (Mine, Book 6)
- Mine Series Box Set Volume 1 (Mine, Books 1-3)
- Mine Series Box Set Volume 2 (Mine, Books 4-6)

Bad Things

- The Devil In Disguise (Bad Things, Book 1)
- On The Prowl (Bad Things, Book 2)

- Undead Or Alive (Bad Things, Book 3)
- Broken Angel (Bad Things, Book 4)
- Heart Of Stone (Bad Things, Book 5)
- Tempted By Fate (Bad Things, Book 6)
- Bad Things Volume One (Books 1 to 3)
- Bad Things Volume Two (Books 4 to 6)
- Bad Things Deluxe Box Set (Books 1 to 6)
- Wicked And Wild (Bad Things, Book 7)
- Saint Or Sinner (Bad Things, Book 8)

Bite Series

- Forbidden Bite (Bite Book 1)
- Mating Bite (Bite Book 2)

Blood and Moonlight Series

- Bite The Dust (Blood and Moonlight, Book 1)
- Better Off Undead (Blood and Moonlight, Book 2)
- Bitter Blood (Blood and Moonlight, Book 3)
- Blood and Moonlight (The Complete Series)

Purgatory Series

- The Wolf Within (Purgatory, Book 1)
- Marked By The Vampire (Purgatory, Book 2)
- Charming The Beast (Purgatory, Book 3)
- Deal with the Devil (Purgatory, Book 4)

- The Beasts Inside (Purgatory, Books 1 to 4)

Bound Series

- Bound By Blood (Bound Book 1)
- Bound In Darkness (Bound Book 2)
- Bound In Sin (Bound Book 3)
- Bound By The Night (Bound Book 4)
- Forever Bound (Bound, Books 1 to 4)
- Bound in Death (Bound Book 5)

Other Romantic Suspense

- Secret Admirer
- First Taste of Darkness
- Sinful Secrets
- Until Death
- Christmas With A Spy

Made in the USA
Monee, IL
02 November 2019